T0193301

Cover Copy

This pirate's latest prize may be love…

With a single pistol shot and the swing of a cutlass, Alice Tupper saves her mistress's life. But no lady's maid in polite society has ever killed a duke—at least, not on purpose. So Alice sets sail for America and her new destiny—only to find herself battling pirates on the high seas. Aboard her rescue ship, The Scarlet Night, she is hailed a hero and earns her place among the crew…as well as the ire of Captain Gavin Quinn.

Gavin chose this pirate's life, but he knows it's no place for a woman, especially one as exasperating—and beautiful—as Alice. Despite his desire for her, Gavin is determined to do the right thing and deliver her to the new world. But Alice's deepest wish is a life by Gavin's side. Will his heart overrule his sense, and will he risk everything to pursue his greatest treasure of all?

WITHIN A CAPTAIN'S TREASURE
A Captains of the Scarlet Night Novel

Books by Lisa A. Olech

Captains of the Scarlet Night
Within A Captain's Hold
Within A Captain's Treasure

Published by Kensington Publishing Corporation

Within A Captain's Treasure

A Captains of the Scarlet Night Novel

Lisa A. Olech

LYRICAL PRESS
Kensington Publishing Corp.
www.kensingtonbooks.com

Copywrite

Dedication

To Benjamin and Timothy

Acknowledgements

I'd like to thank Kensington Lyrical for believing in these stories. They are dear to my heart, and I'm thrilled to be able to bring them to my readers.

I'd also like to thank my agent, Dawn Dowdle and her crew, my editor, Amanda Siemen, and my amazing critique partner, Kathy Hills. You've all made this book so much more than simply words on a page, you've helped me breathe life into these characters. I am forever grateful.

Chapter 1

Portsmouth, England 1686

Alice Tupper refused to look back. As the *Olivia Grace* pulled away from its docking, she didn't line the gunwales with the others waving farewell to England. She stood at the farthest point of the bow instead, pulled her woolen shawl tight about her shoulders, and lifted her face to the freshness of the open sea. Her gaze rested on the thin line where the sea and the sky lay atop one another like lovers—that was where her new life would begin.

"Good day, Mistress Tupper. Ye've stolen my favorite place to stand."

Alice turned and grinned at Captain Fredericks. He was a joyous soul who'd already won the hearts of his passengers. Albert Fredericks reminded her of Father Christmas after indulging in an overabundance of plum pudding.

"I've only sailed twice, but I love standing here as the ship cuts through the water. It creaks and pops and pulls against the rigging like a bridle. When the sails fill, it's as if she breaks into a gallop." She ran her hands along the polished rails and fittings. "I envy you your time at sea. Once I arrive in Virginia, I imagine I'll never sail again." She gave him a quick smile over her shoulder. "Governesses aren't known for their exotic travels."

"Well, then, you're welcome at my bow anytime." He patted her shoulder and leaned close. "Ye can't tell, those children ye've been sent to care for might need to see more of the world than their back porch."

"I hadn't thought of that." She smiled at the dear man. He winked and gave her arm a gentle squeeze.

Over their first days at sea, the other passengers became a tight-knit group, but Alice was hesitant to get too close with any of them. She preferred her books, long hours on deck, and keeping her secrets tucked away. To them she was a simple Englishwoman from northern Weatherington heading to take a new position along the coast of Virginia.

A young girl named Milly made a point to seek her out. The child was terribly lonely but bright as a new copper coin. She'd been sent for by her father, and her excitement to join him in America was contagious. The old woman he'd hired as her traveling companion, however, had spent more time being sick over the rails than she had keeping the girl company.

"It's all so thrilling, don't you think, Mistress Tupper? Two adventurous women like ourselves out on the ocean miles from anywhere." Milly hugged herself. "What do you suppose Virginia will be like?"

"I only know I'm to live on a fine tobacco plantation. Do you think they'll make their new governess learn how to smoke a pipe?" Alice liked teasing the girl. Her pale blue eyes would twinkle with mischief.

Milly giggled. "Or one of those fat smelly cigars with the gold ring around the middle."

"Yes. And I'd smoke it clear to the ring in one breath and blow enough smoke rings to make a chain."

Milly laughed and hugged her. Her companion only groaned and retched.

Alice twisted at the beautiful ring she wore. It was buttery gold, and not made of smoke. She ran her finger over the *A* carved into the face with a tiny pearl cradled in the tail of the initial. Her only true treasure. A farewell gift from her best friend, Annalise. She'd presented it to Alice the night before she left for her voyage.

"Running off to the new world won't erase the pain, Alice. It will only take you too far from those who love you. But if you must go, whenever you feel lost and alone, look at this ring." Annalise placed her hand next to Alice's, *"I'm wearing its twin. This way we will forever be linked."*

Alice already missed her terribly, but Annalise had been wrong. The farther the *Olivia Grace* separated Alice from England's shores, the lighter the burden of her past became. Perhaps it would be easy to erase the events that continued to hang about her neck like a noose.

A spray of chilled sea mist dampened her cheeks. A baptism of sorts. Her rebirth. She licked the salt from her lips and sighed. With each mile, a new Alice Tupper immerged from the tangled mess of the old.

* * * *

More than a week into their journey, the day burned warm and bright. Alice closed her book when the call came from the crow's nest, "Ship off the starboard."

She joined Captain Frederick as he raised his spyglass toward the approaching craft.

"It's an English Brigandine. Mayhap they be in distress. By the size of her, she could be one of those slave haulers."

Soon the ship closed the distance between the two and came alongside. Only half a dozen men stood on the wide deck. A voice called out across the water, "Ahoy, we be the *Delmar*. Permission to board?"

Fredericks called back. "Are ye in some kind of need?" He cursed under his breath. Something in his voice caused a cold shiver to run down Alice's spine.

Boarding ladders slammed across the span between the two ships. The six men from the *Delmar* crossed over. Fredericks approached the boarding party and to everyone's horror, the lead man pulled a pistol and shot the good captain dead on the spot.

Alice stumbled backward as the scene before her exploded. Women screamed and men scrambled, shouting as the assailants from the Delmar fired their pistols at whomever they saw. Her heart hammered. Blood rushed in her ears as she witnessed a tidal wave of brutal, vicious pirates flood over from the *Delmar*. They swarmed the deck like locusts, killing any who dared challenge them.

Time moved in a slow, heinous haze. The crew of the *Olivia Grace* was slaughtered before they could pull their weapons. Milly rushed past and fell as she tried to escape the vicious attack. Alice dropped to her hands and knees searching frantically for a place to hide. Her skirts made crawling near impossible. After tucking into a niche behind a stack of barrels, she prayed to survive.

The tang of blood and gunpowder filled her senses. Acrid smells returned her to the last time she wielded a weapon. The fog of sulfured smoke brought the horrific scene back to her mind. The same fear spurred her on. Tears threatened to blind her.

A high-pitched scream spun Alice around. Two pirates had Milly. Alice rushed them, shouting for them to release her only to be knocked to one side. A brutal blow to the girl's head with the butt end of a pistol knocked her unconscious. The savage pirate tossed Milly over his shoulder like a sack of wheat and headed back to the *Delmar*.

In a surge of ice-cold anger, Alice fought to pull a cutlass from a dead man's chest. She yanked at the weapon until it released. Slipping on the blood-soaked decking, she fell upon another body. The clouded eyes of dear Captain Fredericks stared back at her. Bile rose in her throat at the sight of the cavernous hole torn in the man's neck.

She stifled a scream and scrambled away from the gruesome scene into the grasping hands of another attacker. The pirate gripped her throat with one vise-like hand and twisted her arm brutally with the other, wrenching the cutlass from her grasp. It clattered to the deck along with any hope of escape. He sneered down at her. Rotted teeth filled his mouth. He spun her about and hauled her back against his chest. Putrid breath fanned her cheek.

She shuddered and gagged at the smell of sweat and filth permeating from him. Shoving against him only made his hold upon her tighten.

"Ain't ye a purdy one?"

He groped at her as he slammed her forward against the rails. His fingers raked against her breasts as he pinned her to the side of the ship. Kicking her legs astride, he tore her skirts.

Alice kicked back and twisted her upper body. Her elbow connected with the man's face with a loud *crack*. He swore and spit at her as blood coursed from his nose.

Lunging at her, he knocked them both to the bloody deck. Alice thrashed beneath him. Punching at him, clawing at his eyes, but he grabbed her hands and pinned them over her head. He crushed her wrists with one hand while the other nearly broke her fingers as he ripped her ring from her.

"No." Alice's scream tore from her throat.

"Jones!" A shout stopped him short. Alice used that moment to shove him off her. The man who'd murdered Captain Fredericks stood behind her attacker pointing a pistol at the man's greasy head.

"Get yer sorry arse off the woman. Move whatever we ken use from the hold. Now."

Jones wiped the blood from his face with the back of his sleeve. Moving away, he glared back at Alice.

Alice scrambled to her feet and headed toward him. "Stop. He stole my ring."

The other man only laughed and blocked her with his pistol. "Yer lucky it's all he took." He leveled the gun at her chest. "I be takin' this one," he shouted to the crew as they moved through the scatter of bodies, pillaging things from the dead.

"You, two," he motioned for men. "Show me guest to her new quarters. Mind ye, touch her an' I'll cut off yer fingers."

They flanked Alice, and dragged her over the boarding ladders to the *Delmar*. She was hauled below and thrown into a vile, rank, cave-like cabin. They tied her hands and feet and tossed her onto a filthy, soiled cot, then left. Alice struggled against her restraints in vain. The rancid smell of the bedding beneath her made her skin crawl. Another reeking odor seemed to come from the very boards of the ship.

Blinded from the brightness of the deck, it took a moment for her eyes to adjust to the dark room. She grimaced with disgust at what she saw. The cabin was cramped and cluttered. Food scraps and rotting debris littered a long table. The room had one small window at the back, but between the grime upon it and the myriad of things blocking it the window did little to bring in any light.

Alice's arms ached as she worked her wrists raw trying to release her bonds. She was not going to suffer at the hands of another madman. Panic crested and she screamed until her throat became raw. Collapsing into the soiled bedding, Alice grit her teeth and vowed. She was *not* going to die here.

The door flew open and the man who had claimed her as his own strode in. Arms full, he dumped his bounty amongst the other piles of clutter littering the cabin. He took off the wide-brimmed hat he wore and threw it atop the heap. After fishing a jug from the rubble of chaos on his desk, he lifted it to his mouth. Rivulets of red wine ran down his beard adding new stains to his coat.

He narrowed his eyes at Alice as he wiped his face with the back of his hand. "Aye, a fine bit of skirt. Git along right nice, we will." He drained the jug and tossed it to one side. "I be Capt'n Rasher. Long time since I 'ad the like of ye in me bed."

"I...I'm carrying a child," she lied.

He scratched at the tangled nest of his beard before doing the same to his crotch. "I don't care if ye be carryin' some bastard." He moved closer with a sneer. "We ain't gonna be acquainted fer long."

"Please," she whimpered, "don't hurt us."

He stroked her hair. "Be accommodatin' and ye got nuthin' to fret 'bout. Fight me, and I promise ye, yer babe will be yer last concern." He pushed his jacket open and began unbuttoning his breeches. "Now, be a good lass. Keep yer yap closed and yer legs open."

Alice began gagging. The smells and fetid surroundings made it easy for her to lose the contents of her stomach all over the randy Captain Rasher.

"Ah! Ye bloody bitch." He backed away as Alice continued to retch. "Damn ye, ye scurvied whore." Rasher tried to wipe the vomit off his thigh before he left in a fouled hurry.

Alice spit the sourness from her mouth and glared at the closed door. He'd be back. Her stunt had only bought her time. She had to get off this godforsaken ship before Rasher returned to rape her, and—and what? Fight an entire ship of pirates? Take over the ship? Swim to Virginia? There had to be a way out.

Hours later, the captain slammed his way back into the cabin.

"You'll be wishin' ye ain't seen fit to spew on me." He stuffed a filthy rag into her mouth. Grabbing her hair, he forced her to turn around. His fingers bit into her flesh as he shoved her facedown onto the bed. Alice struggled, screaming against the rag in her mouth and the brutal hold he had upon her neck. She couldn't fight him, not like this.

Rasher pinned her with a vise grip to one shoulder while he raised her skirts and fumbled to release the front of his breeches.

"Time fer ye te learn who be in charge—"

With the tangle of her skirts about her waist, Alice kicked out. Ankles lashed together, she used both feet like a barnyard mule and caught Rasher squarely in the groin. The full force of her kick knocked Rasher back against a pile of debris. A holler caught in his throat and turned into an agonized squeal as he doubled over in pain, clutching at his crotch.

He fell to the floor writhing in pain, cursing her, and gasping for breath. "I'll k-kill ye. Ye sorry b-bitch." He rolled into a fetal curl. "Wait till I get me hands on ye, ye'll wish ye ne'er been born."

An insistent knock rattled the cabin door. "Capt'n, ship off te stern. Followin' close. Be a *plague* ship."

"Aargh, I'm busy. Be gone. Got me own plague right 'ere." He spit at Alice.

Far-off cannon fire caught Rasher's attention. He struggled to his feet, and pointed a dirty finger at her. "I be right back te snap yer bloody neck." Rasher straightened himself best he could and stumbled from the cabin.

Another round of gunfire exploded. Alice listened to the rumble of cannons being rolled into position. Whoever was shooting at the *Delmar* was getting closer by the second. More cannon fire. This shot hit its mark. The *Delmar* lurched as if half the ship was blown away. Overhead, men screamed and scrambled on deck.

The door flew open, crashing into the wall. The same two pirates who had dumped her there earlier yanked her off the bed.

"Capt'n be wantin' ye on deck." They pulled at her to move, but she fell at their feet.

"Cut 'er ankle bounds. I ain't draggin' her the whole way."

Alice was able to spit out the vile rag Rasher used to gag her. This might be her only chance. If she could break free in the chaos, she could hide away in another part of the ship or beg quarter aboard whatever ship was putting holes in the *Delmar*. She forced herself to keep her head and wait for any chance to escape.

One of the men bent to slice at the rope binding her feet. Alice thought to kick him, but with her hands still tied and the other pirate doing his best to break her arms, she wouldn't get out of the cabin alive.

A rough hand began to scratch up the inside of her leg. "She sure be purty." Alice did kick at him then, but he only jeered. "What say we take a quick poke 'fore we bring 'er up?"

"Capt'n's waitin'."

"He's just gonna kill 'er." The man sneered into her face. "He be thinkin' yer a witch that put a curse upon 'im." He raked his hands over her breasts. "Ye don't be lookin' like no witch ta me."

"Leave 'er. Ye want the next back Rasher stripes to be yers?"

"Be worth the whip." He wiped spittle from the corner of his mouth.

"Take orders from yer cock, an Capt'n be havin' it for bait." The other pirate laughed, "If'n he be fishin' for sardines."

The man spun on the other. "Sardines? Must be thinkin' of yer own wee bullocks and twig."

A blast of cannon fire brought their attention back to the matter at hand. "Git 'er te the Capt'n, an' remind me te knock out the rest of yer teeth later."

The scene above was chaotic. Men raced about shouting. Several lay dead. Smoke and sulfur filled the air. A blast from the ship off their starboard exploded, splintering a section of the rail, and rocking the *Delmar*. Alice and her two escorts fell to the deck.

Breaking free in the confusion, Alice scrambled close to the side rail. She tripped over a body but used the dead man's cutlass to slice at the ropes binding her wrists. It took several passes to cut through the rope. A rush of freedom filled her veins. She spoke to the dead man as she stole his blade. "I need this more than you. Sorry."

"There be the witch who's brung the plague down on us." Rasher lorded over her.

"The *Olivia Grace* wasn't carrying the plague."

Rasher pointed his dagger at the attacking ship. "That bloody barge is. Ye cursed us."

The mysterious vessel loomed large and ominous. It was bedecked with tattered black sails. Great strips of sickly green hung from the yardarms. The decks stood empty. Not a soul could be seen. Were the guns firing on their own? It looked possessed, and abandoned.

Better to take her chances with spirits than pirates. Alice pointed her cutlass at him. "You're right. I am a witch, and I've cursed you all to the fiery pits of hell. There's only one way to save your sorry hides. Release me. I have the power to stop the devil ship. Let me go, and you can be rid of us all."

Rasher glared at her. "I be as damned as I plan to git. I'd ratha kill ye."

Alice slashed out with her cutlass. Rasher growled and lunged at her. She swung on him once more as the *Delmar* caught another round of fire and lurched beneath her feet. Alice lost her balance and caught Rasher's hip with the end of her sword. Blood bloomed down his thigh, and he slashed out in anger, missing her as she ducked low to the deck. Rasher moved toward her with his dirk raised high.

Gripping her weapon with both hands, Alice rose to catch Rasher just below his breastbone. She surged upward. Hot blood coursed over her hands. She released the grip as if burned. Rasher's eyes, wide with shock, looked to the cutlass protruding from his front before crumbing to the deck.

More cannon fire shattered a section of rail. Something ripped across Alice's upper arm. She cried out and clutched at the burning pain.

Blasts fired all around her as the approaching ship came alive. The black and green rags fell away as bright red sails rose along with a grinning skull emblazoned on a black flag. More than thirty men materialized out of voluminous clouds of red cannon smoke. It swirled about them as they swarmed the deck of the *Delmar,* looking as if they were arriving from the very bowels of hell.

Alice picked up a pistol and a boarding ax. If the gun wasn't loaded, at least it would buy her some of time. From behind, a hand came down to crush her shoulder. *Jones.* The man who'd stolen her ring. A gaping wound upon his forehead had covered half his face with blood.

He hauled her against him. "Cap'n won't be savin' ye this time, will 'e. Ye've seen to that, ain't ye?"

Struggling against his hold, she spit, "I won't be needing the captain."

With the pistol trapped between them, Alice said a quick prayer and squeezed the trigger. The ensuing blast knocked her hard against the rail, punching the air from her lungs. Powder burns singed her clothes. Jones clawed at the hole in his chest before he died at her feet.

Alice shook her head and struggled to regain her senses. A painful ringing in her ears deafened all else. Dropping to her knees, she began a frantic search of Jones's body.

Holding the ax poised, Alice reached into bloodied pockets until she found what she sought. With a satisfied grin, in the middle of a hell storm, Alice Tupper pushed Annalise's ring firmly back upon her finger.

Chapter 2

The fierce blow of a cutlass knocked the ax from Alice's hand as another pair of strong men subdued her and wrestled her across the watery gap to their waiting ship. She thrashed and screeched and caught one man with a vicious punch of her elbow. No doubt winning him a beautiful blackened eye to remember her by if the blue-tongued curse he spat was any indication.

They hauled her across the decks, through the swirl of red smoke, and down a darkened stairway. Alice strained to see until she was shoved into an aft cabin. The door slammed behind her.

Panic swelled. She couldn't catch her breath. Had she truly fought her way from one pirate ship only to land upon another? At least this time, they hadn't seen fit to bind her.

She searched the room for something to defend herself. The chamber was as different from the filthy cave of Rasher's quarters as mud was to milk. This room was spotless. Surfaces clear and uncluttered. Heavy brass lamps were polished and locked tight in their holders. The bunk was neatly made, and a row of diamond-paned windows curved along the back of the ship and sparkled in the sunlight. Open sea and spice were the only smells.

She lifted an ornate sexton and judged its weight. It might not be heavy enough to kill a man, but it would put a fine crease in his skull.

Alice pulled the tattered remains of her bodice back upon her shoulder. Her skirts had been reduced to rags and what wasn't torn was covered in powder burns and blood. Some of which was hers. Her upper arm throbbed as she pulled the fabric of her sleeve away from the wound. If she didn't tend to it soon, infection was sure to set in.

She crossed the room to a washstand in search of water. The pitcher was dry—but the finely honed razor lying near by—now, that would come in handy.

Amid the chaos continuing to rain down from above deck, booted footsteps heading her way had her poised for attack. A tall man ducked to enter the quarters. His broad shoulders filled every inch of the wool uniform of an English Navel seaman. Gray breeches incased long legs and tucked into tall, cuffed boots.

He glanced in her direction. "Put down my razor."

Like hell. "I'll put it down if you give me a pistol."

Her reply stopped him. "You're in no immediate danger."

"Ha. I've had enough dealings with pirates to believe otherwise. How many times must I defend my life in a single day?"

He removed his leather hat. Without a wig, his blond hair was long, the color of corn silk, and pulled back into a tidy queue. "I give you my word."

Alice wanted to laugh again, but a jolt of recognition stopped her. *It couldn't be...* Stunned, she relaxed her stance and lowered the blade.

"Good." He tipped his head toward her and paused to hang his hat on the back of the door. "I'm Captain G—"

"Gavin Quinn."

Gray eyes narrowed at her. "Yes. How—"

"I should have guessed. Red smoke. The crimson sails." Alice scanned the room. "This is the infamous *Scarlet Night*."

Quinn rested his hands on his hips. "Right again. Have we met?"

"Don't you remember?" Alice indicated her torn, bloodied clothes. "I was wearing the same outfit. Of course, it was more than two years ago. You look exactly the same. Don't tell me I've aged that much."

"Two years? I think I would recall—" He frowned.

Alice knew the moment Quinn recognized her. His eyebrows pushed toward his hairline. "Bloody hell, you're the woman from the cave. Port Royal. The one who shot, then tried to behead a duke to rescue Captain Steele and his wife."

She'd traveled hundreds of miles to escape the blackest moment of her past, and who should she cross paths with? Someone who had a firsthand accounting of the day that continued to haunt her nights. Alice gave him a contrite grin. "That would be me." She held out her tattered skirts. "Alice Tupper." She dipped into a quick, if sarcastic, curtsy.

"Members of this crew still sing the praises of the *great* Alice Tupper. It may make things easier for you." The edge to his voice told her he didn't think there was anything "great" about her, and she was about as welcome as a case of the pox. Quinn reached out to shake her hand. "Welcome aboard the *Scarlet Night*."

The wound of her upper arm bit when she shook his hand. She fought the gasp catching in her throat. It triggered her eyes to water. Alice pulled her hand from his and lifted the tatters of her sleeve away from the gash in her arm. "I'm sure the tale has been embellished along the way."

He frowned again. "You're hurt."

"It's nothing. A scratch."

"From a flying piece of debris, by the look of the wound. It needs to be well cleaned and dressed." He moved to open the cabin door and called down the galley way, "Neo, bring some fresh water."

Alice heard the answering "Aye, Capt'n."

Quinn hung up his coat, stopped to roll his sleeves, and began gathering things: clean linen strips, needle, thread. He poured a single glass of brandy and handed it to her.

"You needn't fuss, Captain. I can tend to it myself."

"If it's not done properly, I'll end up tending a feverish woman."

His distain was palpable. Condescending. She didn't care how striking a figure he made with his dusky-gray eyes and chiseled jaw. Alice's quick dislike for the "great" Captain Quinn heated her cheeks. "I'm betting it's been quite a while since you tended *any* woman." She spoke into her glass before swallowing the brandy in a single gulp. It burned through her like her growing anger.

"Certainly *never* on my ship." He snatched a clean shirt from another cabinet and added it to the growing stack of items. "Women are two things I can ill afford. Nuisance and distraction."

Alice planted her hands on her hips. "Really? Shall I toss my *womanly* self over the rails, or would you rather I throw myself onto your sword? I suppose I should thank you for saving me from the *Delmar*, but I'll not stand here and put up with your…your… arrogance."

The captain stood to his full height and crossed his arms over his chest. "You'll 'put up' with whatever I say. You're not at some garden party. You may have a champion or two aboard my ship, but most of my crew will help you over that rail. And the others—well, they'd more want to throw you onto your back."

Her jaw dropped. "And what *you* have failed to understand, *Captain*, is I am more than capable of handling myself. I neither require your protection nor your champions. Give me a pistol and a cutlass and find the closest port. I'll happily be gone from you and your ship."

"And clothing?" He swept a hand the length of her. "Let us not forget clothing to cover your obvious charms."

Alice clamped her mouth shut to keep from telling him her charms had already gotten two men killed today.

"It will have to be breeches," he continued. "We rarely see the need for skirts." He was close enough for Alice to see the frost of his stormy-gray eyes."

"How uncanny, I was debating the very thing earlier. Skirts are quite cumbersome when you're trying to escape being raped." Her glare locked with his.

A quick knock on the door broke the ice dam forming between them. Alice pulled the rags of her top to cover as much as she could and crossed her arms over her chest. A huge man carried in a hogshead of water with a brass tap in its end. He set it next to the pitcher and bowl. The man's skin was the color of polished mahogany. His scalp was shaved. Wide gold earrings ran through both ears. The play of muscles in his thick arms and across a battle-scarred chest made him an intimidating character. Eyes black as jet pierced her with a stare.

"Thank you, Neo."

"Capt'n." He lifted a wide hand and tapped a quick salute before leaving.

Quinn pulled the stock from his neck and pushed his sleeves past his elbows. "Where were we?"

Alice marveled at the precise efficiency of the man. Every action deliberate and organized. Cool. Restrained. She almost preferred his angry glares. At least there was heat to them. "We were discussing the uselessness of skirts."

He added a drying cloth to the small pile of items he'd gathered. "And what remains of your bodice, as well. Take it off, and I'll see to your wound." She opened her mouth to protests, but he raised a hand to stop her. "It is not something you can do one-handed. If it is your modesty, cover your breasts. I assure you the last thing on my mind is to ogle you. I have more pressing business on deck, so if you could please schedule your scathing remarks for another time, I would be grateful." He poured fresh water into the bowl and carried it to his desk.

Alice narrowed her eyes and clamped her mouth shut. Snatching the shirt he offered, she then turned away and stripped out of what remained of her bodice.

When she'd covered herself with the drape of his shirt, she turned back to him. His eyes held a fury in them. What had she done now?

"Who marked you?" His voice was low.

Alice shook her head. "What?"

He gestured toward her. "You've taken a beating. Fresh bruising about your neck, across your back and shoulders. Who did this?"

She turned to give him access to her wound. "Pirates."

"*Which* pirates?"

She lifted her shoulder and hissed at the pain. "It doesn't matter." She lied between clenched teeth. The adrenaline of the day had given way to the ache of her battered body. She couldn't see the bruises he was talking about, but she was aware of every one.

"It does matter. If it was one of my crew, I'll see the bastard flogged."

Alice shot a glance over her shoulder. Quinn was close. She swore she could smell the sun and salt air on him. She held his gaze. "I saw the bastard killed."

All at once, the horror of the day's events tumbled down upon her. The protective look in his gaze shocked her. He wanted to avenge her attacker? Fight for her honor? When had anyone fought for her? A silent scream echoed in her mind. *Never.* She was always the one doing the fighting. It made her sick to think of it. More men had died at her hand today. More bloodstains on her soul never to be erased. Tears pinched the backs of her eyes, but she refused to let him see her cry. Alice swallowed the lump in her throat that threatened to choke her and turned her face away from him. A hardened resolve straightened her spine. She didn't wince when he stitched her shoulder.

Chapter 3

Quinn studied Alice Tupper's profile. The life of a pirate was a heartless and brutal one. However, his men knew if he ever learned of any offenses toward a woman, he would be the first one to keelhaul the cowardly son of a cur. He might have little use for women—especially aboard his ship—but he wouldn't tolerate any violence toward them.

Even this one. She had a rapier tongue that cut in a blink of those gem-colored eyes. Never had a woman raised his ire as quick. But then, he had seen her bruises, and an anger of another sort flared hot in him. The swift call to defend this woman surprised him.

He took care of her wound taking heed to make his stitches small and neat. She would still bear the mark, but she'd be left with the thinnest of silver lines across the creamy, smooth skin of her arm.

The entire time he poked, prodded for stray splinters, and sutured the wound closed, she didn't flinch. Never shed a tear. Didn't cry out once. A small tremor was the only indication of the shock she must be experiencing. He expected her to crumble into a heap at any moment, but she stood mast straight.

Taking long strips of clean linen, Quinn braced her elbow against his stomach as he wound the bandage around her biceps. Goose bumps rose along her pale skin as he brushed the tender underside of her arm.

Beyond the grime and battle wash, she was rather pretty. Her hair curled over her ear, and in dark spirals at the nape of her neck. The long braid she wore must tame the chestnut tresses.

He smirked remembering the last time he saw her. She was mud soaked and dripping wet from the drenching rains that fell that day. Not a woman who balked at a little dirt, this one. Nor did she faint at the sight of blood. Not even when she was covered in it. Not even when it was hers.

The room was silent save the creak of the hull and the rush of the ocean. After their earlier bickering, the quiet was unsettling.

"Almost finished. Tell me how you ended up on the *Delmar* swinging a boarding ax?"

"I was trying to stay alive. Rasher thought I was a witch. Believed I brought a plague ship upon them. Your ship. He planned on killing me. There were others. More women. I don't know what happened to them."

She adjusted the shirt covering her chest and continued. "We were traveling to Virginia on the *Olivia Grace*. I'd secured a position as governess at a plantation there known as Pleasant Ridge." Her brows knit together. "The men of the *Delmar* struck without warning. They wiped out our crew. Killed all the men."

"You're lucky to have survived. Rasher and his men are ruthless. And desperate by the look of it. Why else would a slave ship attack a passenger vessel?"

She turned eyes the color of spring grass toward him. "Captain Fredericks thought it might be a slave ship."

"Aye. One of the worst." He tied the ends of the bandage together. "The reason why we engaged them. Their treatment of the men, women, and children is the worst we've seen. They suffer horrendous conditions. Rasher loses more to disease and abuse than he brings to the trade market."

"Human cargo. The very idea makes me ill." She grimaced and tipped her arm to look at her bandage.

Quinn nodded his agreement. "I, as well. But this is one shipload we can return to their shores."

Her eyes went wide. "Is that why you captured the *Delmar*? To save the slaves?" The tone in her voice sounded incredulous. Her attitude rankled.

"Yes, why else?" His jaw tightened.

Alice gave a tiny shrug. "You're pirates."

"Privateers," he corrected.

"Still, the trading of slaves is very profitable. I assumed."

Quinn finished tying off the dressing. "You assumed wrong. Some profits aren't worth the cost. Buying and selling of these people is abhorrent. We pirate our usual marks. Our coffers stay full and keep news of our actions from reaching England. At the same time, we're a serious threat to those who ply the African trade. They're cocky. None dare challenge them. Except the *Scarlet Night*.

"We drape the ship in black until we're close enough to strike. Usually, we intercept the ships close to the point of capture and return the negroes before half of them die in those hellish holds. The *Delmar* was farther out than we expected."

"So you bring them back."

Quinn returned the items he'd finished using. "Aye."

"I may have misjudged you." Alice laid a hand over her binding.

He tossed the soiled wash water out the nearest window. "It doesn't matter how you judge me, Mistress Tupper." He latched the window with a snap.

"I didn't expect it would." She shook her head before worrying her lower lip. "Still I'm grateful to you for tending my arm."

Her innocent gesture of biting her lip threw him. It was the first sign of anything less than brazen assertion on her part. Perhaps she wasn't as tough as she pretended to be. "I'm needed on deck. Clean up if you wish. I'll see about finding you some suitable clothing and food. Then we can discuss your fate while you're with us. The men will decide what we're to do with you."

"Do with me?"

"Aye. The crew will vote if you stay. And for how long. Or if you go and when. Were it left to me, you'd be leaving at the first opportunity. The sooner you are off my ship, the better for all concerned."

* * * *

By the time Quinn returned to the deck, the wounded from the battle had been treated, and the remaining crewmembers of the *Delmar* had been gathered and lashed together around the main mast of the *Scarlet Night*. Climbing into the rigging, Quinn swung over the gap between the ships to drop onto the decks of the *Delmar*. His quartermaster, Thomas Bellamy, stood with boatswain, Clyde Jessup, and Henry Robbins, a swivel gunner.

Bellamy shook his head. "Been below, Capt'n. Ain't ne're seen the like of it. Stacked like cordwood. More than seventy dead or beyond hope of ever seeing another day."

Jessup spat upon the deck. "Whole ship reeks of death."

Quinn's lip curled at the smell. He was right. The stench was almost overwhelming. "What of the survivors?"

Bellamy hitched his chin toward the bow of the ship. "Brought 'em up into the light of day and be giving them food and water."

"How many?"

"'Bout twenty. Five be alive, but hangin' by a prayer. Sick 'ave been moved."

"Good." Quinn rubbed his jaw. "Jessup, you and Robbins, take the rest of the captives and get across to the *Night*. Bellamy, you and I have business with Rasher's crew."

Back on the ruby decks of the *Scarlet Night*, Quinn approached the mangy remnants of the *Delmar*. "Gentlemen, good news, you're free to go." Bellamy started to object, but Quinn held up a hand. "Mister Bellamy, release these men, and see they return to their ship. Unharmed."

"This be some sort of trick?" One of the men narrowed his eyes at Quinn.

"No, no trick." He turned back to Bellamy. "See they have food. Water, as well. Two day's worth should be enough. Give them time to see to the dead aboard."

"Two days? We're more 'an two weeks from the closest port."

Several of Quinn's men approached. "Sir, stripped the *Delmar* of every inch of sailcloth, like you ordered."

"Good men, thank you."

"Ye pinched our sails? Ye be maroonin' us on a ship of bloated bodies. We all be dead 'fore we get te land."

Bellamy shoved the man toward the traverse ladders. "You're the smart one, I ken tell. Get movin.'"

"Wait." Quinn stopped the last man. "The women from the *Olivia Grace*. Where are they?"

A sneer crossed the man's filthy face. "Capt'n took his pick. Crew got the rest. Weren't nothin' but shark bait 'fore they got ta me. Some be greedy pricks."

Disgust burned in his gut. It took all Quinn's control not to snap the man's neck. "Get off my ship."

After the transfers were made and the sails set, Quinn scanned the crowded deck.

"Ne'er agreed te take on slaves." Jessup grumbled at Quinn's elbow. "How we gonna fill twenty more bellies."

"Shut that gaping hole ye call a mouth." Bellamy ordered him away. "I hate agreeing with Jessup, Capt'n, but he has a point."

"I'm aware of the situation." Quinn propped his hands on his hips and looked into the blue of the sky. "We're two weeks away from the African coast. Less if we keep at full sail. Until we reach port, nothing goes to waste. Lines in the water for fish. Ale and mead 'til it's gone. Ration the water for the sick. Catch the rain. If need be, there's water in the ballast. Swap it out for sea water if we must, and hope the wind stays with us."

"What about the woman?" Bellamy asked.

"Call all hands. The men have a decision to make." Quinn took to the quarterdeck as the order shouted throughout the crowded deck. The verdict was out of his hands. Alice Tupper's fate would now be put to the crew. Gavin paused as the last men assembled. Having lived his life at sea with clear and concise boundaries, he was suddenly wary of not having the control. All things aboard ship were put to the vote. What if the decision went against her? Would he fight his men if they chose to kill her or offer her up as a spoil of the battle?

"Men, you all earned your shares today defeating the *Delmar*. With victory comes duty to those few slaves we were able to rescue." He outlined the plan regarding food and water as he had with Bellamy. "And there's a vote to be had. We've a woman aboard. Given our articles, it poses a question."

"No question," shouted one man, "toss her over."

"I'll take care of her fer ye, Capt'n," shouted another. Laughter and lewd jibs followed.

Quinn waited. "Some will recognize her name. She's known to those who served aboard the *Scarlet Night* under Captain Jaxon Steele. Her name is Alice Tupper."

The men all spoke at once. "Blimey, Alice Tupper?" "Looked familiar, she did." "Wild chit what saved Capt'n Steele's neck?" "One in the same." "Swings a cutlass like no woman I e'er seen." "See the shiner she give Cole?" "Killed a duke. What was the bastard's name? One did in Cookie Burrows, remember?"

Appreciative murmurs ran through the crowd. Several regaled them with the tale of her daring in Port Royal. Others told what they'd witnessed on the *Delmar*. The fierceness with which she fought. Still, while those men sang her praises, there were a few who argued the curse of women aboard ship. Was *this* woman the exception? Sure as hell didn't fight like any woman they'd seen.

Debating continued until Quinn called for the vote. Majority ruled. Alice Tupper was free to stay. A cheer rose. Above the noise, Quinn added, "Any man lays a finger on her will answer to me."

Talk of Mistress Tupper continued even after the crew had been dismissed back to their duties. Quinn could pick out those men who had served on the *Scarlet Night* for many years. Jaxon Steele had been a popular captain among them.

The day Jaxon tracked him down at that tavern in Port Royal and turned over the ship seemed like a scene from a play. Quinn served for years under Captain Steele, but he'd left large boots to fill. The responsibility wasn't something Quinn took to lightly.

Some had grumbled about the shift of power, but the majority agreed. The crew voted Gavin Quinn as their new captain. Most who objected still had the sense to pledge their loyalty, but as a show of respect, Quinn gave each man the opportunity to re-sign their agreement to the ship's Articles.

A handful left the crew. Given the abundance of ships in Port Royal, it was easy for them to gain new positions on another. Replacements were not hard to find. The *Scarlet Night* had a fierce reputation. They were a force of strength in the Caribbean, and men were eager to join her.

Crewmen like White, Jessup, Summer, and Finch. Robbins, of course, and Bellamy had been aboard for years. They were old hands at how to get every ounce of power and speed out of the ship. When it came to battle, they fought like the very devil. Gavin was pleased they stayed.

Still, they respected Jaxon Steele and his years as captain. Alice Tupper made a name for herself with these men, and they'd never forget what she did.

Quinn moved through the crew. He could also spot those who cared little if Alice was a saint or a slut. She was a woman, and women weren't allowed aboard under any circumstance. He'd keep a close watch on those. Jessup in particular.

The man hadn't stopped grumbling since the vote. He marched up deck holding Bump by the scuff of his neck. "Now we git te deal with a woman? It ain't enough to put up with *this* useless pile of bones?" Jessup pushed the sniffling boy toward Robbins.

"Give 'im a chance. He can't be helpin' it." Robbins checked a reddened lump on the boy's forehead.

"End up dead, he will."

Quinn crouched next to the young orphan lad he'd pulled from the gutters of Port Royal. "What's happened here?"

"Good ole *Bump*," Jessup spat. "Came close te havin' his skull cracked in two. Again. Block got te swingin.' Dinna hear the shouts. Why we got a deaf cabin boy aboard, I'll ne're know."

"He's a good lad. Works 'imself to draggin', Capt'n." Robbins wiped the grim off the boys face. "Needs time te adjust, is all."

Quinn tipped the small pinched face to check the growing knot on the side of his head. "Keep an extra eye on him. Have a man be his ears when the boy's topside. Teach him to keep a sharper eye. Be a shame if we saved him from Port Royal, only to kill him at sea."

"I'll see te him, Capt'n," volunteered Robbins.

"Good man. Mind your duties first. Bringing Bump aboard was my decision alone, but another pair of watchful eyes may just save the lad."

Quinn remembered the day Bump had crossed his path. He had tripped over the lad in the muck of the street. He was filthy, half starved. A woman older than any being he had ever seen had struggled to pick up the child. Quinn gave her assistance and learned about her dear William.

How they'd both come to live in a pirate's den and because William was deaf he was often the victim of brutal treatment. A *"fever when he be only a babe stole his ears."* Barely able to stand on her own, she pleaded with Quinn to help. He decided then and there to take the lad aboard and find him some place among the crew.

He pled momentary insanity when Bellamy questioned him. Through the lad's seasickness and finding some way to communicate with him, Quinn repeatedly asked himself "why?" but he knew the answer.

"Robbins, one more favor if you could."

Robbins rose, and ruffled the thick, unruly hair on Bump's head. "Sir?"

"Mistress Tupper is in need of some clothing. You're a slim lad. Might you have a spare set of britches?"

Robbins shook his head and muttered, "Aye, Capt'n." He rolled his eyes at Bump. "Another damn woman in me pants and nothin' to show fer it. Ain't fair I tell ya."

Chapter 4

When Quinn entered his quarters, he found their famous guest curled up upon his bed fast asleep. She wore his shirt, which tucked beneath her and pulled tight to her body. A length of smooth, pale thigh stretched out beneath. He fingered the breeches in his hands and could picture her legs and the curve of her bottom clad in the snug buff fabric.

It had been a long time since he had a beautiful woman in his bed. And Alice *was* beautiful. The realization threw him off guard. She'd scrubbed her face and let down her hair. Chestnut waves caressed her pale cheek and caught the lantern light.

The ties at the neck of the shirt hung loose, exposing a tempting shadow between her breasts. He closed his eyes to the sight, willing his body to squelch the sudden flare of heat that pooled in his crotch.

His disobedient mind envisioned another fine-milled, garment from long ago, with its row of tiny white shell buttons. Each slipping in turn from their assigned loop from neckline to waist. Parting the fabric, he slipped a hand beneath to stroke the impossible softness of her breast. Was there anything to compare with the silk of a woman's skin? Warm, round. He could still smell the rosewater she used.

Pushing aside the fragile fabric, he kissed his way down to take her tightened nipple into his mouth. Circling the firm tip with his tongue, he swept her nightshift off her shoulders and cupped the opposite breast. She trembled at his touch. Moaning when he began to suckle. Pushing her hand into his hair to hold him to her, she begged him not to stop and covered his kneading hand with her own, urging him on. Arching into her pleasure, she sighed his name. He could almost hear her. *"Gavin..."*

Hands curled into fists. Sweat rolled between his shoulder blades. The pain in his chest competed with the surging ache in his cock. When he opened his eyes, Alice Tupper lay in his bed staring at him. Her bright green gaze held his.

Turning his back to her, he grasped at the shreds of his control. Black anger dimmed the edges of his vision. He pulled a great breath into his lungs. His jaw ticked. It wasn't her fault her eyes weren't blue.

* * * *

Alice woke to Quinn watching her with a queer look about his face. She knew that look. Having seen it on more than one occasion, it was usually followed by her fighting for her honor with some man intent on rutting between her thighs. But then another look flitted across his face before he turned away from her.

"Captain Quinn?"

"Put these on." He tossed her a pair of tanned breeches and kept his back turned. When he glanced back she had started to roll the ridiculous sleeves of his shirt past her wrists. The tails hung to her knees. "They will serve for now. You're still in need of proper clothing. I have a man working to gather things to fit you."

She nodded. "I'm grateful."

He hadn't looked at her. Alice couldn't read him at all.

"The *Delmar* is away." He stated most matter of fact. "We left the remainder of the crew to their dead."

Alice hesitated. Worry made her ask, but she was afraid she didn't want to know the answer. "What of the other women?"

"They were lost." His answer was clipped. The sudden lump in her throat silenced her response. He gave her a sharp look. "Add some seventy slaves and crewmembers, I'd say you are lucky to be standing here. Even if it is in borrowed pants."

The faces of those poor women swam before her vision. Milly. Her sickly companion. So many dead.

"It's been voted. You're to stay aboard the *Scarlet Night* until we can deliver you to Virginia. Many of my crew have heard the story from Port Royal. They're pleased to have you aboard. Some will tolerate your presence, but there are a few whom you should be wary of. You'll earn your keep tending the sick, as well as any other duty I deem suitable. Tonight you bunk here. Come tomorrow we'll have another spot for you to bed down."

He planted his hands on his hips. "We've brought aboard those slaves left alive, some are fighting to stay that way. The ship is crowded; space is limited. You'll be given whatever considerations we can, but I warn ye not to expect grand accommodations. Neither I, nor any member of my crew will be your personal traveling companion. You'll do your chores, stay out of the way, and make no trouble. Do you understand?"

Alice's head was spinning. Her emotions ran from despair to relief to indignation with each passing second. She'd always known a life of servitude, but being ordered about like this rankled her. What did he think she was going to do? Become some demanding shrew? Cling to him like a pampered, sniveling mollycoddled twit. Was he afraid she'd open a brothel and start charging by the hour?

"Aye, aye, Captain." She tapped her forehead.

He narrowed his eyes. "While you are not now, nor will ever be a member of my crew, you will show me the respect due the captain of this ship."

She crossed her arms over her chest and set her jaw. "Evidently such respect only extends to you."

Quinn shot her a warning glance as he began gathering up his logbooks and several personal items. He made a point of taking his closed razor and pointing it at her. "You'd do well to sheathe that tongue, as well. When you're among the men, you'll keep your head down and your mouth shut." Quinn donned his coat before planting his hat upon his head.

Alice notched her chin. "Do I have no say at all?"

"No. You do not. Not unless you think you can make it to Virginia on your own." With his arms full, he moved to the door. "You'll remain here until you can abide by my rules and present yourself on my decks properly."

"I'm curious." Alice stopped him with his hand on the door's latch. "Which camp do you fall into, Captain Quinn? You're not one of the pleased. Are you one of the tolerant, or one I should be wary of?"

Quinn narrowed his eyes. "Disobey me, and you'll have your answer soon enough." He slammed out of his quarters.

Alice fought the urge to hurl something heavy and fragile at the door. The nerve of the man. Frustration won. "Aaahh." She pushed her hands into her hair and dropped onto the side of the bed. "Keep my head down and my mouth shut?" Neither was a practiced skill.

Alice started to pace. "Insufferable oaf. Present myself *properly*. '*Not unless you think you can make it to Virginia on your own.*'" She blew out an angry breath. "And what was the look on his face when he came in? Lust? Revulsion?" Hadn't she always heard of Gavin Quinn's fine character? She remembered overhearing conversations between Captain Steele and Annalise after he transferred the *Scarlet Night* to him. They had nothing but good things to say about the man. Trusted him above all others.

She paced some more. He'd startled her when he first came in. Her defensive walls had snapped shut. Fear was quick to flash into rage. But was it misplaced?

Alice rubbed a hand over her eyes. The faces of the other women passed through her mind. Poor, sweet Milly. What hell had she endured? And those black men and women. Treated like something inhuman. It all added to her fury.

Captain Quinn, while boorish, had done nothing untoward. He'd brought her onto his ship, tended her wounded arm, clothed her. He was prepared to sail her to Virginia, and she'd insulted him, and taken over his quarters. It wasn't his wish to violate her. She was here as a protection until he could gage the crew's reaction to her being aboard. Where was he to sleep tonight? And more to the point, why did she suddenly care?

Alice squeezed her eyes tight. She cared because her future was in his hands, and she'd taken his brash-edged compassion and thrown it back in his face. She cared because she was beginning to despise the woman she was becoming.

Deep fear and mistrust and a cold ruthlessness surrounded her when she was threatened. The speed and brutality with which she could defend herself stunned her. When had she turned into a heartless killer? Alice stopped short. She knew the very moment. It played over and over in her mind. That single life-shattering second when she raised a cutlass high above her head out of fury and not out of fear.

The room closed in on her. Panic nipped at her heels as memories trapped her in the nightmare once more. She crossed the cabin and tested the door, knowing it would be locked and fearing the wave of terror that would follow. But the door opened. Alice peered down the galley way. It was empty. No guard posted to keep her in. Quinn told her to stay here for her safety, not because she was a prisoner.

At her feet, a trencher of food had been left. She hadn't heard it arrive. The smell of rich stew and bread had her stomach protesting the emptiness of her belly. When had she eaten last? She couldn't remember. After bringing the long bowl inside, she attacked the food until she could eat no more.

Wrapping herself in a thick wool blanket she curled up in the oak-paneled niche which served as Quinn's bed. Captain Quinn's distain, prisoner or no, intolerant crewmembers, and a future of deadly uncertainty wrestled within her mind until she couldn't think any more. The gentle roll of the ship and a full stomach lulled her to sleep.

* * * *

Alice snapped awake. The morning burned bright through the sparkling diamond windows. Where had the night gone? She had slept straight through to morning. By the look, the captain had been true to his word and not returned. If given the chance today, she would behave more graciously toward him. Thank him. Apologize for her rudeness. Then perhaps he would apologize for his.

A quick knock tapped upon the door. Alice tried to smooth the unruliness of her hair. A young boy—no more than a child—entered carrying a small pile of clothing and a pewter plate of bread and cheese. He wore a wide-brimmed gray hat trimmed with a froth of white feather upon his head. It was much too large for him. After he placed his burdens upon the desk, he lifted his chin and peeked at her from under the hat. Large dark eyes within a thin pinched face captured hers. He couldn't have been more than five or six years of age. Whatever was a boy so young doing on a pirate ship?

"And who are you?" Alice tipped down to peer beneath the wide brim.

He watched her mouth and frowned before removing the hat and adding it to the pile of clothes. His hair was a tangle of short dark ropes. He turned without a word and left.

"Wait," she called, but the door shut, and he was gone without a word.

She washed using what was left of the water in Quinn's pitcher and looked over the clothing brought to her. The rough-weave, wide-sleeved shirt fit her perfectly and fell to mid-thigh of the snug tan breeches she already wore. A wide leather belt the color of burgundy was loose for her waist but rode low on her hips. Knit stockings fit snug upon her legs, but the tall black boots were too large. Short of going barefoot, they would have to suffice. The crowning glory was the hat. Gray tooled leather with a plume of white curving to meet the band. One side stood proud giving it a dashing look.

Alice secured her hair into a long braid to drape one shoulder and pushed the hat upon her head. Captain Quinn possessed only a small looking glass, to presumably shave, but looking down, she supposed she looked like a proper pirate. Did this mean she was ready to venture above deck and report to Quinn?

The thought of stepping out onto the decks brought a mixture of apprehension and excitement. She wiped at the dampness of her palms across the curve of her thighs. They looked odd in breeches. Alice was pleased with her new attire, however. There was something about a man's garments. She liked the way they moved. The ease of motion. They gave her an unusual confidence no gown could ever give.

Alice made her way along the galley way, her gait had a distinct—what was the word?—swagger.

Chapter 5

Light from above deck lit the dim hallway. The noise of the day's activity beckoned Alice to the ladder. It was an odd sensation, stepping onto the deck of the *Scarlet Night* that first morning. Quinn assured her she was safe, but still instincts had her on edge. She had no weapon. The only things protecting her were the stories told by Jaxon Steele and those witnessing the battle aboard the *Delmar*.

This crew was as fierce as they came. According to Captain Steele, many a ship had simply to see the red sails of the *Scarlet Night* to throw up their hands in surrender.

Stepping into the brilliant light, she dipped her hat to shade her eyes. Around her, crewmen performed their duties. Their actions brisk and orderly. They were rough and gruff in appearance, but much less sinister-looking than those upon the *Delmar*. A few wore the remnants of military uniforms like Quinn. Were they former naval seamen, as well, or had they stolen them from men they'd captured?

Alice weathered several curious looks as she made her way across the crowded deck. One man stopped winding a thick length of rope to tug at the front of his head cloth in greeting. She wasn't sure how to respond other than to say, "Good morn."

She scanned the decks for Captain Quinn but didn't see him. Could he still be below?

"Mistress?"

Alice spun back to find three men. The man who'd addressed her held his hat in his hands. Two others stood slightly behind. One grinned at her like a schoolboy—but with fewer teeth.

"Mistress Tupper. I be damned if it ain't a grand day te meet ya."

"And you as well." She held out her hand.

He stared at her hand with a frown for a scant second before realization lit his face. "Oh, beggin' yer pardon. Done fergot me manners, I did." He pumped her hand and looked back over his shoulder. "Not like we be used to manners, eh boys?" They chuckled and shifted their feet. "Guess now we have a fine lady aboard we need to be learnin.'" He continued to pump her hand, squeezing tighter.

Finally released from his grip, she rubbed at her crushed fingers. "What did you say your name was?"

He laughed again. "I ain't said. I be Finch, Miss. 'N these two be White an' Summer. Wanted to meet ya, is all. We know what ye did fer Captain Steele. White's workin' on a song 'bout ya." Finch hitched a nod in the direction of the grinning man. White's face flamed as red as the sails.

"Mister Finch, Mister White, Mister Summer, it's nice to meet you." She nodded to each. "I don't need a song, but I thank you."

Finch burst out laughing and shoved against his companions. "Did ye hear lads? Misters we be now."

Alice smiled at the trio. White stopped laughing and simply gaped at her. "We can drop all the formality then. Call me Alice."

"Or Tupper?" Finch suggested. Summer agreed.

"Tupper." She tested it on her tongue. She'd never had a nickname. *Tupper.* "I like it."

Finch puffed like a china goose. "Then Tupper it be."

A grizzly man shoved his way through the little welcoming group. "White, quit yer slobberin'. The rest of ye, git back te work." He gave Alice a sharp side glance and sneered at the men. "Women aboard," he grumbled. "Gonna be servin' tea next?"

"Close yer hole, Jessup," Finch snapped.

"She be 'ere less than a day and White be drooling on 'imself. Think he ne'er seen a pair o' tits. Told ye she'd be nothing but trouble." Jessup shoved White aside and moved on. White spun with his hand on the hilt of his knife. Finch grabbed at his arm.

"Let 'im pass. Ye ken the rules." Finch spit in Jessup's direction. "Best keep yer distance, Tupper. Be rotten clear te his backbone, that one."

"I'll remember." She followed Jessup's retreat, narrowing her gaze as he glared at her over his shoulder. "I should find Captain Quinn. I'm to report to him."

"'Course, Miss...I mean, 'course Tupper. Capt'n, be forward on the Fo'c'sle checkin' on those sick darks."

"The slaves from the *Delmar*?"

"Aye. Some be in a bad way."

Alice made her way from one end of the ship to another. Men stopped and watched her walk by, some glared as Jessup had. Most ignored her as they went about their work of securing sails and repairing the minor damage done by the *Delmar*. A tiny tread of fear tugged through her. Quinn had been right. She had to remember where she was. Their decision aside, she was still among a rugged band of pirates and needed to watch her back.

Climbing the ladder to the Fo'c'sle deck, Alice encountered the smell of unwashed bodies, sickness, and death. She put the back of her hand beneath her nose. This was the smell she couldn't identify within Rasher's cabin. It was the smell of suffering.

They'd turned the upper deck into something of an infirmary. Sailcloth stretched overhead to keep the heat of the sun off the wounded men. The bustle of activity hummed around her. Men came and went with practiced efficiency. Lugging this and toting that. At its hub was Quinn. His height and bright hair made him stand out on the sail-shaded deck.

Quinn was the very image of a captain in his navy wool justacorps with the wide cuffs and brass buttons. Against his white shirt, a black leather stock tied snug at this throat and a wide sash of red circled his waist. His baldric of cognac-colored leather held two pistols and his cutlass. He wore a second knife strapped to one thigh. Under the sail cover, he'd removed his distinctive hat and carried it under one arm. His hair pulled back, his skin golden from the sun. Captain Quinn cut a fine figure of a man.

He was deep in conversation with another man. Standing side by side, the contrast between the two was distinctive. Both tall and broad through the shoulders, but compared to Quinn, the other man appeared rough. More coarse. Black seemed his color of choice. Dark hair hung loose to his shoulders. A long scar split one cheek and disappeared into the scruff of his beard.

The young boy who'd come to Quinn's quarters earlier was tucked tight to the captain's side, his intent brown eyes taking in everything within his wide gaze. Quinn took a step, and then the boy took a step, as if he were his tiny shadow. While Quinn had yet to notice her, the child had. Alice smiled at him, but he ducked behind the captain only to steal a look at her again. What was he doing on a pirate ship? He looked far too young to be part of such a dangerous life.

Another young man approached Quinn. He was a gangly youth, all arms and legs waiting to grow into the tall man he was sure to become. There was something familiar in his comely face. Alice had seen it before. When he reached out and tapped the child on his shoulder, the boy nearly leapt out of his skin. Large eyes shot to him, and back at her. His reaction was somehow odd. The young seaman ushered the child toward the aft of the ship.

"Mistress Tupper, so nice of you to join us." Captain Quinn's condescending tone interrupted her musings. His gaze made a slow appraisal of her. She had a sudden urge to cover herself. Heat rushed to her cheeks. Regaining her composure, she removed her hat and stepped closer.

Quinn dismissed the other man with orders to set full sail after introducing him to Alice as his quartermaster, Thomas Bellamy.

"Follow me." Quinn wasted no time with cordial pleasantries. "You're to help with the worst of the *Delmar* slaves."

She did her best to keep in step with his wide strides as he led her farther beneath the tented shade. The coolness under its cover was the only good she could find there. Men lay on low cots, sick and dying. Festering wounds and emaciated bodies. It was worse than she ever could have imagined.

The large dark man, Neo, stood when they approached. He wiped his hands. "Gonna lose two more 'fore the day be done."

"Stay with them. Do your best. I believe they were lost days ago. Make their final hours as comfortable as you can." Quinn slapped a hand on Alice's shoulder. "Neo, this is Alice Tupper. She's to work with you."

Alice started to extend her hand in greeting, but the look on Neo's face stopped her. "Aye, aye," he grumbled as if he'd been given orders to braid the tails of the bilge rats. The side glance he gave her told her he was one of the tolerant—not by choice, by duty. "Come."

She followed Neo through the makeshift infirmary. He pointed to the back corner. "Worst here." Three men were laid out in close quarters. A fourth sat close to one. Alice could tell which two would not live to see the night.

"Bring them more water." Neo pointed to a barrel.

Alice reeled. The smell was beyond anything she had ever experienced. She fought to keep from retching. Moving to the barrel, she clung to its rim to steady herself before finding the wooden dipper. The water tainted by the wood of the barrel was the color of weak tea. She crossed to the furthest man. Eyes no longer capable of sight stared past her as she lifted his head and tried to get the poor man to drink. Water ran down the side of his face soaking the cot beneath. She doubted any of the liquid managed to enter his mouth let alone slip down his throat.

Scanning the area, she spotted a small stock of dressing for wounds. She snatched one, tore the end of the clean strip, and returned to the man. Alice dipped the rag into the water and patiently squeezed water drop by drop between his dried, chapped lips. Silent in her concentration, she repeated the task more than a dozen times.

Alice began to hum softly to the dying man. Words filtered in, and she sang a favorite lullaby she had sung to dear wee James, Captain Steele and Annalise's infant son. She'd traveled hundreds of miles from that sweet-smelling nursery. A world away from the small bundle of love and joy she'd held in her arms and rocked to sleep. As she remembered the babe so far away, her eyes filled.

The tender song slipped from her lips in words this man could surely not understand, but Alice hoped they somehow soothed him. Swiping away the useless tears, she scolded herself for breaking her rule. She'd looked back.

Alice finished her song and was satisfied she had gotten at least a few spoonfuls of water down the man's throat. Soaking the bit of cloth again, she then wiped his face with a gentle hand and left him to rest.

She was startled to find Neo standing behind her, staring down at her. His gaze wasn't frightening, or questioning. He looked at her as if he had stumbled upon some mystical creature he'd never encountered before.

Neo wasn't her only audience. Gavin stood beyond the sailed shelter in the blaze of the sun watching her. Was he waiting for her to balk at the chore? See if she was too squeamish to witness such suffering? Perhaps he didn't trust her amongst his men. He considered her a curse upon his ship, after all.

She muttered to herself. Men were an odd lot, and seafaring men where the oddest of them all. After returning to the barrel, she brought water to the next man. He was in better condition and took the drink with little help. Moving on to the third man, Alice cringed and grimaced as the man writhed in pain before her. Neo stood over him. Another sat close.

Alice lifted wide eyes to Neo. "What can I do?" Neo shook his head. The man was suffering. She had to do something. "What causes him such agony?"

Neo lifted the corner of the sheet covering the man. The sight of his leg beneath was horrendous. Alice had to look away. The shackles holding this man prisoner aboard the *Delmar* had lifted the flesh from his bone, and the infection that now raged was sure to kill him.

Rushing into the sun where the air was less fetid, she took great gulps of air to fight the urge to be sick.

"You've lost all the color in your face. Sit down before you fall." Quinn took her elbow.

Alice straightened and looked back at the tormented man. "He…We need a surgeon. Do you have one aboard? Even I can see he can't survive with his leg like that."

WITHIN A CAPTAIN'S TREASURE

"The surgeon has seen him." Gavin's mouth formed a thin line.

Panic started to well in her. "What is he waiting for? He has to remove that leg."

"He agrees with you, but," Quinn looked back at the man twisting in pain and shook his head, "they'll not allow it."

"They?" She couldn't be understanding. Why wouldn't they allow the doctor to do what needed to be done?

Quinn sighed and held her gaze. "He and his man."

Disbelief flooded her. "He'll die." She lowered her voice.

Quinn held her arm and spoke with quiet concern. "Neo has translated. The man's name is Kgosi. He is a chief, a prince of their tribe. The man with him calls himself Tau. When the surgeon prepared to remove his ruined leg, they stopped him. He cannot be less than a whole man to his people. He's also refused laudanum, as it would tamper with his mind. He couldn't return to them otherwise."

"Without the surgery, he'll not be returning to them at all," she hissed.

"They are a proud people with fierce rules. Tau has wounds of his own, but refuses to leave the side of his chief."

Alice stared back at the two men. "This is insanity. The man is going to die." She turned a pleading eye back to Quinn. "Don't they realize how serious it is?"

"They do." He held her gaze.

"We can't just sit and wait until the infection claims him. There must be something we can do." Alice couldn't believe how calm he was. She indicated the guns tucked into his baldric. "You. You can force them. At pistol point."

He shook his head. "We fought to give these men their freedom. That includes a freedom in their deaths as well."

She stared at him in disbelief. "How can you be so callous?"

"It's not my choice to let the man suffer," he snapped. "He is still of his mind, and this is how he wants to die. I'm respecting the man's last wish." Quinn released his hold on her. "Do what you can and hope his suffering is short."

Alice watched him walk away. Was he asking her to resign herself to this? She wouldn't give up. She'd get Neo to translate. Damn stubborn men. What was wrong with them? Taking a dipper of water and another bit of cloth, she knelt next to Kgosi. His breathing was rapid as he fought through the pain.

Raising dark eyes, he drank some, lifted a hand toward her, but dropped it and turned to Tau. The two exchanged a few words before Tau reached out a long arm and placed his wide hand upon her breast. Alice jumped to her feet in surprise.

Taking a step back, she collided with Neo. "Believed he is seein' visions. Makin' sure ye're a real woman."

"Real enough." She pushed the stray hair away from her face and tugged at the hem of her shirt. "Neo, you speak their language. Tell them—"

"Told them." He stared her down.

Alice threw up a hand. "He'll—"

"Knows." Neo crossed his arms over his wide chest. Legs splayed he resembled a mountain.

Frustration made Alice groan. "I don't understand."

Neo pointed to the water barrel. "Not yer duty te understand."

The situation was impossible. All the water in the sea wouldn't keep this man alive. She might as well scream into the wind for the good her words would do. Her jaw tightened as she brought another dipper of water to Kgosi and helped him drink. Even through his pain, he nodded his thanks.

Kgosi captured her with the deep gaze of his dark eyes. For the briefest of moments he was still. Stepped beyond the pain. As if he'd found a tiny mote of tranquility. And in that single beating of her heart, Alice saw wisdom and pride and a profound knowing in those eyes. He knew there was no hope for him, but he would do whatever was necessary. Suffer whatever pain he needed for his people and his proud culture.

Alice nodded. He was silently asking her to understand, beseeching her to be strong for him. Nothing else. She nodded again, and smiled past the tears he would not want her to shed.

He lifted his hand to touch her cheek. Taking it, she patted the back and placed it gently upon his fevered chest with a silent vow she'd stay close and help in any way they allowed.

Chapter 6

Alice had worked herself into an exhausted knot and curled up against a coil of rope to sleep. Quinn had to wake her. Kgosi was dead and Quinn needed to tell her her vigil was over. She'd been at the side of the sick slave prince for two straight days, but now it was over. Kgosi had died with honor and dignity, and his guardian Tau had stood over him and protected him from all. Another day at sea and they would be able to return the fallen prince to the rest of his people.

During the last days, Alice had shown him the extent of her tenacity. She was indeed a force to be reckoned with. One moment she'd be singing lullabies, and the next she'd be railing at him about how the entire population of men were nothing but stubborn mules. Spooning broth and staring down Tau when he refused food. Cooling Kgosi's skin with damp cloths. Dropping water between dry lips. She never complained once about anything other than the steadfast determination of her patient to die.

Quinn was present when she breached the stoic wall of Tau and tended his wounds while Kgosi rested. She talked to him the entire time cleaning and bandaging his injuries. He spoke to her as well, but without Neo close by, they were lost to anything but each other's tone of voice. At one point, Tau reached out and lifted the thick braid of Alice's hair from her shoulder and made a gentle comment.

"I wish I knew what you were saying." She smiled at him. "Didn't sound like a curse this time. I'm keeping a count. Does this mean you've joined the ranks of men not horrified to have a woman aboard?" She laid a hand on his finished dressings. "I'll take your silence for a yes."

And Quinn wasn't the only one to take notice. Instead of alienating herself from his crew, her actions had only served to win over many of the men. They all called her Tupper now.

Robbins kept asking her for news of Captain Steele and his wife. Or as she'd corrected him, it was Lord Steele, now. He had become a marques. Quinn had to admit, when he'd heard Alice tell Robbins of Jaxon and Annalise's blessed life and dear infant son, the ensuing slice of envy had stung deep.

Alice was steadfast in her work. She'd spent every minute above deck. Sleeping little and eating less. Even Neo had good words for her. She'd only lost her temper and composure once more in his presence, and that was simply out of frustration for the certainty of Kgosi's outcome.

Even Bump had taken a fancy to her. Alice had ruffled his hair once in passing and Bump had begun following her about her duties as a duckling attaches himself to a mother duck. In fact, there were only a handful of men left not impressed by her. Jessup was leading the pack.

Had Quinn had a change of heart as well? He frowned as he watched her sleep and noticed the new sprinkling of freckles across the bridge of her nose. Why was it so hard for him to acknowledge her presence and be done? Carry on as if having her here was of no consequence? Why had he spent the last two days finding every excuse possible to keep her within his sight?

She was his last thought at night as he lay in his bed, and his first thought come morning. Even that he could explain away given the oddity of a woman aboard, but it was more than a sense of protection for her.

No, it was the dark, dream-filled hours within those long nights that caused the most unsettled thoughts. He'd been correct. The vision of her in tight breeches continued to haunt the cloistered part of his mind. And his body. Damn it, he was only human. He'd shielded himself from women for a dozen years, and here was an ordinary woman thrust into an extraordinary situation. Of course he'd pay attention to her—to all the soft curves of her, and the memory of a tender pale thigh.

Gavin rubbed a weary hand over his eyes hoping to erase the vision in his mind. He could make all the rational explanations necessary, but the truth of the matter screamed louder than an angry gull. He was captivated by the good Mistress Tupper, as was most of his crew. If he were to keep his head, he needed to stay more than a fair distance away from her. The sooner they turned this ship in the direction of Virginia, the better.

Quinn knelt by her side. "Tupper?" He quelled the urge to brush the stray wisps of hair from her cheek. "Alice?" He lowered his gaze to her lips. They appeared impossibly soft. A more powerful urge to test them coursed through him.

Lifting his eyes in a slow sweep of her face, he was surprised to meet the green of her gaze. "You're awake." Their closeness made the hush of his voice all the more intimate. "I need you…" He cleared the sudden dryness of his throat. "You need to know about Kgosi."

"I guessed." Alice brushed her hair away from her face and sighed. "Is it wrong to be grateful?" She worried her lip.

"No." He fought to keep from reaching out and stroking a finger along that lip.

"I'm saddened by his passing, of course, but I can imagine him strong and vibrant now. Young and proud for eternity." She glanced past Quinn. "Are Neo and Tau seeing to his body?"

"Aye." Her continued concern touched him. For him, death was as common as breathing. It was a daily occurrence. Perhaps she was right, he was callous. Time had hardened him. Life had hardened him. For all her bravado, this was still no place for her. The sooner he could get her away, the better.

"Another to commit to the sea. How many does that make?"

Looking into her wide eyes, he couldn't recall the figure. Too many. "Kgosi's body will not be buried at sea. We're close to the coast of Africa now. His people will want to honor him in their own way."

Alice nodded and stretched her back. Quinn nearly groaned at the innocent yet sensual gesture. He shifted his body to still its impulsive behavior. She scanned the remaining cots. "The rest are doing much better. Proper food, water, and fresh air have done their work."

"None have worked harder than you." Gavin stood and offered her his hand. "You've proved your worth these last few days."

Alice shrugged one shoulder as she got to her feet. "Earning my keep. You've worked as tireless as any. I see why your crew respects you."

"Perhaps you'll find your way to your quarters now. Not a large space, but you'll be able to sleep on a proper cot and have a bit of privacy. Luxury aboard ship."

"I don't need luxury." She brushed at the seat of her pants.

"Solitude is the only advantage of the space I've found for you."

She straightened her shirt and adjusted her belt. "I didn't displace someone, did I?"

"Storage is all." As Alice tidied herself, he couldn't look away. It was as if she were dressing before him. Never had anything so innocent affect him so sensually. It had been a long time since he'd shared company with a woman. He'd forgotten all the small ways they could beguile a man.

Picking up her ridiculous hat with the feather, she gave him a small smile. "I should thank you."

Clearing his throat, he shook his head. "Best see it before you offer thanks. You're dismissed from duties for twenty-four hours. After we've delivered Kgosi and the other survivors back to their shores, we set sail for Virginia."

"Virginia." She blinked at him and fiddled with her ring.

Something in the tone of her voice caught him as strange. "That was your destination."

A frown creased the space between her eyebrows. "Yes, I... It's strange. I somehow got it in my mind I'd never get there."

"Where did you imagine you'd end up?"

Alice looked toward the bow of the ship and lifted her one shoulder again. "I've been too busy to give it much thought."

"You've still got weeks."

She met his gaze and stood a bit taller. "Then a new life in Virginia."

Her forced determination struck him as odd. "Isn't it what you wanted?"

"So much has happened." Alice glanced once more to where Kgosi had lain. "It's hard to know exactly what I want."

The long journey should erase any doubts in her mind. And in his. "As I said, you've time to work it out."

"In the meanwhile, what's my next duty?"

"For the remainder of your time aboard, you'll be giving our gunnery master a hand in the armory. It takes a sharp mind. You'll do well. His name is Malcolm MacTavish. He's a beast of a Scotsman. Red tartan. Braids in his beard. Smells like sulfur. He's the brilliance of the *Scarlet Night's* red smoke."

"You used it during your attack on the *Delmar*." She nodded. "Stunning effect. How's it done?"

Quinn snorted. "You'll have to pry that bit of information out of MacTavish's dead fist. He shares his secret with no one. Until then...."

He moved closer and crooked his finger. Alice's eyes widened. A grin tugged at the corner of his mouth as the lad came from behind her. "Bump will take you to your quarters."

Was that relief on her face? "Your name is Bump?" She dipped her head when she spoke to him, looking the child in the eye, waiting for an answer which would never come.

"Aye, it suits him." A few pointing gestures and the lad seemed to understand what he wanted. Quinn patted the boy's shoulder and urged him forward. Bump slipped his hand in Alice's and tugged on her to follow him. "He's not much of a talker given the fact he can't hear a word you're saying."

As Bump pulled her away, Alice shot a hard look back over her shoulder. "Why on earth is a deaf child living aboard a pirate ship?"

Quinn folded his arms over his chest. Ah, the makings of another battle for another time. Why was he deriving so much pleasure out of fighting with this woman? Better to fight than to explore other pleasures, surely.

He mimicked the way she shrugged a shoulder. "Someone needed to show you to your quarters."

* * * *

Of all the flippant... "Did you see the look he gave me?" Alice spoke to the back of the child's head. Of course he didn't see. "What is the man thinking? You're a child. You shouldn't be aboard even if you could hear. Who's taking care of you? Protecting you?"

"Good morn,' Tupper," Finch called out as they passed.

Alice checked her anger. "Good day, Mister Finch."

A round of chortles followed as Finch posed like a fine gentleman, raised his battered hat from his balding head, and swept it in a grand gesture as he bowed.

"Bloddy arse, quit grovelin' 'n get back to work." Jessup gave Finch a mighty shove.

Alice pulled Bump to a halt. "I apologize, Mister Jessup, if I've disrupted your station. I was simply saying good day." Bump gave an insistent tug upon her sleeve, but Alice held her ground.

Jessup turned on her. "Sayin' g'day, was ye? Next ye'll be teachin' these sots how to knit a tidy cozy fer their teapots. Or how to hold their pinkies when they drink their grog." He roared at his own joke.

"Actually, I was wondering if *you* could show me a few things."

Jessup stopped laughing and narrowed his eyes at her. "I ain't fallin' fer any of yer games, missy."

"No games. You see, I've shot a pistol a few times now, but for the life of me, I don't know the first thing about reloading one. And maybe you could tell me the best way to retrieve my cutlass after I've buried it deep in a man. I've had a devil of a time with that as well. Any helpful tips?"

Jessup spat at her feet and moved closer so he could sneer down at her. The smell of his breath reminded her of Rasher.

He growled low. "I ain't gonna teach ye nothin' Stay out of me way and ye won't get hurt. Keep crossin' me path, and I be showing ye how fast I ken load me pistol. Bitches die quick as a man. Yer gonna regret tryin' te make me out te be the fool."

Bump nearly tore the sleeve off her shirt yanking her away from Jessup until the man tried to backhand him. Alice notched her chin and pulled the boy behind her. "Touch him and you'll regret it just as quick." She smiled into his ugly face. "I'm not afraid of you, *Mister* Jessup."

She turned and followed Bump as he pushed through the small crowd that had formed around them.

"I reckon you'll be regretting' that too," he shouted at her back.

Bump didn't stop tugging on her until they'd reached a short door toward the bow of the ship. He left her only long enough to shimmy up a barrel and snatch a lantern. Handing it to her, he then turned and opened the door.

The quarters were as tiny as Quinn had suggested. The sliver of a room had been achieved by hanging a bit of sailcloth between her and a storage hold full of kegs and trunks and coils of fat rope. It was only as wide and deep as necessary for a cot, a three-legged stool, and a rickety table, which kept the door from swinging fully open. "Ah, home."

A tray sat on the table with some bread and cheese and a mug of rum. She offered some bread to Bump, but he shook his head, looking anxiously toward the door.

"Don't you worry about Jessup. He's just a rooster fluffing his feathers." She bent her arms and waved them like she was flapping her wings. Bump's eyes widen. Alice gave her best *cock-a-doodle-do* and strutted about. The boy ducked his head and gave a little snort of laughter. She pointed above deck and flipped her hand as if she were swatting at a fly before patting his shoulder.

Bump nodded and gifted her with a small grin before he hurried out.

Closing the door behind him, Alice discovered the crude latch and lock that appeared to be newly added. She gave a silent prayer of thanks. For the first time since she had come aboard, she began to relax.

Under the table she discovered a short ewer of water with a bit of cloth hung over the handle. "A bed and private bath? Pure luxury indeed." She grinned.

After the last few grueling days, Alice wasn't sure which she needed most. Food, sleep, or a clean face? The rumble of her stomach answered her question. As she ate and drank the sweet rum, she stripped out of her clothing and let down her hair. Using precious little of the chilly water, she wiped the grime from her face and body. Even the icy water was wonderful.

Closing her eyes, Alice sighed. Remembering days past tugged at her heart. When she returned to England with Jaxon Steele and Annalise, she wasn't called back into service as Anna's maid. They wouldn't hear of it. Instead, they treated her as a treasured member of the family. She ate in the dining room and slept in her own chambers. Spent idle hours before Anna had their babe reading and riding through the miles of fields surrounding the manor.

When she'd return, rose petals would be added to her bath. Fat bars of lavender soap and thick drying clothes waited alongside the deep copper tub filled with steaming water. Alice would sink down into the blissful warmth with only her head and the tops of her knees peeking out of the festooned water.

It was heaven. Yet she couldn't help but think, standing naked in a room little larger than that copper tub and washing with only a few handfuls of frigid water was almost as close. Beyond his insufferable rules and regulations, and questionable decisions where Bump was concerned, Quinn saw fit to give her what few comforts he could. A lock, a bed, and a bath.

"Luxury, indeed."

Chapter 7

A pounding startled Alice out of a deep sleep. The last thing she remembered was wrapping herself in a rough wool blanket and stretching out along the taut canvas of her cot. Bone-deep weariness claimed her, and gentle rocking combined with the song of ship's wood creaking and the rush of water against the side of the hull had lulled her into a dreamless slumber.

Another pounding. "All hands."

Was it still night? Without a window, it was hard to tell. She raised the oiled wick on the lantern until the smoke began to soot the glass.

The blinding of the morning's sun answered her day or night question when Alice arrived on deck. She hadn't the chance to secure her hair before she jammed the hat upon her head. *Land.*

Ribbons of sand stretched into turquoise water. Palms and shorter trees stood twisted and bent into the steady winds bringing the *Scarlet Night* closer. They'd reached the coast of Africa. A handful of men had come down to the water. Given the times, Alice didn't think they were there to welcome them.

The *Scarlet Night* anchored off shore, as there were no docks within the tranquil quiet cove. Men were placed in twin longboats and ferried to shore. Word must have spread as the first boats landed. Men and women soon lined the beach.

Quinn called all hands to show respect for Kgosi and his people as they left the ship. The prince's body would be the last to leave. Before lowering him into the waiting boat, Tau approached her. Saying a few words, he touched his chest and offered her a small bow. Alice looked once again to Neo for translation.

"He owe ye a debt."

Alice held up her hand, "That's not—"

"To deny is to insult," Neo clipped.

Instead, Alice nodded her understanding and watched the proud man walk away. "Thank you, Neo. I'm grateful for your knowledge."

He jerked his chin toward the final boat heading for the beach before walking away from her. "They're grateful for yer kindness."

As the shrouded body of their leader returned to their shores, the people stood shoulder to shoulder in silence. One by one, they dropped to kneel in their reverence for their prince as he was carried past. His were a noble, proud people. Alice wondered if they would ever know how much he had suffered for them.

When the beach cleared, Quinn dismissed the crew and gave orders for the *Scarlet Night* to get back underway. The canvas overhead snapped as the sails were set, and each in turn caught the wind. Alice lifted her face to the cool rush of air as the ship lurched beneath her. Rigging creaked and ropes hummed from the strain of holding the great ship back when she wanted nothing more than to break free and become the wind herself.

"Next port, Virginia." Quinn came to stand beside her.

Those three words brought a rush of jumbled thoughts and emotions. Anticipation, relief, fear. The most shocking was disappointment. What was wrong with her? Virginia was her future. Her safe, fresh future without the anchor of her past weighing her down. A new life. What she wanted and needed. Why was she debating this?

Because it was all a lie. When she stepped on shore again, her life would be one of deceit and dishonesty that would dog her every step. Here she was free of the deception because every man onboard the *Scarlet Night* knew the truth. That was what was different, the illusive sensation she couldn't put a name to. She was free here. Freer than she would be anywhere. They knew all her crimes and respected her for it. Told the tale like some gruesome bedtime story.

Like changing her skirts for breeches, she had stripped away all the pretense of what she wanted the world to believe. In doing so, she had become what she was truly meant to be.

Oh my God, I'm a pirate!

Alice shot Quinn a look of shock at her realization. He had his gaze fixed upon the horizon. Her heart pounded. This was foolishness. She was insane. Quite mad—and she could prove it.

Standing there, the desire to be a pirate and serve upon the *Scarlet Night* paled only slightly to another desire that washed over her like a rogue wave. It was sheer craziness to want Gavin Quinn, of all men, to sweep her into his arms, crush her against his chest, beg her to stay with him, and then capture her mouth in a searing kiss. Insanity made her want to pull the lacing from his hair and…and ruffle his pristine appearance. She suddenly needed to untidy him.

To keep her hands from acting on such a ludicrous suggestion, she twisted at her ring. Good Lord, what had come over her? Gavin Quinn and a life of piracy? Perhaps there had been something in last night's rum. Next, she'd be swinging from the rigging and singing a sea shanty. She stifled an amused cough. Heat rose to her face. Her ears threatened to burst into flames. She must be the color of a bloody radish.

Gavin looked over at her. "Are you unwell? You're flushed."

Alice tipped her chin and tried to hide beneath her hat. "Yes. No," she stammered. "I'm, fine." She put the back of her hand to her burning cheek. "The sun is warm today, don't you think?"

"We're standing in the shade of the mainsail. Are you ill?"

"That would explain it," she conceded before raising her chin and meeting his gaze. Alice was quick to lower hers, convinced the clear gray of his eyes could see deep into her soul and read the wild ramblings of her mind. However, focusing on his mouth was a mistake. It only made the urge to kiss him stronger.

"Tupper?"

Watching his lips form her name tipped her world. She released a slight gasp. He grabbed her arm to steady her. He smelled of spice and salt air.

"Rough seas." Alice came close to laying a hand to his chest, but checked herself. His buttons winked in the daylight. Without his baldric, the crisp white of his shirt fairly glowed.

He frowned. "The waters are calm."

Not mine.

Gavin gave her arm a squeeze. "It's fitting you're off duty. Take the day and rest."

She held his gaze for a scant moment longer than was prudent. "Is that an order, Captain?" Her voice turned low and breathy. Alice cleared her throat.

Gavin cocked one golden eyebrow. "If it needs to, so be it."

Oh yes, he was much too tidy. Her lips twitched as she stifled a grin. "Aye, aye," she whispered.

Walking away with a newfound brazen attitude put an extra ounce of sway to her hips. Was he watching her? She didn't look back to check, but took off her hat and slapped it against her thigh. The sea breeze lifted her hair. *Are you watching now?*

Back in her speck of a cabin, Alice finished off the rum from last night. She was wound tighter than a child's spinning top. Pacing in a room three strides deep only added to her growing frustration until she flopped into her cot with a groan and covered her eyes with her arm. She had to stop this ridiculous thinking. Her. A pirate? And the captain? When had flirting with him become an option? Gavin Quinn was about as attracted to her as a mule was attracted to a moth.

She played out the comic scene of seduction in her mind. After a day of swashbuckling and pillaging, she'd return to their luxurious cabin, lush with carved oak furniture and deep feather ticking upon the large, four-posted bed. Stripping out of her battle-stained clothing, she'd stand naked before the finely painted pitcher and bowl to bathe, creating handfuls of silky bubbles from the thick bar of perfumed soap.

Gavin would enter. His pistols still smoking from the battle. Not a hair out of place. His gaze taking in the scene before him. A look of pure, heated lust spreading across his handsome face. Crossing the room in two wide strides, he'd take the sponge from her hand and toss it heedlessly over one shoulder. His fingers would spread a swath of rich suds across the curve of her breast. She'd melt beneath his touch. Arch her back and sigh.

All at once he'd be naked. His clothing vanishing as if by magic. She'd boldly appraise his manly gifts. There'd be a mere second of disenchantment. Confusion. Uncertainty. Weren't men's…um… *shoulders* supposed to be…bigger? Hard to envision, not knowing. The other maids in Weatherington used to boast about their lovers girth. Hung like a horse did not describe what she was imagining. She always suspected they lied. How would men's pants fit if they were sporting huge barnyard appendages? Besides, size didn't matter, did it? He was perfect in every other way. Given her lack of experience, whatever size his *shoulders* happened to be would be more than adequate. Who wanted a horse anyway? No her. This fantasy had taken an odd turn. Alice rubbed a weary hand over her eyes. Where was she? Oh, yes… Naked. Soapy.

Sweeping her into his arms, he'd place her on the bed and lay his body next to hers. She imagined golden hair carpeting his chest and she'd rake her fingers through the crisp curls while his hand continued to caress her breast. "Kiss me," he'd whisper, "I order you."

"Aye, aye, my captain…."

His mouth would lower toward hers with a slowness that was shear torture. It would make her ache with the desire to taste his lips upon hers. Arching her back she'd rise up desperate to end the torment of waiting. Feeling his warm breath brush across her mouth, her lips would part in sublime anticipation.

A blast of cannon fire lifted Alice from her cot. Her heart nearly leapt from her chest. Sweat made her clothes cling to her. She trembled as a rush flooded her limbs. Good God, they were under attack.

The scene on deck was a familiar one, like a recurring nightmare. But instead of the *Scarlet Night* being the one under attack, the brilliance of red sails told her they were the ones attacking. An unfortunate ship had crossed their path, and their crew was doing their best to fight them off.

"Fire!" The roar of the port-side cannons made her ears ring. Pirates filled the rigging of the *Scarlet Night*, their howls and screams raising the hairs on the back of her neck. They were a frightening swarm of bloodthirsty men waiting for their chance to lay claim to the other ship.

Red smoke curled around her boots. The smell of sulfur burned in her nose as each cannon was swabbed, reloaded, pricked, and maneuvered back into place. Powder monkeys ran sacks of black powder waiting for the next round of fire. The entire procedure like a well-choreographed dance.

Through the chaos, Quinn stormed toward her. "Get below."

In the bow, Robbins maneuvered his cannon and fired a shot across the other ship's bow. Alice ducked. "I can fight."

Quinn shook his head. "Not on my ship."

"You've seen me in battle."

"I've seen you swing blindly and get lucky. Go below." He grabbed her arm and shoved her behind him as he drew his sword.

The two ships moved closer. Boarding ladders swung into place. The crew began firing smoke pots onto the other deck to disorient their prey as they shot their muskets into the fog.

She tugged at him. "Give me a weapon and I'll prove you wrong."

Gavin growled through clenched teeth. "I've no time to argue with a bullheaded woman, get below, that's an—"

"Oh my God, Bump." Alice caught sight of the boy scrambling up the rigging.

Gavin followed her line of sight. "He's high and away from the battle."

Her jaw dropped at his lack of concern. "High and away?"

The crew started to swing across the open water to drop down upon the deck of the other ship. The battle was on. Through the smoke, the clang of blade meeting blade rang out.

"I'll not tell you again—" He pointed toward the ladder way.

The fight intensified. The other crew was not backing down. Several made it past the initial flood of pirates and fought their way onto the decks of the *Scarlet Night*. Quinn pulled his cutlass and a long dirk from his boot and ordered again over his shoulder. "Go."

Alice hadn't taken her eyes off the child clinging to the rigging. Her heart clogged her throat. Either the child would fall to his death or be killed by a random shot. She had to get him down and to safety.

"Bump, come down," she shouted above the fray. What was the use? The boy couldn't hear her. She'd have to go up after him. Before she could get there, another had taken notice of the lad and had same idea, but this man was not a member of the *Scarlet Night* crew. He pulled a dagger, narrowed his gaze, and began to climb for the child.

Panic roared in her head drowning out the bedlam of the battle around her. Her vision tunneled. Rushing to Quinn's side, she dodged the swing of his left arm as he finished off his opponent. She yanked one of his pistols from his baldric, turned, aimed and fired. Bump's attacker fell against the net of rigging before dropping to the deck. She shoved the smoking gun into her belt. The heat of the barrel scorched her blouse and burned her skin, but her only thought was to get to the boy before he lost his hold and careened to the deck below.

Quinn grabbed for her. She wrenched herself from his grasp and rushed across the deck. His angry shouts followed her, but somehow Bump had seen her and she didn't stop until the child was safely in her arms.

Turning, she met Quinn's furious glare with one of her own. He yanked his pistol from her belt and balled the front of her blouse in his fist.

"My cabin, and stay there, or I'll throw you from this ship." He ground out the words through a clenched jaw. "Now." He jerked her toward the ladder way before releasing her blouse.

Blood still pounded in her ears. Angry tears threatened. The battle on deck was drawing to a close, but the battle to come was going to be epic.

Chapter 8

A lead ball zipped so close to his ear, the breeze brushed Quinn's cheek. Lucky for him he had another loaded pistol strapped into his baldric, and he put a quick end to the man firing at him. Fury raged hot through his veins as the surrounding skirmish with the Spanish carrack reached its ultimate end. Victory was theirs.

In the end, thirty men begged quarter. They'd lost ten in battle, including their captain and first officer, and the decision was made that Tom Bellamy would assume command of the ship called *Ala de Cuervo* or *Raven Wing*. The rich bounty was secured and orders given to divide the spoils, see to the wounded, and set the sails of the *Scarlet Night* once more.

Quinn's anger hadn't lost any of its fiery edge as he stormed toward his quarters. The nerve of that…that *woman*. Had she been a man, he'd have her stripped, lashed to the mast, and be adding fifty stripes to her back. Her presence was treading on his last nerve. They were in the midst of a battle. Lives were at stake. Hers. Hell, his. If she continued to draw his attention, he was sure to die.

She'd already attracted too much of his notice every time she stepped topside. It was bad enough she continued to strut across his decks looking like some seafaring siren in britches and boots. He blessed and cursed her each time she left his company because, for the life of him, he could not stop himself from watching her walk away. The tilt of her backside, the sway of her hips, the stretch of her legs. He was powerless. And now this.

Slamming into his quarters, Quinn found Alice sitting with the lad who was asleep in his bed. When the door hit the wall, Alice sprang to her feet.

He planted his hands on his hips and shouted. "If you *ever* disobey an order given by me again, you will hit the water so fast you'll think the ship disappeared beneath you."

Pink stained her cheeks. "I was not going to stand by and let this child be killed."

"This child is *my* responsibility."

She cocked her head as if she hadn't heard him properly. "And how responsible is it having a child on a pirate ship? How long has he been here? What possessed you to allow him aboard?"

Quinn threw his hat atop his desk. "I'm the captain of this ship. I don't answer to you."

When he turned to remove his baldric, she stepped in front of him. "Does it give you the right to put an innocent child in harm's way?"

He snapped. "He wasn't in harm's way until you called attention to him."

Alice flung her arms wide. "It was a good thing someone was paying attention. He'd be dead now."

"You could both be dead now," he bit out the words between clenched teeth.

"All I needed was a weapon, but again you're too narrow-minded to listen to reason."

Quinn slammed his baldric on its hook. "So you took mine."

The chit had the decency to tuck her chin and look guilty before glaring at him again. "I did what I had to do."

"I was in the middle of a battle." His jaw ticked as his hands curled into fists. Had she been a man...

She shrugged a shoulder at him and looked away. "You weren't using your pistol. I needed it. I took it."

Forget flogging, she should be keel hauled. "You're lucky you're a woman."

She spun back. "That has nothing to do with this argument."

"It has *everything* to do with this argument. And it's the only reason why I am not hanging you by your wrists and whipping the hide off your back," he bellowed.

At his shout, she shot a looked over her shoulder as if checking to see if his yelling had woken Bump.

"He's *deaf*." Quinn flipped a hand at the boy.

Her green eyes flashed at him. "My point exactly."

"And one of the reasons he's here at all." His jaw pulsed. It was a wonder his back teeth were still intact. "When I first saw him, he was bleeding, lying in the gutter amongst the filth in Port Royal."

A frown softened her glare. "I remember seeing the urchins there."

"A woman claiming to be his grandmother told me his name was William. She was too old and weak to protect him." Quinn crossed to the bed and lifted the boy's hair. A line of pink showed a fresh scar. "The older he got, the worse the beatings. She begged me to take him." He tucked a blanket around the boy.

"Another week in Port Royal and he'd been dead. First week aboard, I was sure he'd die anyway. Sick, lost, unable to communicate. But he's smart, and strong. He learns quickly. It surprises me how much he understands."

"In battle, the most dangerous place for him is on deck. If he can't get below, he's been taught to climb the rigging. Others watch over him. It's more than he had in Port Royal."

Alice sat next to Bump and stroked his back. "The poor babe."

"Don't do that." His words earned him another fiery glare. "Coddling won't help him. This is his life now. He needs to be tough."

Alice stood and crossed her arms over her chest and stood in the sassy way she had with one knee bent and one foot crossed over the other. She let out a long breath. "I'm sorry."

He hadn't expected an apology.

"Don't look so surprised. I'm not so stubborn I can't admit when I've been wrong. I acted on impulse."

"And put both of you in greater danger." He laid his pistols on his desk to be cleaned and reloaded.

When he looked back, she'd planted her hands on her hips. "Are we both alive and well?"

"Yes, but—"

She indicated the guns. "And did I, or did I not prove I could shoot a pistol to defend myself?" She notched that infuriating chin.

"A pistol you stole from me within a hairbreadth of the slice of my dirk."

Alice held out both her arms and did a slow spin. "Am I cut?"

Quinn gave her a slow, thorough, head-to-blessed-boot evaluation. Warmth spread within him. "No," he snapped. Was he talking to her, or giving himself a warning?

"Will you admit that perhaps you were wrong as well?" She cocked her chin.

"No." Mimicking her stance from moments ago, He crossed his arms over his chest and lifted a defiant chin.

"But—"

He dropped his hands and moved dangerously close shaking his head. "This is one argument you will never win."

"Why not?"

He locked his gaze with hers. "I'm the *captain*."

She opened her mouth to speak and Quinn did the only thing he could think to stop her. The thing he'd debated doing for days. The one thing he couldn't stop thinking about. He kissed her. Hard. Like a slow match to black powder, a flash of pure longing shot through him.

* * * *

Gavin folded the eleventh letter and returned it safely to its appointed envelope. He rubbed at his eyes before raking his hands into his unbound hair and holding his head to keep it from hitting his desk. What time was it? He didn't care. It mattered not. Sleep would continue to elude him. Even now, closing his eyes, the rush of memory was still too vivid.

He'd kissed Alice Tupper to shut her up, but the moment his lips met hers, the inner turmoil of his mind and his body began to shout loud enough to drown out any rational thought. He'd shocked her at first. Holding her by her shoulders, his mouth had claimed hers. She pounded a fist to his chest a second before taking firm hold of his lapels and standing fast.

Her mouth had been opened to no doubt fire another shot in his direction about her need for a cutlass and pistol. Gavin used the advantage to ravish the sweetness of her lips. But then Alice unleashed a much more lethal weapon—she slid a hand up to caress the nape of his neck and she kissed him back.

Before the smoke cleared, he'd wrapped his arms around her waist and hauled her brazenly against the growing ache in his trousers. He tipped her back, curving his body over hers, making her slip her arms tighter about his neck.

When sanity reigned, they righted and separated as if they'd been burned. Her erratic breathing matched his own. His heart worked at a full gait to pump blood to his ready cock. Their eyes locked, and before he could come up with a single sensible word to utter, Alice spun on her heel and left.

Bloody hell. What had he been thinking? He hadn't. That was clear as a May morn.

Gavin looked at the small stack of letters now lying before him. Beth's letters. Letters she'd written when he'd gone to sea as a green-horned lad of twenty.

They'd only been wed a little over a month. He hated leaving her in their doorway, but she didn't want to stand on the dock and watch him sail away. *"I'll not whimper and sniffle with the other women. I plan te give ye a proper kiss right here, Gavin Quinn, and here I'll be standing te kiss ye again when ye come home to me, safe and well."*

As he'd promised, he returned safe and well fourteen months later, but the only thing waiting for him was a stack of letters and a pain so deep he nearly died. Would have. Gladly. But his father-in-law had dragged him back into the world of the living, and convinced him to return to the sea where he belonged.

More than a dozen years had passed. A dozen years of sailing from one corner of the ocean and back again. Trading his honor for a life of piracy. Fighting. Scraping. Waiting. Knowing the next battle would be his last. Or hoping it would be.

Twelve years and he'd never betrayed Beth's memory until today. Yes, there had been women in that time. A few. When the needs of his body overruled his head. But he never let any of them close enough. Not until now. Alice had somehow slipped past his rock-solid defense.

He gathered up Beth's letters and put them to rights. Each in line with the next. All thirty of them. And the last, still bearing the marks of his hand as he crushed the pages in his fist. The one he'd only been able to read once. Even it sat in its proper order within the thirty envelopes. *My darling, Gavin* written on the face of each. He tied the thin length of black leather to hold the small bundle and returned them to his desk drawer. Next to them lay a fine cut crystal bottle of brandy tucked securely into its appointed cubby. The matching glass caught the light of the ceiling lantern.

His hand hovered. How many demons was a man to fight in one night? He slammed the drawer shut, rose, and snatched his coat from its peg. Perhaps he'd find the clarity he sought pacing the decks, feeling the sea air on his face. He sure as hell wasn't going to find it at the bottom of a bottle.

Night had its last hold on the sky. The gray of dawn's push lightened the horizon as he headed toward the bow. Another had beaten him to the spot, however. The nemesis of his sleepless night already stood there.

Gavin moved to stand next to her. Words failed him. She gave him a long look before averting her gaze. Evidently, words failed her, as well. A reluctant grin tugged at the corner of his mouth. His kiss may have been successful in silencing her after all.

Her eyes made a quick scan of his person. "You're mussed."

He shook his head. He'd made his conclusion too soon. "Pardon?"

"Your hair's unbound, you're unshaven, unbuttoned, no stock or sash."

"I wasn't aware there would be an inspection." He rubbed at the night's growth on this chin.

Alice lowered her gaze and was quiet for a long moment. "I didn't mean it as a criticism." She met his stare. "I rather like it. You look rakish."

"Rakish? Interesting word." She looked as lovely as the last time he'd seen her. In that second between their kiss ending and her bolting from his quarters.

"Pay me no mind." She tugged the blanket wrapped her shoulders a bit tighter and pulled a deep breath.

If only I could. "What brings you on deck so early? Didn't you sleep? Or are you prepared to complain about the size of your bunk?"

"No. My private little corner is all I could want. I just needed a bit of fresh air."

"Aye." He nodded a slow agreement, but he didn't believe her for a moment. How long were they going to dance around the subject keeping both of them from their rest?

"Did *you* sleep well?" She slid a glance his way.

Gavin began to say, "like a babe," but the words stuck in his throat. "Well enough." He went back to watching the horizon. "I had a bit of reading to do last night."

"Now I'm envious. Of all the things I've lost since leaving Weatherington, I miss my books the most. Not that I've had much leisure time to read, but in the middle of the night...."

"When you're sleeping sound and well...." he teased.

She shot him a grin. "Exactly."

"You're welcome to look through what I have. Most are dry naval tomes, but we did secure some new books from the Spanish ship yesterday. Bound in leather, trimmed with silver at the corners. I haven't had a chance to examine them fully, but they were listed in the accountings."

"I'd love to see them."

"They're in my chambers. Come by after eight bells. Read whatever you wish."

"Your chambers." Her words hung in the air. She kept her gaze upon the sea. "Should we talk about what occurred the last time I was in your chambers? The kiss—"

"A lapse." Like her, he studied the stretch of dark water in front of them.

She snapped her head to stare at him. "A lapse?"

"In judgment." Quinn buttoned his coat and faced her. "What took place yesterday was a result of high emotions from both parties involved. It won't happen again."

"It won't." She continued to study him.

Was that a question or an agreement? At the moment he didn't know which he preferred. "Indeed, not."

Alice lifted her hand, tipping the palm. "Perhaps it would be best if we forgot the entire incident?"

He gave a curt nod. "That would be wise given the circumstances."

"I agree." She turned away from him.

No argument. No clipped words. He pushed away from the rail. "Our first meeting of the minds."

Alice studied the toes of his boots. "It was bound to happen."

"Very well." He wished he could read her mind. Perhaps it was best he didn't know. "I've morning duties, and you have orders to report to MacTavish. I'll leave you to carry on."

"Yes. Carrying on." Alice didn't move. She murmured. Contemplative. At least they're last words to one another didn't include raised voices. He should be more pleased.

"One last thing." He met her gaze over his shoulder. "Have MacTavish fit you for a weapon."

Chapter 9

Gavin had not exaggerated about Master Gunner, Malcolm MacTavish. He was a beast of a man. Not overly tall but broad as a barn with legs as thick as tree trunks poking bare from beneath a wool plaid. The tartan must have been a bright red before it saw most of its days in the company of black powder. It swept up over one shoulder of a loose, collarless shirt. His sleeves were rolled back past his elbows showing forearms carved from stone and larger than her thighs.

"Excuse me, MacTavish?"

"Blast." He startled and spun on her holding a short knife. When he saw her, he made a face as if he'd been given something sour. "Aw, now what do I need with the likes of ye, I ask ya? Have ye lost yer way, lass?" He pointed to the table with his knife. "Ye should ney be sneakin' up on a soul workin' wit things that explode. Rid me of a year of me life." He turned back to his work. "I'm busy. Be gone wit ya."

Alice stood where she was. MacTavish turned back narrowed his gaze. "Do yer ears flap o'er? Dinna ye hear me tell ya to git?"

"The captain told me I should report to you for work."

The hulk of a man tossed down his knife and planted his hands on his hips. "Oh no, he dinna. No, he dinna. I'll snap his neck, I will. I swear. What have I done te deserve the likes of you? I won't be havin' a lass down here. Blow us all te kingdom come, ye will. No." He gave a short jerk of his head and retrieved his knife. "There, I said it. No. Ye can tell our fair-haired captain I'll have none of it." He flipped his hand toward the door. "Yer dismissed."

"What if I swear on my mother's grave I won't blow us up?" She glanced around the place. It was chaos with pots of powder and piles of all manner of things spilling into each other. Pistols sat awaiting repair, swords leaned against a whetstone. Lead shot molds and crucibles littered the far table. "Couldn't you use an extra set of hands around here?"

He snorted. "Wee lassie hands? I doubt it."

"One day," she bargained.

"No."

"Half a day."

He glared at her. Alice read the moment of silence as a good sign and kept pushing. If he wouldn't let her stay, he sure as hell wouldn't agree to give over one of his spare pistols. "Eight bells. If I don't change your mind by eight bells, I'll leave you in peace." She crossed her arms over her chest so he wouldn't see the slight tremor of her hands and stood her ground.

MacTavish narrowed his eyes and peered into her face. "Tell me, have ye a bit of brain behind them bonnie green eyes of yers?"

She met his stare. "I think so."

"Ken ye be readin' a scale?"

"Yes." She didn't dare blink.

He grunted and indicated a pile of cloth with the tip of his blade. "See 'em squares of cloth?" She nodded and he pointed again. "Put two grams of that powder there onto each square and tie the corners snug."

"The black powder?"

"Nay. The gray powder. Dinna ya see me pointin'? If yer not gonna pay attention...."

Alice raised her hands in surrender. "Two grams. I got it."

"Aye, and not a mite over."

"Aye, aye." She nodded and grinned.

"Don't ye be 'aye, aying' me lass. I ain't yer captain. Quit yer sass and git workin'."

Alice set to measuring out the appropriate amount of powder until she had exhausted the small pile of linen squares. MacTavish spoke not a word, but he'd glance in her direction every few minutes, gave a satisfied "humpf," and return to his work.

She'd finished by the ringing of the noon bells, and had tidied the area where she'd worked. By the eighth bell, she'd stopped and stood waiting for his decision.

MacTavish moved past her to the small pile of powder sacks. He plucked half a dozen and checked each in turn on the scale. "Come back after yer noon meal 'n I'll give ye more te do."

"You'll not be sorry."

"I'm already sorry. Git away 'fore I change me mind."

Alice brushed the remains of soot and powder from her clothing and moved away from the ship's magazine.

She soon found herself standing back in the same spot she'd stood the day before. After she and Gavin's "lapse." She skimmed her fingertips over her lips. Yesterday they'd tingled. Alice had never been *lapsed* quite like that before. It had been her suggestion they forget it happened, but she wouldn't forget.

They'd been angry at one another, and in the next instant, his mouth had crushed down upon hers. It was nothing like the slow, languid promise of the kiss in her dreams. It was as if he'd touched a flame to black power. The instant flare had rocked her to the soles of her boots. No, she'd never forget.

Alice took a deep breath. She regretted nothing except running from Gavin's quarters like a frightened rabbit. All night long she'd imagined the scenario of what might have happened had she stayed. Kissed him again. Would he still consider the knee-melting embrace to be a momentary slip of his resolve?

What did it matter? It happened, it didn't happen. Their kiss was water past the hull. Gavin didn't want an encore. He made that fact clearer than fine glassware. And she had stood in the bow at dawn and agreed. Brushed it away as if it meant nothing to her.

She was here to get a book. Not anything more. So why did her stomach feel as if she'd swallowed a jar of sparrows? *Stop being foolish and knock on the door.*

"Come." Gavin sat at his desk bent over a ledger. Hair queued, stock in place. Not an unstarched wrinkle. He didn't look up when she entered.

"You're busy. I can come back."

"No." He rubbed a hand over his eyes. "I've tallied this column four times, and I've come up with four different totals."

Small chests of coins sat open on his desk. Another held gold and silver chains, jewels. She picked up a stunning emerald-and-gold necklace and admired it in the light. The stones were clear and bright and nested in a filigree of solid gold. "What a beautiful piece. There must be a most unhappy queen somewhere. She's been stripped clean."

Opening the collar of her shirt, she laid the piece to her neck. "Can't you imagine her? Velvet gown and satin slippers, with her hair piled high on her head." She moved to Gavin's small shaving mirror, and tried to see how it looked. "What do you think?" She swept the braid of her hair and twisted it up. "Does it suit me?"

Gavin didn't answer; he watched as her fingers stroked the face of the largest gem. He cleared his throat and looked away. "Aye. It suits you." He shifted in his seat and concentrated on his tallies.

The way he'd stared made Alice suddenly self-conscious and foolish. She would never be the kind of woman to wear such a costly piece of jewelry. Returning the necklace to the desk, she laid it back exactly as it had been. "No wonder the Spanish crew fought so hard." Her hand swept the cache. "All this must be worth a fortune."

"Unfortunately for them, the queen will never get the chance to get it back. We'll sell the gems, melt down the gold. We don't see beauty past what its worth. We're thieves." Gavin gestured toward the built in cabinet along the back left wall. "You're here for a book. I warned you, however, I can't imagine books of sea routes and battle accounts will interest you." He indicated a flat-topped chest with brass latches. "The Spanish books are there. Useless if you don't speak the language, I'm afraid. You're free to read whatever you can find."

She opened the hutch doors. The familiar smell of fine leather, paper, and ink made her smile. "It will be wonderful to have something to read." She ran her finger along the spines reading the titles. *Pilgrims. Navigations. Seafaring Prose?* She slipped the slim volume from its place. "I didn't image you fancied prose."

Alice traced the title pressed in gold upon the leather cover before lifting it to her nose and breathing deep. She loved the perfume of fine books. "Captain?"

Gavin watched her with an odd look upon his face. "I'm sorry. I...my mind must still be on my ledgers. Did you ask me something?"

"You fancy prose?" She held up the book for him to see.

"I don't recall seeing that before."

"It was hiding amongst your naval strategies. A rose amongst the thorns."

"Hidden treasure." His eyes held hers for a long moment before he looked away. "You should keep it."

Alice caught something in his tone. He'd been acting strangely since she tried on the emeralds. Hidden treasure? Were they still talking about the book? "Don't you want it?"

Gavin shook his head and kept working. "It doesn't belong on a ship like this. Amongst a crew of castoffs and freebooters. It should know a life of quiet civility." His voice was clipped and cool. "Take it with you."

Alice stared down at the book in her hands. No, they were not talking about the book anymore. All her fears, all the uncertainty crowded in on her. "What if a life of quiet civility isn't the place for it either? Perhaps its destiny is to be here on your shelf where you can find it whenever you wish. It would be wrong to cast it aside before you've learned to appreciate it. You might regret such a hasty decision."

"It doesn't belong." Gavin didn't raise his head or even glance in her direction. His words hung in the air like smoke after a cannon blast.

Alice blinked away the sudden blur of tears and cleared the catch in her throat. "No, I suppose not. You're right, it has no place here." She held the book to her heart and closed the hutch. "I've kept you from your work long enough. Perhaps I could look over the Spanish books another time. I'll stow this treasure in my quarters and return to my duties. Thank you."

She had to leave before she said or did something she'd regret. But he spoke the minute her hand touched the latch. "How are you getting along with MacTavish?"

Alice closed her eyes. *MacTavish*? Did he want to completely humble her today? "I've convinced him I'll not blow us all to our deaths. I warn you, though, he's none too happy with you for sending an unwanted lassie into his lair."

"He'll come to appreciate my decision."

The muscle in her jaw ticked. "And perhaps he and I will become the best of friends. Braid each other's hair over a few pints of ale. Trade recipes. He's sure to share all his secrets with me." She stopped.

The rush of sarcasm wouldn't lift the sudden heaviness of her heart. What was she thinking? Quinn was right. She didn't belong here. Like a book of prose. Or a fancy necklace. She couldn't be melted down to become anything of worth. At least not to him. He was right. She'd never belong. So they shared a kiss. One angry kiss. She was foolish if she believed it meant anything else, or made any difference.

Alice opened the door and didn't look back. "I'll bet MacTavish doesn't fancy prose, either."

* * * *

Returning to the magazine, Alice buried herself in clearing the space, and worked to tidy several corners. The tangle of swords was a melee of sizes and styles. Rapiers, sabers, cutlasses. She'd observed the gathering of swords and all other weapons after a battle. She lifted a beautiful sword with an elegant basket grip. It strained the muscles in her arm to raise it.

"Yer not fit for a hanger. The blade's too long fer ye." MacTavish returned still drinkin' his noon ration of ale.

"What would you suggest?"

"I'd suggest ye git out of me armory, but seein' I'm stuck wit ye...." He rummaged through a back corner and pulled out an oilskin-wrapped bundle. "A shorter boardin' blade be what ye need." He handed her a gleaming sword, its blade sharp and oiled. The brass guard finely etched with what looked like a monogram.

Alice ran her finger over the lettering. "What does this stand for?"

"J. A. S." MacTavish sat on a short barrel and rested his mug on a bare knee. "Been told the tale of how ye survived weeks of torture an' dragged yerself from the bottom of the sea to save Captain Jaxon Steele, och, pardon, *Lord* Steele and his wife from the hands of a murderous duke. You emptied three of yer pistols into the man, but he kept coming at ye weldin' a dagger. Then ye dodged the slice of his blade and took off his head with one swing of yer cutlass. An' while his head was rolling around the floor still hollering that he was gonna kill ye, he walked another eight steps before falling into a pool of his own blood 'n expirin'."

"That's the tale they're telling?"

"White told me. Says ye come screamin' in like a banshee an' rushed into the fight seconds before the madman was to cut Steele's heart from his chest."

Alice shook her head. "White exaggerates."

"It's what Robbins said. Claims *he* saw the duke's head and it was still attached. Mostly."

Alice dropped onto a low stool and covered her eyes. No wonder they're making up songs. They've worked the truth into a tale as tall as the mast. If she denied it, would MacTavish even believe her? She didn't want to call out White as a complete liar. The others must realize the story had been embellished.

MacTavish jerked his chin in the direction of the sword. "J. A. S. Jaxon, whate're be his middle name, Steele. Only fittin' ye have one of his blades."

Alice cradled the sword in her lap. "The A. stands for Alexander." She should set them all straight, tell them the truth, but what purpose would it serve to spend her remaining time on board defending and denying what happened in that cave on Port Royal.

Yes, she'd shot the duke. Once. After the gun she'd raised had practically shaken from her grip and only after she'd wiped the terrified tears from her eyes. She could barely recall squeezing the trigger. Her aim was to shoot him in the leg. It hit his shoulder and spun him around. The shot didn't kill Duke Wolfsan, true, but it brought him to his knees. Wolfsan hadn't been about to cut Jaxon's heart from his chest. He'd been about to rape Annalise while he forced Jaxon to watch, however.

Everyone believed she'd saved them. Truth was, Jaxon had freed himself from the ropes binding him. He could have fought Wolfsan himself even if Alice hadn't shown up when she did. She was no hero. How she hated that word. She was a murderer.

At least the tale had been true in one thing. Killing Benedict Wolfsan wasn't something she had to do; it had been her choice. From some cold, dark place within her, she decided the man had to die, and she wrestled a cutlass from its scabbard and charged the man with it raised over her head to do just that.

She could still feel the force of the impact when the blade met the side of the man's neck. It reverberated up her arms. Where had she found the strength to inflict such a blow? Blood sprayed across her body. Hot across her cheek. She remembered the smell and how dark it was. It stained her clothes, her hands, her soul. That instant had altered the path of her life forever.

This sword would be a constant reminder, but wasn't it better to face the memories rather than bury them and live in fear of them? It was time she accepted there were things she couldn't change. "I'd be proud to carry Jaxon Steele's blade."

Let White and the others have their tale. Let Gavin convince himself there was nothing between them, that the passionate kiss they shared was an accidental slip of the tongue. She was strong enough to know the truth.

Alice held up the blade so it caught the light. It felt good in her hand. She tested the swing and looked to MacTavish. "Could you choose a pistol for me, as well?"

Chapter 10

The rest of the afternoon, MacTavish's grumbling had given way to a grudging respect. True or not, he believed enough of the story to bear her presence in his armory. She'd spent the rest of their day loading black powder into the cloth sacks the powder monkeys ran to each cannon during a skirmish.

MacTavish had even taught her how to prepare a proper slow match. He'd only cursed at her twice. As they both emerged on deck after six bells, however, MacTavish cursed again.

"Dammit, we be in for a time of it." He turned on his heel and headed back.

"What are you talking about?"

"Pay attention, lass." He pointed to the rush among the crew. Even though the winds and the sea were calm, everything on deck was being lashed down. "Now be looking off the starboard. See the color of the sky? Got one hell of a storm droppin' in on us, and it be comin' fast and hard. Follow me. No time to be jawin'. We got powder to cover and barrels to secure."

After tying everything to the spars of the ship and making sure all the precious powder was covered tight, Alice and MacTavish struggled against the growing pitch of the *Scarlet Night* and made their way to the upper deck.

The winds had risen. Waves crashed over the bow. Orders shouted from man to man as the crew scrambling to clear the decks and secure the sails. Day had turned to night as the fierce storm bore down upon them. Lightening split the sky. Rain and seawater seemed to come from every direction at once. MacTavish shouted for her to get herself below and buckle in for a wild night.

Alice headed toward the forward ladder. She clung to the ropes to keep her footing and not be tossed out into the churning sea. The sails had been lowered and lashed except for the top mainsail. A handful of men gathered below struggling with the ropes and riggings.

The *Scarlet Night* fell into a deep trough and Alice soon found herself grabbing for the first solid thing she could reach. Jessup.

"Tupper, there ye be. Been lookin' fer ya. Need ye climb up an' free up the buntline."

"What? Climb the rigging?"

He pointed straight up and shouted into her ear. "The buntline. It be snagged on the end of the yardarm and ye gotta release it or the ship be fittin' te roll in these winds."

Panic made her voice catch. "M-me?"

He narrowed his eyes at her and sneered. Rain plastered his hair to his skull. "Ye thinkin' ye be part of this 'ere crew, ain't ya? Every man's gotta climb the riggin'. Every woman, too. Now, climb. That be an order." He grabbed her arm and shoved her toward the climbing ropes.

A howl of wind whipped the words from his mouth but she saw clearly, "Now."

Alice looked up the tall rigging and saw the tangled rope on the topsail flapping wildly at the top of the mast. It looked miles away and on a beautiful calm day, it would have been a frightening prospect of climbing to such a height, but in the middle of a storm? She shot Jessup another questioning look. The smirk upon his face told her all she needed to know. He knew she wouldn't do it. Counting on it, he'd crow for weeks if she refused.

Alice glared at him, handed him her sodden hat and bent to remove her boots. Swallowing her fear, she started to climb, concentrating on the thick rope before her. One hand, one foot, she made her way up the wet, slick lines.

"Don't look down, don't look down," she chanted.

A gust tipped the ship and she lost her footing. She let out a scream and clung to the ladder with all her strength. After what seemed like a week, she somehow regained her hold.

Alice ignored her own strict orders and looked down. More crewmembers had gathered to watch her kill herself. Finch and Summer started after her, but Jessup pulled them down.

Screwing her eyes shut, she fought the nausea and paralyzing fear. Damn her stubborn pride. Damn Jessup. There was no turning back. The sooner she got up there, the sooner she could use her shiny new pistol and shoot him.

One hand, one foot. The next few yards were done in a surreal slow motion. Each blow of the wind, each wave crashing over the decks filled her with a fresh terror. And the hardest part was yet to come. If she lived to reach the topsail, she'd need to crawl out across the yardarm to slip the tangled rope off the end.

The storm surged. Wind howled in her ears like a caged beast. The muscles in her arms and legs burned. But from somewhere a renewed sense of panic mixed with a rush of irrational, insane determination. Alice climbed the remaining distance and swung her leg over the yard.

Laying her body along the ridge of the pole, she crept inch by painstaking inch along its length clinging to any hold she could find. She shook so her teeth chattered. Each sway of the mast had her hanging on for dear life bracing for it to sway in the opposite direction. Tears, rain, and the icy spray of a furious ocean blinded her, but she dared not release her hold to wipe at her eyes. Exertion and fear had sapped her energy. The muscles in her limbs shook with the effort, but somehow she made it to the end.

Alice fought to free the tangled line. Each time the wind howled, the mast would swing, the rope would pull taut and refuse to move. She needed to time the release on the downside of each blow, but at that angle the sail would flap and the roll of the ship would threatened to toss her off.

Finally, the rope released its hold. Was that a cheer she heard from below? She wasn't about to look as she was too busy mustering enough strength and courage to get the hell down. It took a moment riding the yardarm like an unbroken horse before she gathered her will and began to back up.

* * * *

Quinn handed over the helm to the most skilled helmsman on the crew, First Mate Simons. Man was small in height, but he had arms like forged steel. Quinn set course due north hoping he'd read the sky right and they could dodge the worst of it. He needed to do a last sweep of the ship to make sure all was secure.

A small crowd of men stood at the base of the main mast. What the hell were they doing? The sail needed to drop or the mast would snap in these rising winds. Through the driving rain, he could see a man had been sent up to release the line. He couldn't make out who it was.

Moving closer, he saw Jessup in the crowd below. How many men did it take to bring in one sail? The others should be at their stations or secure below.

At last, the line had been freed and sail secured. The ship still rolled and pitched, but the release of that sail would give them a better seat through the storm. Quinn strained to see who'd been sent up. The man had balls;

he'd give him that. Not too many would risk a climb in these conditions. He watched as the seaman reached and began to descend the ladder.

Good Lord. Damn it all, that was no seaman; that was Alice!

An angry burst of wind and wave knocked her off the last few feet of rigging and she hit the deck. Hard. Quinn wasn't the only one to rush toward her, but Alice picked herself up, notched that damn chin of hers, and leveled a look of cold defiance at Jessup. She picked up her boots and the remnants of her now shapeless hat and marched past the small assembly. Summer and Finch slapped her on her back and praised her nerve. She acknowledged no one.

Quinn watched her walk away. He shot a glare back at Jessup. The man had gone too far. He'd pay for his part in this. Shouting orders for the deck to be cleared, Quinn spun on his heel to go after Alice. He had a few choice words for her as well. What was she thinking? She could have been killed. The woman's nerve needed to consult with her sense once in a while.

He closed the space between them with long practiced strides but slowed as he realized Alice was in trouble. Navigating a rolling deck, her steps faltered. She was close to the ladder way. Could she have climbed the main mast and risked her life only to fall down the steps to the deck below and break her neck?

She struggled to keep upright and reached out to grasp the knotted rope line at the top of the ladder. Gavin did not break stride as he came up behind her and caught her. Wrapping a steadying arm around her waist, he lifted her against his chest, and carried her down the stairs.

From this angle, the rest of the crew would never know their fierce, brave Tupper had fainted.

Chapter 11

The ship bucked and rolled within the storm as Gavin carried Alice back to his quarters. He had an awkward hold on her, but he didn't stop until they were within his cabin and away from prying eyes.

Entering the dark space, he lowered his sodden burden upon the bed before lighting a single lantern. The light swayed and pitched in its brass mooring, throwing odd shapes and shadows across the room.

Gavin rode the rock of the ship with his feet splayed and hands upon his hips. He fought to control his breathing as well as his emotions as they swept from anger, to fear, to relief, and back to fury. She could have been killed in a dozen horrifying ways. Fallen to the deck. Swept out to sea. Hung in the ropes. He could have lost her. The thought punched the air from his lungs.

He knelt next to the bed. The wind had torn her hair from its braid, and it obscured the view of her lovely face. He brushed the wet strands aside. She'd lost her boots and one stocking on her trip from the deck, and her clothing was soaked through. The linen of her shirt left no imaginings as to the shape and curve of her breasts.

Gavin stroked her cheek. "Alice, open your eyes." Those beautiful eyes that could be the cold green of deep ocean water or spark like those emeralds in a certain light. "Open them and glare at me. Curse me. Insult me. Dammit, save me. Save me from myself." Good God, he loved her. Like the towering waves of the storm, that thought hit him harder than the last.

The ship rose and fell as it creaked and popped against the battering of the sea. A drop into a deep wave nearly tossed her from his bed.

Her eyes opened and she frowned. "Where?"

"You're fine. You fainted."

She sighed, shook her head, and smiled. "Dreaming...." Her eyes closed again.

"Alice, this isn't a dream."

"It is." She stroked his chest. "You'll see. I'll want you to kiss me, but I'll wake up just before your lips reach mine." She lifted her hand to his cheek and opened her eyes once more. "Why are you wet?"

"Because in your dream, and I've just saved you from a storm."

Another roll of the ship caused her to grab hold of his shoulder. "Wait. The storm...this is real." Wide eyes met his.

"So is this." He lowered his mouth to hers.

Alice tightened her grip on his shirt and gasped into the kiss. She arched beneath him and he slipped an arm about her, pulling her closer, locking her to him, and steadying them against the pitch of the ship. Alice trembled in his arms. Her hold upon his shoulder released as he savored the softness of her lips. Teasing. Tasting.

Slipping her arm about his neck, Alice pressed into his embrace. When the heat of their bodies joined the dampness of their clothes, his resolve turned to steam.

Then she breathed his name. "Gavin...."

He pulled back, looking down into her beautiful face. The ship rode wildly around them, but everything seemed to slow in that fraction of time. Alice looked up at him with those emerald eyes. Her chest fusing into his with each breath.

She shook her head. Was she saying no? Gavin's heart dropped along with the *Scarlet Night* into a deep trough. A wave slammed the side of the ship. He looked away, sure she could see deep into his soul. He'd fallen again. Lost hold of his control.

"Gavin...." She still clung to him. He looked back into the smolder of those green eyes. "Don't... Don't push me away." His gaze fell to her mouth. "Please don't stop. I want you—"

His mouth crushed out any more words. Desire flashed white hot behind his eyes. He ravished her mouth. Sweeping his tongue between her lips, she moaned with pleasure and returned the deepening passion of the kiss.

Alice reached for his hand and placed it boldly upon her breast. He kissed down the side of her neck as she pressed into his hand, filling it with the round firmness of her. The tight peak of her nipple strained against the damp linen. She tugged at the ties of her blouse, but the wet material and her impatience tangled the lacings. Her groan of frustration turned into a cry of pleasure as he suckled at her breast through the fabric.

Soon the desire to run his hands over her bare skin, see her, taste her, turned desperate. He pulled the belt from her hips and tossed it to the floor. The ship rocked, and the heavy buckle raked across the floor.

Alice tugged at his hems. He struggled out of the clinging garment and let it drop. She touched him then. Stroked feather-light fingers over the planes of his chest. Brushed the flat of his nipples before rising up and laying a kiss over his heart.

Her shirt soon joined his. Followed by her single stocking and trousers. The lantern swung its light in wild swaths across her body. With her hair in disarray drying around her, the dark tresses allowed a seductive view of her breasts peeking between. She was the most beguiling creature he'd ever seen. He left her only as long as it took to remove the rest of his clothes.

The ship tipped. Alice's belt scraped across the floor to the other side of the room. When he lifted his gaze to hers, her bemused expression beguiled him. Riding the sway of the ship, he slipped in next to her and kissed the delicacy of her collarbone. "What has you so amused?"

"You." She trailed her fingers into his hair and sighed as he kissed a path along her neck. "You're different than I imagined."

"You've thought of me like this?" Gavin nipped at her earlobe as he cupped her breast in his hand.

"Yes. No. I'm afraid I underestimated the size…of…of your shoulders."

"Did you?"

Her gaze dipped lower before Alice ran a hand up his arm. "Yes, I didn't give your *shoulders* their proper justice at all."

He eased her onto her back. Taking his time to memorize each view as the lantern made its sweep. "And here you are as lovely as I thought you'd be."

"You've thought of me?"

He kissed her before answering. "Daily."

"In your bed?" she sighed.

"Nightly," he whispered as he traced a path along the soft valley between her breasts.

Her breath caught as he skimmed her belly. "Imagined what you'd do with me?"

"Hourly," he growled. His hand slid over her hip and down the length of her smoothing the roundness of her behind and urging her to raise one knee to rest high along his waist. He watched her face. Pleasure closed her eyes as she arched into his touches. "I imagined this." He lowered his head and pulled her taut nipple into his mouth as his hand continue to play over the ridges of her ribs and splay across the flat of her stomach. He kissed his way to lavish equal attention to Alice's other breast.

He rose to kiss once more at the pulse point of her throat and just below her ear as his hand slipped lower. "And this…."

The hardness of his cock played havoc with his patience. It pulsed against her hip. Wet heat bathed his fingers as he slid them between the slick folds of her sex. Beneath him, Alice gasped with pleasure and clutched at his arms, her nails raked his back.

Never had a woman responded to him quite like her. She whimpered her eagerness and cried out to him once more not to stop. She opened her thighs wider and raised her hips to meet his touch as he teased and stroked the satined flesh.

The storm that raged around them was nothing compared to the storm raging within him. Blind desire drove him. He needed to be in her. Feel the heat of her surrounding him. Bury himself within her and end this torture. Find his release before he exploded.

Gavin moved between her thighs. He could wait no longer and pushed into her with one strong thrust, tearing through the thin barrier of her maidenhead before he even realized what the slight resistance could be. The tightness of her and her sharp cry of pain brought the shattering truth to his passion-fogged mind. *Virgin? Alice was a virgin.*

He froze within her, afraid to move and cause her more pain. His body screamed, fit to burst. Her nails bit into his arms.

"Oh dear God. I didn't know." Panting, he struggled to make sense of it. He peered into her anguished face. Tears ran into her hair. What had he done?

Shaken, he began to pull away, but she clung to him. "No. It's all right. I'm...all right. Please." She pulled him to her and kissed him, held his face in her hands. "I want this. I wanted it to be you." She kissed his neck and slipped her arms about him holding tight. "Please."

Alice began to move beneath him. She gave a small lift to her hips. Gavin groaned as his still-hard cock ached for his release. He pressed back into her. Gently. He kept the rhythm slow, rocking with the sway of the ship. His strokes grew stronger, deeper, faster.

Alice cried out again. This time it was one of surrender, one of passion. She tightened around him as his own body spiraled out of control. The years of denying his needs rose and crashed like the waves upon the hull. His last thrusts sank as deep as her body would allow before he found his release.

When it was over, he pulled out of her and left the bed. He found his pants in the shifting light and donned them before his breathing had returned to normal. Anger followed so quickly, he had doubts his breathing would ever be normal again. The ship still fought through rough seas, but experience told him the storm outside was beginning to ebb—the one within him, however, was far from finished. He secured the last button on his breeches and turned on her.

She sat in the middle of his bed looking every bit a ravished woman. Hair loose and mussed, lips swollen and pink, a rosy blush across her skin. She clutched a blanket to her chest. One perfect breast escaping cover.

"Where are you going?"

"Why? Why didn't you tell me you were a virgin?" He shoved his feet into his boots.

"I didn't think it mattered—"

"It mattered to me." Gavin stood with his hands on his hips. Blood still pulsed through his limbs. His cock. God help him, he couldn't look at her without wanting her again. What was wrong with him? How could he be incensed and drawn to her in the same breath? Because it did matter to him. *She* mattered to him.

He'd been selfish. His body had been in control tonight, and he'd carelessly taken her virtue. If this insanity continued, it would only be a matter of time before he planted a bastard in her if he hadn't already. A fine new life he'd condemn her to. He'd done enough damage. This had to stop. Now. It had already gone too far. He hung his head and watched as the heavy buckle of her belt made another slide across the room.

Gavin stepped on the belt's tail, bent, and gathered her sodden clothes. "Get dressed and get out." He threw them on the bed before grabbing his shirt and coat. "I want you gone before I get back."

Chapter 12

The door slammed behind Gavin. What happened? One minute he was kissing her throat and positioning himself between her thighs, and the next he was hurling her clothes at her and ordering her out. Out of the room. Out of his bed.

Confusion had Alice staring at the back of the door. He couldn't have left like that. He'd get two paces down the galley way and realize he'd made a mistake and he'd be back.

As the seconds ticked by, the sting of his rejection burned deeper. Alice covered her face with her hands. She could still sense him, touching her breasts, stroking her, filling her. Her body pulsed with the pleasured ache of knowing a man. So this is what all the fuss was about.

Part of her was grateful. Gavin, being more experienced, obviously knew how to please a woman. Alice sighed. The way her body reacted to a swirl here, a kiss there. With each caress, tiny sparks of light danced upon her skin. When his hand slipped lower and his fingers moved upon the sensitive flesh between her thighs, she never imagined anything could feel like that.

The pain of his first thrust didn't surprise her. She'd heard from enough women to know what to expect, but what happened after the initial pain lost its burn had been stunning. The power of him. His strength. The smell of his skin. His...*shoulders*.

But now, throwing her clothing at her. He'd changed her feelings of pleasure to ones of guilt. She felt shamed, used, dirty.

Alice moved off the tangled bed and started to dress. Her clothes were cold and damp as if they held Gavin's icy rejection in the weave of the fabric. She shivered into them, sliding the trousers over the new tenderness of her body. Where were her boots? She clutched one sock in her hand. The other had to be in this room, but searching was to no avail.

She had them when she marched past Jessup. Alice dropped back onto the side of the bed remembering the terrifying event. She'd climbed the bloody mast. It must be her night to soar to new heights only to fall hard to the deck when it was over. Alice gave a bitter laugh and swallowed the sudden lump in her throat. Scanning the room again, it still didn't answer the question of her boots.

Well, she wasn't going to sit here any longer. At the door, she gave a final look about. The room was as it had always been. Neat, tidy. Except for Gavin's bed.

Alice eased her way into the hall. The storm had quieted, and she didn't want to announce to anyone below decks where she had spent her time. The latch closed with a soft *click*, and she paused and dropped her forehead to the rough boards of the door. Why did this cut so deep. How could she let herself care so much? *Stand up and gather your self-respect if not your damn boots, Alice Louise Tupper. It was nothing to him. Damn it. Move. Do not cry.*

She sucked in a deep breath and pushed away from the door. Turning in the direction of her bunk, she saw him. *Jessup.* His dark eyes narrowed at her before doing a slow appraisal of her. A smile curled one side of his mouth as he looked from her to Gavin's door and back.

Could this night get anymore humiliating? Notching her chin, she put one bare foot in front of the other and moved to pass him.

He muttered low as she made her way past, "Whore."

Alice forced herself not to break stride. Never stumbled. Behind her Jessup laughed. The grating of it echoed in her ears until she reached her quarters and locked the door behind her.

Jessup? Why couldn't it have been anyone else? By morning, the entire crew would have heard how she rode out the storm in Gavin's bed. Or would he keep his mouth shut for fear of Gavin's retaliation? Jessup couldn't know Gavin tossed her out. How long before he figured out his captain's whore wasn't even that? Swimming to Virginia might yet be an option.

Lighting her lantern, Alice choked back a sob. Her boots, tall, polished, and proud, stood next to her cot. They'd been shined and buffed to a soft glow. Her lost sock, neatly folded, hung over the top of one. Had her heart not been carved into neat slices, she could almost laugh at the bitter truth. He cared more for her footwear. "Damn you, Gavin Quinn. I'll never be able to put on another stocking without thinking of you, you b-bastard."

It was then she caught sight of Bump curled up under her cot. Alice crouched down and laid a hand on his arm. Wide, dark eyes met hers. "What are you doing under there?" As he crawled out from under the bed, Alice saw the gash under his eyebrow. Dried blood crusted on his cheek and stained his clothes. She reached out to him. "Oh, Bump."

Setting him on the cot, she soaked the washing cloth with the last of her water and began washing away the blood. "It doesn't look too bad." She knelt and laid the cool cloth on the lump. "How long have you been hiding here?" Lifting the cloth, Alice surveyed the damage. "Don't think you'll need to have the surgeon stitch you up." She wiped his face and gave him a reassuring smile. "You'll live."

Bump slid off the edge of the cot and laid his head on her shoulder. Pulling the child into her arms, he jerked as she tightened her embrace and scrambled away. Alice's already bruised heart ached for him. "I promise I would never hurt you."

Alice shifted to sit upon the floor and held her arms wide. He eyed her warily but after a long moment of hesitation, he curled into her lap and rested against her. She didn't try to hold him, but began to stroke his back. "My poor babe." Setting her chin on the top of his head, she sighed. The gentle magic of the child's weight leaning against her began to heal her heart. "Whatever you do, sweet one, don't tell Captain Quinn we coddled."

She closed her eyes and began to hum.

* * * *

Alice reported early for duty in the magazine. Damage from the storm was minimal due to their hasty precautions. MacTavish marched in and stared her down.

He crossed burly arms over his barrel of a chest. "I know what ye done last night."

Alice went still and swallowed hard. How could he know? Did it show? An old cook back in Weatherington used to say she could see the look in her maid's eyes when they'd been lifting their skirts to the grooms in the barn. Said it was like they wore a flag of their sins across their face. Now that she thought about it, the old cook did look a bit like MacTavish. Chin whiskers and all. "What are you talking about?"

"In that cocka of a storm." He shook a thick finger at her. "Don't be playin' coy wit me. I ken all about it."

She turned her back on him. "I don't know what you're going on about. Can we please work?" Maybe she could distract him. "Tell me how you make red smoke."

"Nice try, Lassie."

Alice shot a glance over her shoulder. Fine. If MacTavish knew about her night with Gavin, then the whole crew had been told. She might as well face it. "Damn, Jessup," she mumbled.

"If'n it be any comfort, Jessup'll be getting his."

She knitted her brows. "Not from me, he won't."

"He did ye wrong. Makin' ye climb the riggin'. Crew's not takin' that light."

Relief washed over her. "Oh, *that*."

"Yer daft as a hatter, but I got te be handin' it to ya. Took some stones, it did, gettin' up there in those seas." He tipped his head and narrowed his gaze. "Was there some other foolishness happen in the storm?"

Heat flared in her cheeks. "Of course not."

MacTavish raised a shrewd eyebrow. Alice looked away. "I'd prefer to forget last night ever happened."

"Ye keep actin' like this, ye're gonna make a name fer yerself."

"Oh, I know the name," she mumbled remembering Jessup's parting word.

"Might just earn the right te learn me secrets, ye keep it up."

Alice smirked. Jessup was most likely spreading her secret all over the ship. "It was a one-time thing. A mistake I won't be foolish enough to repeat."

Neo ducked into the armory. "Tupper, on deck."

"Why?"

"Capt'n's order."

As Alice followed the wide back of Neo topside, she worked on keeping her emotions in check. She didn't want to see Gavin and couldn't let him see how much he'd hurt her.

Ahead, a group gathered at the base of the main mast. Gavin's bright hair was a beacon in the sunlight. Alice looked away. Beside him, stood Jessup. His hands were bound, but he spat on the deck boards as she approached.

"Tupper," Gavin began. Alice studied the stock about his neck. If she looked into his eyes... He continued. "It's been decided amongst the crew. A great wrong was committed against you last night." Around him, several men muttered their agreement. "It falls to you as an honorary member of this crew to levy the punishment against the guilty man."

A great wrong. A great wrong. The words followed one another around and around in her mind. She closed her eyes and gave her head a quick shake. "I don't understand."

"Jessup did ye dirty, Tupper," cried Finch. "Ye 'ave te say what his punishment be."

She looked at Finch in disbelief. "Why me?"

Alice could feel Gavin's gaze upon her. "You're to impose his penalty."

Jessup glared at her. She saw the muscle jump along his jaw. When she met his stare, the corner of his mouth tipped in a knowing sneer. If she called him out for what he'd done, he'd tell everyone she was a whore and drag her into the muck right along with him. It would be the only way he'd save face among the crew. There was only one other solution.

"I hold no ill will toward Mister Jessup."

"Tupper, he could'a killed ya," Robbins sputtered.

"But he didn't. I was asked to do what any other seaman on this ship would have been asked. There was no wrong done to me." Alice risked a quick glance in Gavin's direction. "Not by Mister Jessup. He should be released."

Jessup's glower grew darker at her absolution. She had him, and by the murderous look in his eye, he knew it too. If he said anything about her and Gavin now, it would appear he was concocting stories to justify what he'd done. No one would believe him. She'd outsmarted him. Disgraced him in front of the crew. In front of his followers. If she hadn't been an enemy before, she was now. "If that's all, I'd like to return to my duties."

Alice didn't wait to be dismissed, but as she attempted to leave, Gavin stopped her.

"If that's your final say."

She replied to the toes of his boots. "It is."

"Then so be it, but as captain of this ship, I charge First Mate Jessup with endangering a member of this crew, thereby putting the ship and the rest of the crewmembers at risk. Mister Jessup, you are hereby on half rations for the next fortnight."

Jessup's glare turned black with rage. As she walked away, she could almost feel the heat of his fury burning into her back.

Returning to the armory, MacTavish handed her a beautifully carved baldric of thick black leather. "Sharpened the blade there and shortened up the belt te fit."

Jaxon Steele's sword sat in a matching tooled scabbard tipped in silver, which hung off the wide strap. And the pistol MacTavish chose for her sat clean, oiled, and snug in its holster.

"You made this for me?"

"Were ye plannin' te carry yer weapons in yer pocket?" He narrowed his eyes at her. "Now don't be gettin' all soft on me. Just take it."

Alice slipped it over her head. The position of the sword and gun were easily within reach. She pulled the pistol, and pointed it at the door.

Not too heavy. It fit her hand perfectly. As though the two were destined for one another.

Closing one eye, she aimed for a knothole in the door. "Teach me to load."

Chapter 13

Gavin's watchful gaze followed Alice as she moved through the crowd. Back straight, her hips with their easy sway. She hadn't looked at him. Not in the eye at least.

He wasn't the only one watching her leave. Jessup's growing hatred toward her had increased tenfold. The man should be grateful. Were it up to Gavin, he'd be dragging him across the keel this morning. Alice's actions had only endeared her to the rest of the crew once more. They'd watch for any retaliation from Jessup and stop him. They were quickly becoming her champions. Next, they'd be voting her captain.

When he'd returned to his cabin last night, the sight of his rumpled bed cut him deeper than any blade. The perfume of her skin clung to the sheets making his body hard for her all over again. He'd spent hours navigating the *Scarlet Night* through the last of the storm reliving each torturous touch in his mind. Every caress. The taste of her skin. He wanted to go to her, beg forgiveness, and sweep her back into his arms. His hunger for her had only increased.

But then he had seen the blood. The proof of her virginity there on his bedding. Guilt and anger gnawed at him. If Alice was playing some sort of a game, it was a dangerous one. One that could only end badly. First climbing the bloody mast in the middle of a rage, then giving herself over to him without a word and with no thought to what lying with him had done to her future. They were both mad.

It had to stop. Now. As difficult as it was, he needed to speak with her. Opening the door to the magazine, he stared down the barrel of a pistol. "Were you expecting me?"

Alice lowered the weapon and looked away. "If I were, the gun would be loaded."

Behind her MacTavish snorted. Gavin grabbed her elbow. "We have unfinished business, you and I."

"I'm on duty."

He steered her toward the door. "Not until we settle things." He kept a firm pressure on her arm moving her through the crowded decks.

"Where are you taking me?"

"My quarters."

Alice tried to jerk away from him and pulled them both to a stop. "Say what you have to say."

He snapped. "My quarters."

She looked him in the eye. First in anger. Then something else flitted across her face. Was it fear? Regret? Hurt? It caught him like a blow to the gut. "My quarters," he insisted in a gentler tone.

* * * *

The bed was made. Gavin's cabin was once again pristine as if last night never occurred. The door closed behind her, but she couldn't face him. Was it his goal to humiliate her more than he already had? Unfinished business? What more could he want?

Behind her, Gavin gave a short sigh. "We need to discuss last night."

Alice continued to stare at the bed until she closed her eyes against the images already burned into her memory. Crossing her arms over her chest, she dropped her chin.

Gavin continued. "Why didn't you tell me you were an innocent?"

"I'm hardly innocent."

"I took something I had no right to take."

She lifted a shoulder. "You are a pirate. Isn't that what you do?"

Gavin grabbed her arm and spun her around. "Don't be glib, woman."

"I'm glad to be rid of it." Alice pulled out of his grasp and crossed to the windows to concentrate on the ship's wide wake.

"How can you say that?"

Her patience snapped and she spun on him. "What did you expect of me last night?"

"Not to discover you were a virgin." He threw his hands wide.

Alice planted her hands on her hips. "Why? Do you think I frequent men's beds?"

"No, of course not. I thought… I assumed. You'd been a prisoner of the Duke of Wentworth. Wolfsan had a vile reputation. He left a trail of destroyed, dead women in his path."

She nodded. "You thought he raped me?"

Gavin clamped his jaw and let out a long breath. "Yes."

Anger flared. Would Wolfsan's stain upon her ever be gone? Would she fight it forever? Her breathing hiked. To link what she survived with the duke to what happened with Gavin made her ill. "He tried. There's a scar on my thigh. Here." She lifted a knee and showed him the position of the slivered line that was a constant reminder of her time with Wolfsan. "This is as far as he got. He preferred torture to foreplay and started to monogram me by carving his initials into my skin." She jerked at the neck of her shirt and tipped her head. A thin line marked her throat. "This is his work as well." She straightened her collar. "Needless to say, I killed him before he got the chance to finish what he started."

"And you survived the crew of the *Delmar*?"

"I lied, vomited, kicked. I shot one, stabbed another. Had you not shown up when you did, my *precious* virtue wouldn't have lasted another hour."

"What happens when you begin life in Virginia? When a man wants you for his wife?"

Alice gave a bitter laugh. "I have no such illusions. If, by chance, there was a man who wanted to wed me, hearing my story he'd assume as you did. But the fact I killed my attackers would no doubt disturb him far more than the absence of my maidenhood." She went back to staring out the windows. "I can't see what difference it makes to you. I won't demand you marry me if that's what you fear." Alice turned to face him. She met his gaze. "Last night…was nothing." The lie turned to dust on her tongue. "Another lapse in judgment."

His head jerked back as her words struck. It should have made her feel victorious to give back some of the hurt he'd given her last night, but it didn't. It only hurt her more. Made her hollow inside. When had she become so hard? Where had she learned how to wield her tongue with the same force as her sword? She was beginning to hate the woman she had become.

Gavin pulled a bottle of brandy from his desk and poured himself a drink. Tossing it back, he grimaced at the bite of the liquor and leveled a dark glare at her.

"Was it yet another lapse in judgment when you decided to climb the mainsail in a full gale?" He took another drink and waved the glass at her. "I see you found your boots. Do you recall how you lost them? Or how you ended up in my bed?"

"No, I—"

"After your stunt—"

"Stunt?"

"You notched that damn chin of yours, glared at Jessup and proceeded to faint at the top of the ladder way. I caught you about the waist and carried you. No one knows you didn't walk down those stairs on your own."

Alice twisted at her ring. "Then I should thank you for saving more than my neck. All I'd gained in climbing the rigging would have been lost had they seen me collapse."

Gavin slammed down his glass. "Gained? Are you insane? Whatever possessed you? You could've been swept out to sea or thrown to your death."

"I was ordered," she shot back.

"By Jessup. I'd be striping his back right now had you not stopped me."

Alice threw up her hands. "I couldn't refuse. No other member of your crew would have been given that option."

The muscle in his jaw pulsed. "It's not the same thing, and you know it."

"Jessup has hated me since I arrived. He has no loyalty to Captain Steele. He doesn't care who I am. I'm a cursed woman aboard this ship. I silenced him and put an end to it. I'll continue to do whatever necessary to survive until I can reach Virginia." Alice understood his anger, but she was alone in this. She'd fought Wolfsan alone. Boarded the *Pennington* alone. The decisions were hers, as well as the consequences. Stopping Jessup's reign of abuses had been her battle, not Gavin's.

"Everything I did last night was to secure my place on this ship."

Gavin's head snapped up. "Does that include warming my bed?"

Alice was unprepared for the blow mere words could inflict. "You twisted my words." Past the pain, a deep sadness engulfed her and threatened to drown her. Any hope she had clung to regarding his caring for her were dashed. She swung back. "If you'll recall, *Captain,* you were the one to carry me to your bed."

Gavin poured another drink and spoke into the glass. "You could have stopped me."

Alice closed her eyes to keep him from seeing her pain. "Could I?"

"You just finished telling me how you stopped men in the past who were much more intent upon having you than I."

Ice encased the shattered remains of her heart as she forced herself to lift her chin and look him straight in the eye. "Yes, I stopped them, and then I killed them, but none of those bastards was ever vile enough to call me a whore." Alice crossed to the door. "At least Jessup is honest in his hatred toward me. It seems my imagining about your cock wasn't the only thing I was wrong about."

Alice looked down at her chest as she made her way back to her post. Was there blood? There should be blood when someone cut out your heart.

Moving though the crowded deck, her vision blurred. Everything slowed as if she were trudging through murky water. She was numb.

Looking forward, there was sea as far as the horizon and beyond. There was nothing left to do but pray the winds held and the voyage to the new world was swift. Short of throwing herself overboard, Alice's only hope now was to survive the next few weeks and be rid of this ship and *all* who sailed upon her. She would keep to herself, work herself into exhaustion so she could sleep at night without the dreams of what would never be, and stay clear of the good captain.

She and Annalise had played a game as children. They would become invisible. Keeping out of sight and anticipating each other's moves, they stayed one step ahead of each other. Stealth was a honed gift, and she planned to use it to lose herself within this ship. It had helped when she tracked Wolfsan into Port Royal and ended him. Evading Gavin couldn't be any more difficult.

And for the next several days, it was child's play. Gavin came looking for her in the armory. Alice ducked behind a stack of crates.

"Where's Tupper?"

MacTavish shifted. "Over there... She just be there talkin' te me. Must 'ave slipped by."

From her vantage point she could see Gavin's frustration. He scanned the armory. Twice. "She came this way. I've been trying to track her down for days."

"Been here 'ard at work. Quiet mostly. Does what's asked of 'er." MacTavish stopped what he was working on and wiped his hands on his kilt. "What ya be needin'?"

Gavin rubbed at his eyes. "Nothing. Forget it."

"Then why ye lookin' fer her?" MacTavish's broad back blocked Alice from seeing his expression, but she knew the tone in his voice and could imagine the narrow-eyed glare he was famous for using.

Gavin growled and turned to leave. "I'm seeing things. Carry on."

Alice waited until Gavin closed the door and returned to her workspace. "I've finished trimming the wicks and filling the smoke pots. Aren't we casting shot today?"

MacTavish leapt from his stool. "Lassie. Scared te crap out te me. Capt'n lookin' fer ye."

Alice bit back the laugh. "Oh, sorry."

"Were ye here te whole time?" The Scotsman rubbed at his eyes. "I'm losin' me grip."

Alice patted his muscled arm. "You're fine. Should I start melting the lead?" She bit the inside of her cheek to keep from smiling. The ever-sharp MacTavish didn't miss anything.

He narrowed his eyes at her and planted his meaty fists on his hips. "What game ye be playin' at, lass?"

"Don't know what you're talking about." Alice crossed her arms over her chest and studied the toes of his worn boots.

"I ken smell it. Ye be up to somethin'."

She lifted one shoulder. "I'm doing my chores and keeping myself from trouble."

"Well, none ken fault ye fer that." He got almost nose to nose with her and stared her down. "But I smell somethin' rotten."

Alice blinked at him. "When was the last time you washed your kilt?"

* * * *

While Alice chose to evade Gavin's notice, over the last days, she gained a small shadow. One who was becoming dearer to her by the day. Bump had no trouble finding her wherever she may be. He wouldn't venture into the armory, but she had come to expect he'd be waiting for her at the end of her day. Sometimes she would find him curled up in front of her door. Other times she would be crossing the decks, and he would simply appear at her side. They shared their evening meal together. It was Alice's favorite time of day. They started off sitting in silence, but soon Alice took to telling him stories of her and Annalise's adventures when they were his age. He didn't hear a word, but it didn't matter. He would watch her and on rare occasions treat her to a tiny glimpse of a smile.

The night of the storm when she found him hiding under her cot, he had crawled into her lap, but that had been the only physical connection she'd made with the boy short of the occasional ruffle of his hair or a pat on his back. He was careful to never get closer than arm's length. His unreasonable panic at being hugged had her worried. What must his short life have been like to incite such a response?

This night, however, he wasn't waiting in his usual spot. Alice slipped into the galley and gathered bread and ale. Still she didn't see the boy. Tonight, she guessed, she'd be dining alone.

Moving into the dim below decks, she spotted him in a dark corner. His eyes were round with fear.

"There you are." It was then she noticed the hand gripping the boy's shoulder, and the knife against the boy's chest. Jessup stepped out of the shadows. Alice's blood chilled. "What the hell do you think you're doing?"

"Hard to decide which of ye needs cuttin' worse." He jerked Bump back against him and tightened his hold.

Cold fury flashed behind her eyes. "Let him go."

Jessup shook his head and pressed the blade against Bump's throat. "Done enough listenin' to ye. Ye made me the fool fer the last time. Now ye be listenin' te me."

Alice's hands were busy holding bread and ale. If she dropped them to draw her pistol, Bump would be dead before she could cock the hammer.

"Sick of hearin' about the *great* Tupper. Ye're nothin' but a fukin' slut. Makin' everyone think yer better 'an me." His voice was low and menacing. "Think I don't ken what yer doin'?"

She tried to talk him down while keeping a close watch on his knife hand. If he so much as drew a drop of that child's blood... "I'm not doing anything. I swear. Let Bump go."

Jessup went on as if she hadn't spoken. "Stood there, all high and mighty. Takin' me balls wit ya when ye strutted away like some common whore. Got the crew laughin.' They all be laughin.'"

Alice inched forward. "I want nothing to do with your balls. They wanted to flog you."

"Ye think I ain't had me back striped afore?" he spit before jerking Bump back against him again, adjusting his hold.

Each move he made caused her gut to twist. Jessup wasn't going to listen to any explanation. "Hurt the child and they'll do more than that."

He laughed. "Din ya hear? Lad slipped o'er the rail. Lost 'im we did. Couldn't even yell fer help."

Fear crept under her skin. If she could get him to loosen his hold on Bump, she could blind him with her ale.

"Then it be yer turn. I'm gonna split ye from stem te stern and feed yer heart to the sharks."

"Going to claim I slipped over the rail as well?"

"Tupper's disappeared?" He laughed. "Don't know nothin' about it." Jessup jerked his chin at her. "I been watchin.' Ye've been disappearin' all week. Think yer smart. Leadin' the capt'n around by his cock. He'll thank me."

A group of three boisterous seamen came down the ladder way. Jessup cursed under his breath and pushed Bump at her. He sneared into her face. "Don't be countin' on seein' many more days. Talk 'n ye'll not live long enough te take yer next piss. It be a mighty small ship, an' I ken all the hidin' places. Ne'er see me comin.'"

He gave her a sharp shove. Bump took off like cannon shot.

Chapter 14

Alice bided her time. There was no chance she would let Jessup's threat against her and Bump go unreported. Quinn had to know. Not for her sake, but for the boy's. She could defend herself, but Bump was helpless against Jessup's plot. He couldn't even cry out. The thought froze the blood in her veins.

Jessup was on third watch. It was her chance to slip into Gavin's quarters and wait for him to return. Entering, Alice's breath caught. His quarters were in total disarray. Clothes littered the floor, the once-clear desk lay cluttered with parchments, maps, and discarded food. The bed barely looked slept in.

What was happening? She sat behind his desk and tried to make sense of what she was seeing. She'd never known Gavin to drink anything stronger than weak ale, but the scattering of empty bottles told another tale.

A tumbled stack of yellowed letters caught her eye. Beautifully scrolled writing upon the face of the envelope captured her attention. Pale, faded brown ink read, *"My Darling, Gavin."* A deep hollowness filled her belly.

Alice lifted one of the letters, turning it over in her hand, noting the wear. With gentle care, she opened it.

Dearest Gavin,

I miss you desperately, my love, my husband. It has not been a day since you left my arms and I wonder how I will bear the long months without you. I will keep the thought of our last few blissful days within my heart. Never have known such joy and passion, my darling. I'm counting the days until we can be together again. I love you with all of my heart and soul,

Your faithful wife, Beth

A wife. Counting the days until his return. Alice's stomach twisted. Her eyes shot to the door, but fear at being caught could not stop her from reading the next letter.

Like the first, the pages were faded and worn and filled with love and longing. Beth was busy making their house a proper home for him.

Another letter contained within the beautiful faded writing the sheer joy and excitement with which she announced she was carrying their child.

Alice dropped the letter to the desk as if the words struck her. She covered her eyes. A wife and a child. She had seduced another woman's husband. Why hadn't he told her?

The question needn't be asked. The answer was clear. Like the issue of her virginity, there was no discussion before they fell into bed in a blind rush of lust. No regard for either's circumstances. They were strangers driven together by their own careless desires.

Curiosity kept her reading. Beth's touching words spoke of her growing excitement over the babe, as well as her growing waist. Her father had built a beautiful oak cradle with tiny ships carved into the wood waiting by the hearth for the baby's arrival. Just as she would be waiting for Gavin to come home to them. Beth hoped the baby would have Gavin's fair hair. If it was a boy, she hoped he would be tall and handsome like his father.

One letter was written on the day Beth first noticed the fluttered wings of movement in her womb. The words stung Alice. Envy soured in her stomach. Would she ever experience the miracle of that magic sensation? She remembered Annalise's wonder over the same thing as she carried wee James. The urge within her to carry her own child surprised her. It wasn't something she'd given much thought to before now. Pure folly to even imagine it.

Another letter dated several months later was filled with Beth's impatience. She was anxious to see her child, and eager for the return of her husband. Her words sounded angry as she lamented over her awkward bulk and sore back, and her growing resentment that Gavin was not there to share some of the burden. But the next envelope overflowed with apologies for the previous one. It burst with her unfailing understanding as to his duty's call. Spoke of her pride in him. More and more she was convinced she was carrying his son, and she wanted to pass on Gavin's strength and conviction as well as his name.

This letter like the rest ended with love and devotion and signed, *"Your Beth."*

Alice slipped the next letter from its envelope.

My love,

Your son has arrived. I fear he carries my impatient nature, as he was not due for weeks. But he already bears your adventurous spirit as he chose the height of a storm with which to make his appearance. He is tiny, but perfect, my darling. I have given him a fine, strong name. I've named him Gabriel. I cannot wait for you to come home and meet our beautiful boy. Hurry back to us, my love.

  Your Beth

He has a son. Closing her eyes, Alice could picture the babe. Cherub-faced with pale, feathery hair. Would he have Gavin's gray eyes as well? Chubby legs, dimpled hands and feet. She could imagine him toddling out to welcome Gavin home. A lump of jealousy caught in her throat. Tears pinched the backs of her eyes. She didn't think she could bear reading any more, but the dwindling pile of notes seemed odd. Only three remained. The last looked as if it had been crushed.

  She opened the next letter.

Gavin,

  I pray I find the words to write. Our Gabriel, our sweet beautiful son, has been lost to us. Three days past a fever claimed him. I never left his side, but he was so small and slight. He fought bravely, but it was all in vain as God has called our angel back to Him. I fear I shall drown in my grief. My heart lies cold in my chest, shattered into a million shards. I am so sorry. I go over each minute in my mind worrying there was something else I should have done. Something else that could have saved him. I can think of nothing save the pain I feel pulling me into its dark depths of despair. I wish I were dead as well. B.

Tears ran unchecked down Alice's cheeks as she read the words. Her heart broke for Beth, for Gavin. The poor babe. She cried for them all. Alice read the next letter through her tears. It was more heart wrenching than the last. The writing appeared shaky and spoke of the blackness of Beth's heartache. She blamed herself for the baby's death and was losing her soul to the overwhelming waves of grief and guilt.

  Only one letter remained. It didn't look like the rest. The pages were wrinkled, but were not worn like the others. The ink hadn't faded. Alice wiped her eyes and read.

My dearest Gavin,

  I can no longer bear this pain. The blackness surrounds me, engulfs me, and I cannot wipe it from my soul. I need to be with our baby. I'm his mother and it is only right I go to him and care for him and love him as I was prepared to do. I cannot live without him. I don't want to live without him. I pray you understand. You're strong and brave and I know you will survive without me. Your life is with the sea. My life is with my son. I hope when you remember me you will only feel the depth of my love for you. A love like ours can never die. I'm sorry, my darling. I know no other way out of this darkness.

Please forgive me. Beth

Alice covered her mouth as Beth's words reached eerily off the page and deep into her heart. "Oh, dear Lord, no...."

"What the bloody hell do you think you're doing?" Gavin slammed his door.

"Gavin." His anger radiated from him like the sun. Alice scrambled to replace the letter into its envelope. "I'm sorry... I came to talk to you and... I had no business—"

"Get out."

Alice was on her feet. "Please let me explain. I—"

"I don't want to hear your explanation. I want you gone."

She took a step toward him. "B-but I understand now."

"You understand *nothing.*" His hands balled into fists. The muscle in his jaw flexed. As furious as he was, she wanted nothing else than to hold him. Love him. Somehow, soothe the anger and pain he held tight.

She stood her ground and met the heat of his anger until the wash of tears distorted his image. "I-I understand why you pulled an orphaned deaf child out of the gutters of Port Royal."

Gavin's breath rushed out of his lungs as if he'd been punched. "You had no right to read those letters."

"I know. And I'm sorry. So very sorry for all of it."

"I don't need your pity." He searched through the clutter of bottles until he found one not empty and used a dirty glass from his desk to pour a drink.

"I don't pity you. I ache for you. I can't imagine your grief." Gavin had turned his back to her. Shutting her out. Pushing her away again. "I've no excuse for what I've done. I don't blame you for adding this to the long list of my offenses, but I came here to talk to you about Bump. And now I understand—"

He spun on her. "You understand nothing."

Gavin wasn't listening. She was afraid he wouldn't hear her passed his anger, but she had to try. "Jessup has threatened to kill him."

He lowered his glass and stared at her. "When? What has he done?"

"He was waiting in the shadows when I came down from the galley earlier. Holding a knife to the boy."

Gavin slammed down his glass. "I'll take care of him. I should have keel hauled the bastard when I had the chance. Now I'll just put a bullet in him."

"And hang for murdering a member of your crew in cold blood? There's no proof other than my word. Bump can't tell anyone what happened. No one else heard Jessup threaten him."

"What else did he say?"

"It's not important. What's important is that we keep an extra watch on Bump. Jessup can't have another opportunity to hurt him. The boy can't defend himself. If he was able to sneak up on him once...."

"Jessup threatened you as well, didn't he?"

Alice dropped her gaze. "I can look out for myself."

"That's not what I asked."

She met his angry stare. "I can look out for myself."

Gavin took a long moment. He turned the glass in his hand. Tipping the amber liquid to catch the light. "He would be eleven now."

"Gabriel?"

"Yes."

There hadn't been a year on his letters, only the month and day. November twelfth was the babe's birthday. "I'm so sorry, Gavin."

"It was a long time ago." He drained his glass and looked around the room as if he was just now seeing the mess he'd created.

"Eleven years, two years, I doubt if time matters. There are moments which never leave us. Define who we are. Change us forever." Alice lifted her eyes and met his. "I think we're more alike than you realize." She tidied the letters and began gathering up the empty bottles. "We're both trying to outrun our past."

"I don't see how one compares to the other."

"Perhaps they don't. But each drove us to who we are. Turned our lives into a battle to go on." Alice took a deep breath before continuing. "I killed Wolfsan. I *chose* to kill him. Not in defending myself, but because he was evil. That coldhearted act has haunted my every step since. Its mark upon my life stained my soul. I keep trying to escape the memory of that day, but I can't. All I can do is fight to survive."

"You may be fighting to survive, but I have no wish to."

"If that were true, you'd have placed yourself in front of a loaded cannon long before now." She swept her hand over the letters. "You're stronger than that." Every fiber of her being wanted to go to him and ease his pain. She loved him. Now more than ever. She understood why he continued to keep her at arm's length. It all made sense. His distance. The solid sense of duty he carried like a stone around his neck. The fierceness of him in battle. It all made perfect sense now. "None of this was your fault, Gavin. You couldn't have prevented any of this."

He held her gaze for a long moment. "Maybe not, but I can prevent what's about to happen to you. We are three days outside of reaching land. Until you are safely on shore, I have your back. Don't hide from me. And don't make me walk this ship another time looking for you, wondering if you've been killed and thrown overboard." Gavin ran his hand through his hair and retied his queue. "Bump will be watched. I'll see to it. Jessup won't get another chance to harm him. I promise."

"Thank you." She moved past him toward the door, but he caught her arm.

"Tupper." He averted his gaze. "Alice...." His voice rasped. "No one has ever read those letters other than me."

Gone was the anger. The walls had crumbled. Gavin stood there for the first time showing her the vulnerable, wounded man he had spent the last eleven years hiding. Bleeding in private. Her heart ached with the rush of sorrow. She reached out to touch him. Silently pleading for him to meet her gaze, When he did, Alice searched his beautiful eyes, willing him to know how much she respected him, and honored what he shared with Beth and their life together. If she told him she'd fallen in love with him, would he think it was out of pity?

Alice laid a hand over his heart. "I understand."

Chapter 15

Fingers of a rosy dawn trailed across the morning's sky. Gavin paced the decks keeping an eye on all the comings and goings. Alice had reported to MacTavish. He'd seen her go, and so had Jessup. The man spit in her wake and fingered the hilt of his dagger. It took everything in Gavin not to draw his pistol and shoot the bastard on the spot. Bump was with Robbins per his order, but only Gavin was watching Alice's back. If he had to wear the ruby paint from the deck boards to do so, he would.

Neo met him mid pace. "Boy's safe."

Gavin kept and eye on Jessup. "Let's keep them both safe. Once Tupper is clear of the ship, Jessup will have no use to make Bump his pawn, but until then."

"Man won't scratch his balls without someone noticin'."

Gavin's hand still itched to pull his pistol, but Alice was right. Until Jessup tried something again, he had no recourse. "He touches her, I'll hang those balls from the crow's nest."

Neo gave a low rumble of laughter. "Still attached?"

"Depends on my mood." His eyes never left Jessup's back.

Three more days. They were close to sighting land. Gavin could sense it. With the winds holding in their favor, it could be sooner. Then Alice would be out of harm's way. From Jessup and from him.

After last night, he could no longer deny his feelings. Finding her at his desk reading Beth's letters had infuriated him, but that soon gave way to a surprising sense of relief. Alice knew and there was a lightning to the burden he'd carried alone for all these years. With that came another blow, however. In three days, he'd lose her too. The circumstances were different, of course. Unlike Beth, if he could keep her safe from Jessup, Alice would still be alive, but the pain at losing her would still be as great.

Last night he'd bared his soul to her. Never had he allowed anyone to see past his carefully erected walls. Not even Beth had seen him this broken and vulnerable. Instead of feeling shame, he was strangely moved. Alice loved him. He read it in her eyes as clear as if she had shouted it from the bowsprit. Her compassion was genuine. It only strengthened his decision to see her safe. Even if it meant he'd never have her.

Out of the glare of the rising sun came cannon fire. The *Scarlet Night* was being fired upon. Men rushed the deck on full alert as Gavin raised his spyglass. The fire of the sun burned through the length of brass. A ship bore down on them. She was riding high. The black flag they flew only identified them as pirates. Waiting for the moment their mast crossed through the sun's glare, he knew who was upon them.

Crown's Curse. Gavin shouted to the crew. "Drop the reds. Warn that bottom feeder, Capt'n Gantry, who he's shooting at." The sails were lowered; the bones were raised. Gavin looked through his glass again expecting to see the smaller ship veering away. No. "Bloody hell. Gantry's looking to make a name for himself. Forgets who he's challenging. Take him down. No quarter!" The *Scarlet Night* was full and slow. They'd never outrun them. "Hard to port!"

Gavin caught Bump as Robbins rushed past to his position as forward gunner. Sweeping him high, the boy positioned himself secure in the rigging. Gavin's gaze swept the decks. He didn't see her. "Run the port guns."

He saw Alice then behind the rush of the powder monkeys. Another cannon blast from the *Curse* gave him no time to send her below. A high-pitched whistling announced the speeding chain shot that clipped the top of their forward mast, shattering it like kindling.

Bump! Gavin raced beneath the raining debris and held up his arms, willing the child to understand and jump. The boy didn't hesitate and leapt from the crumbling lines mere seconds ahead of the top portion of the mast and sail as it toppled toward them.

Curling around the boy to protect him from the impact of wood, sail, and rope, Gavin braced for the impact. But a sudden force from the starboard side propelled them hard into the gunwales. He looked back to watch the yardarm crash to the deck. One side crushed the gunwale above his head. Had he not been shoved tight against the ship's side, both he and the boy would be dead.

They scrambled out of the rubble into the face of the battle. Gavin in his fury gave the order to open full gunfire against their attackers. "Aim for their rails, then bury the bastards." Both rows of cannon were run to port and with practiced timing and precision they fired one after another with little time between each loading and firing in perfect rhythm. Their target could not begin to defend themselves. Greed and inexperience had brought them in too close. There was no chance for *Crown's Curse* to retreat before the unrelenting cannon fire blew them to bits.

In the melee, he'd lost sight of Alice. Through the rush of men and clouds of smoke, he couldn't find her.

* * * *

Alice crawled out from beneath the ruins of the forward mast. Her cheek burned and the tender flesh under her eye was beginning to swell. She spotted Bump and nearly cried with joy at the sight of him. Gavin was ordering the guns to fire. A bruised cheek meant nothing as long as they were alive.

She didn't think when she saw the top of the mast careening toward them. There hadn't been time. It was only by luck the sail brought her down rather than wood or iron.

Sweat and blood ran down her cheek as she grabbed Bump's hand and skirted the rush of battle to get them below. Her heartbeat pounded in her ears, and the rush was making her dizzy. Stopping with the boy, she pointed repeatedly to her chest and to the hatch. "My quarters. Go." He scrambled down the ladder way ahead of her. Through the swirling smoke, she tried to pull in deep breaths to clear her head before rushing to follow him down.

Hitting the deck below, Alice had only taken two strides when strong fingers latched onto her arm and swung her about. Gavin's hand plunged into her hair and pulled her lips to his in a crushing kiss. The battle raged above as he pinned her against the wall and ravished her mouth. Shock entangled with passion as the depth and intensity of the kiss overtook her.

Gavin broke the kiss as quickly as he'd started it and stared into her face. "You could have been killed." His chest heaved as he wiped at the blood on her cheek, but his words weren't edged with anger. He appeared stunned. Grateful.

Alice laid her hand over his. "I wasn't going to lose you both."

"Lock yourselves in your cabin so I know you're safe. I'll come for you when it's over." He stared deep into her eyes before kissing her hard again and leaving.

Alice placed shaking fingertips over her lips. Her head still spun. He wasn't pushing her away or railing at her. *I'll come for you.* For once, his words weren't a threat; they were a promise. A tender promise that filled her heart. On shaky limbs she made her way to her quarters.

"Wasn't that sweet…." Jessup spit as he stepped out of the dark. The blade of his cutlass caught the light. "Still playing Quinn's whore."

Alice froze to the spot. She didn't see Bump. He must have made it past Jessup. Without Bump as his shield, it was just him and her. Alice liked those odds. She notched her chin. "Jealous?"

"Ha. Like I'd stick my dick in the likes of ye. Rather dip my wick in some barnyard sheep than fuk a conniving, backstabbing bitch like you."

Alice pulled her sword. "Poor sheep."

"Shut yer mouth, whore, before I cut out yer tongue." He shook his head. "Too bad yer a stubborn bitch. Didn't Capt'n tell ye te stay below? Hadn't been topside, ye'd ne're gotten killed in the battle."

She snorted. "I'm not going topside."

Jessup stared her down. "Figure I can drag yer scrawny carcass up them stairs after I'm done killin' ya."

Alice braced herself. She never blinked. "I doubt you could drag your ass the length of your dick." She held up her free hand, indicating a short distance between her thumb and index finger.

"Bloody bitch," Jessup growled and swung wide. Alice stopped his blade with her own. The force of the blow radiated up her arm. "I'm goin' split ya in two." His next blow came from above. Alice dodged to the left.

He backed her into a corner. Adrenaline pumped through her. His blows were too strong. Too fast. She cursed herself for not pulling her pistol first, but she was still so slow cocking the hammer, she'd be dead before she aimed.

Jessup sneered at her as he pinned her cutlass beneath the power of his. "Nothin' more to say, bitch?"

Alice struggled against the force. "B-behind you."

He laughed foul breath into her face. "I ain't fallin' fer that."

Neo lifted Jessup like a child's toy and knocked him to one side. He pulled Alice behind him as Jessup came off the floor swinging wildly. "I'll kill you, too."

Neo pulled a short knife, but Jessup caught him and cut a vicious slice across his arm. He came up sharp with an elbow, connecting with Neo's face. His knife clattered to the floor as he let out a holler and clutched at his nose.

Panting, Jessup grinned at them both. "Ain't no match fer me, a woman and a stupid—"

"Drop the sword or the first shot goes straight through your skull." Gavin held two pistols aimed at Jessup's ear. "Alice, weren't you headed somewhere?"

"But, Neo—"

Gavin didn't take his eyes off Jessup. "Neo? Do you need Tupper's help?"

The man spit a wad of blood on the floor and stood up to his full height. "No, sir. Think I be givin' ye a hand, though."

Jessup looked back and forth between the two men. He hadn't dropped his weapon.

"Alice, go." Gavin voice was cold as ice.

Her legs shook as she rushed to her tiny quarters. Behind her, she expected to hear the shot, but none came. Locking the door, she crumbled to the floor. Bump was at her side in an instant. Large brown eyes watched her with concern until she smiled at him. Still no shot came.

Bump brought a wet cloth and placed the dripping rag against her cheek. Water and blood soaked her shirt. The coolness was a blessing after the initial sting. Minutes ticked by. Still no shot.

Above them, the familiar din of post battle signaled another victory for the crew of the *Scarlet Night*. Had Jessup won as well? If anything happened to Gavin…

A pounding on the door rattled the lock. Alice jumped up. The handle jiggled, and her heart threatened to beat its way out of her chest. She pushed Bump to hide under her cot.

"Alice, open the door."

Gavin. Relief washed over her. She grabbed the back of Bump's shirt, stopping him before hurrying to open the latch.

Alice flew into Gavin's arms. He held her tight to him. Pulling away, she looked him over, running her hands over his arms, the tear across his chest. None of the blood on him appeared to be his. He caught her hands. "I'm unharmed."

Relief bloomed in her heart. "I kept waiting to hear your pistol fire. What happened?"

"Jessup's dead." Gavin cupped her cheek. "Neo found Jessup dead at the bottom of the ladder way. He fell sometime during the skirmish with the *Crown's Curse* and broke his neck."

Alice raised an eyebrow at the lie. "He fell?"

"Like a sack of wet sand."

Bump pushed past the two of them. Habit had Alice calling after him, "Wait."

"He can't hear you, remember? Threat's over. He'll be fine." Gavin gently fingered the wounded flesh at her cheek. "Thanks to you." His thumb brushed the curve of her lip. "We owe you our lives. You could have been killed." He said softly, "Again."

The sweep of his thumb across her mouth sent a delightful shiver through her. "You stopped Jessup, we're even."

"Neo stopped Jessup." Gavin's gaze scanned her face. He tucked her hair behind her ear.

"He was hurt."

Gavin tipped her chin. "The man has a scratch on his arm and another broken nose. Jessup broke it the last time, too"

"I should go tend to him and thank him." She didn't move an inch.

"You're not going anywhere." He had a low husk to his voice.

"Must we always argue?" Alice shivered as he skimmed the front of her throat with his fingertip. "Couldn't we talk about something else?"

"How about we don't talk at all." Gavin tipped his head and lowered his mouth to hers.

Chapter 16

Gavin took her hand and led her to his cabin having only one more thing he needed to say. Something about her quarters being too small for bilge rats to mate in, and he wanted her "desperately" in his bed. Or something to that effect.

Perhaps he whispered something about how much he wanted her as he brushed her wounded cheek with a feathered touch and showered her face with tender kisses. She couldn't recall. When he ran the tip of his tongue between her lips, urging her to open her mouth to him, she could barely recall her own name. But then, he sighed it into her mouth.

Alice was swept away at the tender beginnings. This was nothing like the crushing kisses in the hallway. Tossing his baldric aside he removed hers as well before pulling her to him and kissing her deeply. Her heart soared. She wrapped her arms around his neck and returned his kiss, pressing her body along the long length of him, leaving no doubt to the fact she wanted him as well.

Gavin pulled away, breaking the kiss that began sweetly only to reach white hot in a matter of seconds. "There's no storm tonight." His chest rose and fell under her hands. "I wasn't gentle the first time."

Her lips tingled. The kiss had ignited her longing for him. She couldn't deny it any longer. Alice reached for him impatiently. "You didn't know."

"But now I do." He eased her long braid over her shoulder and undid the bit of leather at its tail. "Let me show you how it should have been."

Alice stroked his cheek. "I regret nothing."

"After tonight, neither will I." He loosened her hair from its braid and ran his fingers through its length. He was intent on his actions. The thought of what was to come made her tremble. She ran her hand up his arm and down to caress the hard muscles of his chest.

He unbuckled her belt and tossed it aside, lifting her shirt from her. "Beautiful." He swept his hands over her skin, smoothing and awakening every part of her. Gavin traced the scar about her neck. A sob caught in her throat as he laid loving kisses along the silvered line that had been etched onto her skin by Wolfsan's evil.

Cupping the fullness of her breasts, he slid his hand to encircle her waist. Her breath came in shorter gasps as each fingertip sparked a trail of delicious warmth along her flesh.

Gavin knelt before her, skimming her behind and down her thighs, before slipping her feet from her boots and stockings. He released the buttons holding her breeches and peeled the snug garment from her.

Alice held tight to the tops of his shoulders so she wouldn't topple over. His touch was magical. She was on fire as he turned her around and smoothed the skin of her back, her ass, her legs. Gavin's mouth followed the path of his hands. Grasping her thighs, he laid a warm kiss upon the small of her back. Alice's knees buckled as the sensation shot straight to her sex.

He stood, sweeping her hair to one side; he kissed her neck as he filled his hands with her breasts. The roughness of his palms teased the firm peaks of her nipples while he tasted the curve of her ear and nipped at its lobe. "Gavin," she whimpered.

Her thighs trembled when he pulled her back against him. Alice didn't know how much more of this delicious torture she could take. He hadn't removed a stitch of his own clothing, yet she could feel the hard, hot ridge of his erection. She moved against him seductively, making him moan deep in his throat as he continued to kiss a path along the top of her shoulder.

"Can you feel how much I want you?" he whispered against her skin.

Alice couldn't speak. She nodded and gave an anguished sigh. He pulled her tighter against his rigid cock while one of his hands slipped down past the slight curve of her belly to cup the curled nest of hair between her legs. Alice covered his hand with her own, urging him to end his sweet torture. "Please, Gavin."

She cried out with pleasure as he slid his fingers deeper. "You're wet for me," he growled low into her ear. "Does that feel good?"

"Y-yes...." When he pushed two fingers into her, the first waves of pleasure rippled through her. Her legs weakened as her body succumbed to his bold caress and shuddered with anticipation. "Gavin...."

* * * *

He had only begun to make love to her. Gavin wanted to touch and taste and caress every inch of her, imprinting her forever upon each of his senses before he sank his cock into her heat and found his own release. It would be the last time.

Then he would drive her away. Away from this ship and this life. Away from him. He would make her surrender her body and her heart, then set her aside. Force her to hate him. It was the only way to keep her alive and well, and give her some chance at a normal, happy future. But for this day, this night, she was his.

Alice turned in his arms still trembling. She kissed him and loosened the lacing at his neck. Laying a kiss in the dip at the base his throat, she unwound the ruby sash about his waist and let it fall to the floor.

Gavin pulled out of his shirt as she rained quick kisses over the breadth of his chest. Each one a tiny flame. When she ran her tongue over the flat of his nipple, the surge to his cock had him clutching at her hips and grinding her against him.

"Mmmm…you taste like the sun and the sea." She continued to suckle and tease his sensitive flesh while her hand reached between them, slipping beneath the waistband of his breeches until her fingers circled him.

"Alice." He captured her face and pulled her mouth back to his. Her fingers stroked his throbbing cock from tip to base until he thought he was sure to lose himself. He backed her toward the bed and removed her torturous hand from his trousers. "Not so fast, or I'll be finished before we start."

"I'm sorry. I don't know how—"

"No. Don't apologize." He laid her on the bed. "I don't want to rush." Kissing along her neck, he dipped lower to capture the rosy tip of one breast between his teeth. He sucked it between his lips. "I want to savor every moment. Every morsel."

Alice arched her back. "I won't survive," she drew a sharp breath.

"I promise you will." Gavin left her only as long as it took him to remove his boots and breeches releasing his impatient cock from its linen prison. He had her back in his arms in an instant reveling in the sensation of skin against skin, pinning her beneath him as he ravished her mouth.

He would make this an experience neither of them would forget. Perhaps the memory would soothe some of the hurt still yet to come. Gavin refused to think about that now. Tomorrow would be soon enough. She was here now. In his arms, in his bed, in all her naked glory, responding like no other to each touch, each kiss.

His hands played across her pale skin. The night of the storm, he'd been in such a hurry to drive his cock into her he hadn't noticed how soft her skin was. How it was the color of rich cream. A handful of golden freckles sprinkled along her collarbones. Gavin kissed each one.

The firm peaks of her nipples caught his fingertips as he continued his exploration. His mouth followed the trail.

"Gavin...." Alice sighed as she held his head, tugging at a fistful of his hair as she purred her delight. Her body writhed like the swell of the ocean in a slow wave beneath him. He reached lower as he moved down her body, circling her navel with the tip of his tongue, kneeling between her raised knees. His fingers barely brushed the dark curls between her thighs. Her knees fell open as she rocked her hips toward him. "Oh, please...," she begged.

He looked into her pleading eyes and shook his head. Her chest rose and fell with each pant until she dropped her head back with a frustrated groan. Gavin kept up his sweet torture. He kissed one knee before licking and kissing his way down her thigh. Alice gasped and knotted the bedding in her fists.

He moved to her other leg, burning a similar path. Then he saw it. Just as she'd said. The scar marring the perfect sweep of creamy flesh. He traced the silvery curve with the tip of his finger while battling past his lust-filled haze to the tidal wave of murderous rage toward the man who'd marked her.

At his touch, Alice went still. Laying his palm over the scar he met her gaze. "He's lucky he's dead." Her eyes shown with a sudden wash of tears before he lowered to kiss the mark away. If not from her skin, maybe from her soul.

Alice let out a sob as she gripped his shoulder. He pressed her legs open wider before putting his mouth to her sex. Her sobs turned to cries of pleasure as he licked and sucked upon her.

"Oh God, Gavin." She tugged at his arms, but he held firm, pleasuring her with sweeps of his tongue and deep strokes of his fingers until she cried out for him to stop. She pulled him up her body, positioning him, wrapping one leg about his waist. "Please, now." She pulled him down to kiss his mouth.

He wanted nothing more than to bury himself in her heat and end both their torment, but he ignored her pleas and eased into her slowly, inch by inch. Alice clutched at his back. Her nails scratching his skin. Gavin pulled back and pushed into her tightness again. Sinking deeper and deeper with each plunge.

Alice arched and rocked her hips to meet his thrusts. Gavin dropped his forehead to hers as the building of his release pushed him faster and harder. Alice cried out. She tightened and convulsed around him, pulling him deeper, pushing his body past its zenith until he joined her in an incredible climax. His body poured into her, their souls met, and she clung to him until they both spiraled back to earth.

Gavin brushed at the hair clinging to her damp cheek. Her legs still circled his waist. Still joined, he didn't want to pull away. He didn't want this to end and nearly cursed the finality of it. Of them.

Their labored breaths danced between his last kisses until he broke the spell and rolled away from her. Alice tucked into his side.

She draped her arm over his chest. "I don't know what to say. That was...so... When you... I have no words."

He covered her hand with his own and smiled. "Had I known that was all it took to render you speechless."

Alice shoved against him as she laid a line of kisses along his jaw. She nuzzled his neck. "I'll take a vow of silence and we can stay wrapped in each other's arms from one edge of the Atlantic and back."

"Alice," Gavin steeled himself. Only one of them would be crossing the Atlantic again. She'd despise him for it, but it had to be.

Alice continued, "Where will you be taking me? I never reached Port St. Maria, but I understand it's beautiful there. We can have the repairs made to the *Scarlet Night*, bask in the sun during the days, and at night—"

"We're not changing course. We anchor off the coast of Cape Henry by nightfall tomorrow."

Alice rose to look into his face. "We'll make repairs there?"

"No." A fist turned in his stomach at what was coming. He lifted his hand to cup her cheek and soften the blow, but came within a hairbreadth of touching her. Unwavering, he looked her straight in the eye. "The plans have not changed. When the *Scarlet Night* docks, you will be taken ashore. It is a short coach ride from there to the Whitmore plantation."

Her eyes registered disbelief, and hurt, before she turned away. "I thought...this...." Her hand swept the bed. "Everything has changed."

"Not everything. Taking you back into my bed doesn't change the facts. A life aboard this ship isn't fit for you." He moved away from her. The hurt in her eyes was more than he could bear. He swung his legs over the side and sat on the edge of the bed with his back to her.

"You don't want me to stay with you?"

He closed his eyes. "That was never the arrangement."

"Arrangement," she repeated woodenly.

Gavin left the bed and slipped into his breeches. He couldn't look back at her. If he told her the truth—that losing her would kill his already wounded heart—she wouldn't leave. One word of caring would anchor her to him forever and to a life of constant danger and peril. How many times had she cheated death today alone? Better to have her hate him and live.

He bent to slip on his boots. "I admit, I did give a second's thought to keeping you here. If for nothing more, than to warm my bed." Behind him, she gasped. He'd hit his mark. "After the unfortunate issue of your maidenhood was dispensed with, you became a lovely distraction."

"Is that all?"

"What more did you expect? Oh, of course you have my thanks for saving my neck this morning. Bump's as well. I'd say ample compensation should be given for your heroism, although foolish. I am indebted. I believe a certain share of the bounty captured from the Spanish ship is due you." He lifted his gaze to hers at her gasp.

"You want to *pay* me?"

Gavin issued his final shot. Loathing himself with each word. He indicated the bed with a sweep of his hand. "You've earned it."

Chapter 17

Fury, not earth-shattering passion stole the words from her mouth. Hurt and humiliation jockeyed for position in her heart. Gavin's words vibrated through her brain as she climbed out of his bed.

Retrieving her shirt, she then pulled it over her head. In the time it took her to don her britches, she'd chilled an iced shell around her heart. How could she have been so foolish to believe Gavin wanted anything more than what he found between her legs? Pay her?

Her emotions had overruled her good sense. This raw, burning pain in her chest was a proper reward. Gavin Quinn was like the rest. Worse. He made her believe she was wanted. Said the words. He'd taken all he would take. She'd been stripped clean and laid bare like one of his captured merchant ships. He'd get nothing else from her.

Gavin sat at his desk, the perfect picture of indifference. Alice eyed the heavy brass sexton she'd hefted to use as a weapon the first time she'd entered this room. She wanted to use it again for the same purpose until the realization stopped her dead. She loved him. Deeply. Profoundly. The fact she could do nothing to stop her feelings hit her like a cannon shot.

"How much farther until we reach Virginia?" Her voice droned oddly flat to her ear.

Gavin didn't even lift his eyes. "Twenty-four, possibly thirty-six hours."

Alice was done. Broken. She wouldn't fight or beg. Wouldn't give him the satisfaction. He wasn't going to hurt her anymore. She notched her chin. "I'll be ready."

He nodded. "It is for the best."

"Yet another thing we've come to agree upon." When his eyes met hers, the sudden lump in her throat threatened to choke her. "T-the sooner I get away from this ship, the better."

"I knew you'd see the sense in it." He went back to his logbooks.

She refused to battle for his love, but there was one fight she still had to wage. "I'll be taking Bump with me."

He never lifted his gaze. "No, you won't. Bump stays here."

"If I'm not safe on your precious ship, neither is he. More so."

Gavin looked at her as if she were some pitiful dolt. "Think about what you're proposing. A single woman arriving at a plantation in Virginia with a dark-skinned child?"

She shrugged. "I'll say I've adopted him."

"No one will believe you."

"I don't care what anyone believes," she snapped.

Gavin shook his head. "Bump stays with me."

"I'm the closest thing to a mother the boy will ever have. He loves me."

"He can't afford to love you. He's a pirate." The muscle in Gavin's jaw jumped. "There's no room in his life for love. He's a child; he'll get over it."

"You make it sound so simple."

Gavin met her gaze. "It's not simple. It's essential." Was he still speaking about Bump? "I'm sure he'll keep fond memories of you and your time here, but this is his life."

A cold, hard life full of struggle and violence and danger with no room for joy and affection. Love wasn't something to give or received. It was something to survive and snuff out. Burying it along with your heart. Gavin would be the perfect teacher.

"I, too, will never forget my time here, Captain Quinn."

Alice left Gavin, and maneuvered her way slowly and woodenly through the crowded deck. Crewmen removed most of the damage from the attack of the *Crown's Curse*, but they were busy running new rigging and sail to compensate for the loss of the upper portion of the forward mast.

"Good show, Tupper." "Another feather in yer cap." Men slapped her on the back as she passed. "Capt'n be one lucky bastard, he be." "Hear how ole' Jessup got his?" "Bought it slipping down te ladder? Worse be drowin' in yer mug o' rum." "I want te meet me maker at te end of a bloody blade." "Or under a buckin' whore." Raucous laughter followed. Each man added his final wish to the colorful list of how they'd like to die.

MacTavish was hard at work preparing for the next battle when Alice pushed into the magazine.

"Lass. Dinna expect ye back here."

Alice pushed past him. "There's work to do."

"Afta what ye done already, I guessed ye'd be takin te yer bed."

"Not you, too." She shot him an impatient glance. "Can we please forget about it?"

His eyes widened. "Would ye luk at that shiner."

"I'm sure I'm a beauty."

Lisa A. Olech

"I'm betting Capt'n and the boy won't be forgettin' what ye did. That was some quick thinkin.' Pure amazin' yer only standin' the'r with a black eye. The mast could've smashed ye like a rotten turnip."

"Can we not talk about it?"

"Fine, if ye ain't got time to hear me singin' yer praises...."

"Do you want my help filling these powder bags? Virginia is a day away."

"Capt'n'll miss ye when yer gone."

The shaft of pain cut straight through her. "I'm certain he's as anxious as I am to see me off this ship."

"Ye blind in that eye as well? I've seen the way the man looks at ya. Can't keep from watchin' ya."

"He's worried I'll disobey one of his rules."

"He ain't thinkin' about no rules when he looks at ya. I ken that fer sure."

Alice closed her eyes. "You're wrong."

MacTavish snorted. "I've been around the horn more times than ye've got teeth. I ken a thing 'er two about affairs of te heart."

She spun on him. "Since when did you become some gossiping old fishwife?"

"Fish wife, is it now? What's got into ye? Ye're as prickly as a blow fish with te bends." He snorted and turned his back on her. "An' here I was thinkin' ye might be worthy of the secret of the smoke."

Bracing both hands upon the worktable, Alice dropped her head. "I'm sorry, MacTavish."

"What's nibblin' at ye? Come on, out with it." MacTavish narrowed his all-seeing gaze upon her.

She was quick to side step him as her reserve began to crumble. "I can't talk about it."

He raised his hands in surrender. "Fine. I know when te keep me nose out of a powder keg."

"Let me lose myself in work for a while. What do you want done first?"

Alice worked until darkness forced her to stop. Her back was knotted and she was covered in a fine black film. All the pots that needed to be filled had been and she'd tied more than three score muslin pouches with the proper amount of precious gray mix.

As he had every other night, Bump waited for her outside the armory. He took her hand and began walking toward her tiny cabin, but she stopped. She couldn't go back there. Not tonight.

The air was clear and warm. Seas were calm, and reflected an ocean of stars above them. Alice found a spot against a coil of fat rope and sat down. She patted the place next to her and waited for Bump to sit.

Leaning back, she lost herself in the beauty of the sky until the boy leaned against her. She wanted to sweep him into her arms and crush him to her chest.

"I don't want to leave you. Not here. But where I'm going, life for you would be as hard. Harder. I'm scared for you. I'll never see you again. See you grow up. I'll always worry if you're safe. You have to promise me you'll be careful. Promise you'll grow into a strong, fine man. Promise you'll not forget me. Because I will never ever forget you."

Alice looked down to find him watching her. He lowered his gaze to her mouth. "I love you, sweet boy."

Bump blinked at her and frowned. Alice closed her eyes and tipped her head back. How could she get him to understand? Maybe it was better he didn't. But then he leaned his head against her shoulder and wrapped a thin arm about her waist. The stars above blurred behind a rush of tears that filled her eyes and ran into her hair.

* * * *

"Land!"

The call came down after eight bells the next day. A cheer rang out amongst the crew. Alice strained to see. Before long, she spotted the thin strip of earth barely visible along the horizon. Virginia. The next chapter of her life. Her destiny.

While the crew scrambled, Alice stood in their midst and felt lost for the first time since she'd been aboard. She should be doing something. Preparing. Saying her farewells.

When she woke this morning, Bump was no longer at her side. Her body was sore and stiff from sleeping against a pile of ropes. And Gavin… she hadn't seen him since she left his cabin. He had to have heard the call. He'd be eager to get her under way. She'd wait until the last minute to say her good-byes to him. Maybe by then she would have found the right words to say.

The thin strip of land grew. Alice twisted at her ring and ran the gambit of emotions. Anticipation, fear, hope, sadness. Why did it seem like her journey to this new land, new life began three lifetimes ago? This is what she wanted. Her destination. This is why she left Weatherington. She'd set off with determination and a sense of adventure. When had her fortitude disappeared?

She fingered the tiny pearl nestled in her ring. Her tether to Annalise. What words of advice would she offer Alice?

"Tupper?"

Behind her stood her three men-at-arms. Finch, Summer, and White. All three stood grinning at her.

"Gentlemen."

They snorted and jostled each other until Finch gave the others a shove and they sobered. Finch took off his hat and gave her a serious nod. "Tupper, we got te talkin'. Them an' me. As yer official landin' crew an' all, we be thinkin' ye can't go ashore lookin' like some castaway."

White shoved him, hard. Finch stumbled to recover. "Not that ye don't look fine. Ain't what we be sayin'." He worried the brim of his hat. "What I mean, is ye should leave dressed like a lady."

White pushed a parcel at her. "Made ye this." He studied the toes of his dirty feet.

"Made? What is it?"

"It be a skirt."

Alice unfolded it and held it up. The simple garment was made in panels of rugged fabric stained a dark tan. Down the back were three stripes of stiff red cloth running from waist to hem. The *Scarlet's* sails. "You made me a skirt? I don't know what to say."

"Ain't the latest fashion, but beats the hell out of borrowed britches." Finch jerked his head. "Summer come up wit the idea. Used tea to get the brown color. White's a mender and scrounged the scrap. An me, I be the right height."

Alice held the garment to her waist. "I can't believe you did this." She shot a look at Finch. "Wait. You're the right height?"

Summer snorted. White rubbed his nose to cover his grin. Finch shoved them again. "Needed to ken how long to cut the stripes." He crossed his arms over his chest and leveled a look at her. "We be the same size to the floor, you an' me. White measured each bit off me."

Alice bit her lip to keep from laughing at the image of Finch as a dressmaker's model. "I'm touched. I can't thank you enough."

"Yer mighty welcome, Tupper. Been a fine thing havin' ye aboard. Come, lads, we've work ta do loadin' the skiff."

"How long before we reach port?"

"Oh, we ain't heading ta port. Too risky. We be anchoring down shore. Capt'n put us three and Simons in charge of haulin' ye to the beach. Me and Simons is to see ye as close te town as we dare."

Gavin had set everything in motion. "How long before we leave?"

"Couple, three hours, at most. Got a hell of a head wind comin' off an' wit the one mast broke we be movin' some slow. Be happy when we turn back and the breeze be at our arse."

"That gives me plenty of time to change." Alice clutched the skirt to her chest. "Thank you again for my gift."

As the three moved away, Alice shook her head and laughed at the image of three of the fiercest fighting, blood thirstiest pirates brewing tea and stitching a lady's skirt with Finch as their model.

Heading toward the gangway, she crossed paths with Neo. His face was swollen. One eye nearly closed. A bandage on his arm stood out against his dark skin. "Neo."

"You be gone soon."

Alice gave a slow nod. "That's what I hear."

He took her hand and placed something in her palm. "Take this." It was an ivory-colored curve capped in gold hung on a rough chain. "Tao give to me. I give to you. His name means lion. This is a lion tooth. Te bring ye strength and courage."

"I can't—"

"I give, you take."

"Neo," she ran her thumb over the beautiful piece, "I owe you my life." She laid a hand on his bandage and lowered her voice. "I couldn't have fought him much longer. You—"

Dark, bottomless eyes held hers. "Jessup fell."

Alice nodded her understanding. The subject was closed. What had transpired wasn't for her to know. It was done. "You are one of the finest men I've ever met. I know you weren't among those who approved of my being aboard, yet you fought for me. Risked your life. I saw how you ministered to those men. Honored them. I'll never forget."

He curled his large calloused hand around hers, closing it over the tooth. "Fair winds to ye, Tupper."

Alice followed his strong back as he walked away before she continued to her room. Entering the small space, she remembered the last time she was there. Gavin, passionate, joking, kissing her until her knees went weak. She still hadn't seen him. Would he see her off? Say good-bye?

Pouring cool water from the pitcher, Alice then began washing the grime from her face and neck. Unbraiding her hair, she finger-combed through the tangles. She stripped out of her breeches and stepped into her skirt. It was heavy and the seams scratched at her skin. The waist was too large, but the length—the length was perfect. Alice grinned again thinking of Finch.

With the tails of her blouse untucked, and the large buckled belt secured across her hips, she was ready to meet her new life. The heavy lion's tooth hung about her neck well below her breasts. She tucked it into the fullness of her shirt.

Neo said it would bring her strength and courage. Alice prayed he was right. She was in need of a healthy dose of both.

Chapter 18

Alice left the tiny sliver of a room she'd called her own for the last time and nearly tripped over the boy seated outside her door.

"Bump, there you are. I was worried I wouldn't see you before I left."

The child jumped up and ran a hand down the new skirt she wore and smiled. Alice crouched down and put her hand on his shoulder, returning his smile. Ruffling his hair, she put her hat upon his head. He didn't understand and tried to give it back, but she placed it on his once more, shook her head, and pointed from the hat to him. "It's yours now."

Bump beamed from beneath the wide feathered brim before running off with his prize. As he scampered away, she prayed God would watch over him.

Back topside, the men stopped their chores to notice her walk past. Alice shot back over her shoulder. "You'd think you'd never seen a lady in a fine skirt before." Many said their good-byes and wished her well.

She found Robbins and returned his breeches. "I thank you for the use of your trousers."

"Least I can brag 'bout all the fine women been in me pants." He smirked and blushed to the roots of his hair.

"One day you'll don a fine pair and I hope you'll remember me." Alice patted his arm.

"I ain't likely to forget ye, Tupper." Robbins nodded.

"And you'll keep an eye on Bump for me?"

He bobbed his head, again. "Aye, I will. Ye ken count on me. Always."

They were closer to shore now. The order to drop anchor would come anytime. Alice moved away from the bow. Watching the land grow larger and large in her sight was setting off nerves and emotions she was struggling to sort.

"Would ye look at you?" MacTavish stood with his hands on his hips appraising her. "I'd have ye in a fine tartan pinned o'er ye shoulder, but I imagine that'll do."

Alice smiled at the burly Scotsman. "Only Scots wear tartan."

"Aye, but on rare occasions, we're allowed te bestow an honorary Scotsman badge of honor."

"You'd make me an honorary Scot?" She raised her eyebrow. Tough and grizzled like an old bear, MacTavish had a tender side to him few saw and even less dared to acknowledge.

"I might." He jerked his head back toward the magazine. "Follow me, lassie."

"If you pull a kilt out of a bag—"

"Nay, just come wit me." Stopping inside the armory he closed the door. "I ain't a man te get sentimental. But ye've been a fine thing te happened on this here tub. Ye work hard and yer brave. And ye put up wit te likes of me." He tugged at the braid in his beard. "Might bloody well miss ya."

Alice was tempted to tug at his beard as well, but knew better. "I might bloody well miss you, too."

"I want ye te have somethin'. Ya know, te remember yer favorite Scotsman. Have I ne're told ya where I be from, lass?"

"I don't think you have."

"I be from a bonny part of the highlands. A tiny village called *Sròn an t-Sìtheinn* means nose of the fairies. Our tartans be a fine red color fer a reason, ya see. There be these rocks there that burn a bloody brilliant red fire."

"The red smoke." She clapped her hands together.

"Shhhh." He opened the door and peered out. "Keep yer voice down, lass. None be knowing 'cept me—now you."

Alice lowered her voice. "Why are you telling me?"

He planted his meaty fists on his hips. "Ye been askin' near every damn day."

"I never thought you'd actually do it," she countered.

"Must be havin' a weak moment." The corner of Alice's mouth curled into a smirk. MacTavish frowned at her. "What be that look fer?"

"Malcolm MacTavish, beneath your brawny, burly, grouchy exterior"— Alice put on her best Scottish accent—"ye be nothin' but an ole' softy."

MacTavish's face flushed crimson. "Ye be takin' that back."

Alice crossed her arms over her chest and shook her head. "I will not."

"If ye were a man—"

"You'd never have told me."

He laughed and nodded. "Ye got that right. An' I'd ne're be givin' ye this." From the rugged leather sporran tied about his waist, MacTavish took a small square of his beloved red tartan and a small leather pouch. "I be givin' ye the secret and a wee bit of me powder. Toss a pinch into a fire and ye'll have a grand show. And I give ye a bit of me fine wool.

Wear it pinned near te ya heart. It'll bring ye luck." He pushed both items into her hands.

The gesture touched her bruised heart. "MacTavish—"

"Ye be stoppin' right there. I'll be havin' none of the mush yer fittin' to spout."

"Can I say thank you?"

He sniffed. "Ye did, lass. Now be gone wit ya."

"Just when I think I may like you, you go and show your true colors." Alice laid a hand on the steel of his arm. "Then I like you even more. I promise to keep the tartan near to my heart and your secret safe."

He gave a gruff nod and opened the door for her. Outside she looked at the items in her hands stunned at the generous nature of these men. Alice tucked her front shirttail into her belt to create a reticule of sorts and moved toward a certain spot in the bow. Virginia stretched out before her. Land filled the horizon. She was here.

"We'll be dropping anchor soon." Behind her, Gavin's voice wrapped around her. "I can't accompany you, but will send men to escort you."

The ache in her heart closed her throat. She could only nod.

Gavin was silent for a long moment. "All that is left is to wish you safe journey, Mistress Tupper."

Alice straightened her spine. "The same to you, Captain."

"I see a bit of the *Scarlet Night* will be leaving with you." He'd moved closer. His voice a low whisper in her ear. "Her sails have never looked lovelier, but I believe I prefer you in breeches."

Alice closed her eyes. She wanted to scream for him to stop. Turn and slap his face. She wanted him to grab her and kiss all the pain and confusion away, and to tell him how much she loved him. How getting off this ship was going to kill her. Instead, she gripped the railing before her until her knuckles went white.

The order rang out to drop the sails. Shouts throughout the men and the loud release of the ship's anchor chain rattled like a death knell to her.

"It sounds as if you've arrived." Did his voice seem strained? "I'm leaving you in Simons's capable hands."

His warmth left her side. He'd stepped back. "Good-bye, Alice."

She stood stock-still, not moving, not speaking. Gavin's boots thudded on the deck as he moved away. She refused to allow the flood of tears threatening to drown her. Momentum shoved her against the rail as the *Scarlet Night* pulled rebelliously against her heavy tether.

If she didn't move, held her breath and closed her eyes tight, perhaps she could make time stand still. She could stop the sun and the tide and languish in this precise second of in-between. For the space of time it takes a grain of sand to drop in an hourglass, she could freeze this moment and exist within its minute boundaries.

But her lungs still pulled breath; her heart still beat out its perpetual rhythm. Time moved on against her wishes. The crew's activity behind her and the wind upon her face were gentle reminders she needed to move on. There was a new life and a whole new world awaiting her. It was what she hoped for long ago, and here it was, close enough to touch.

She shelved her past away. Tucked it back into the far corner of her memory. Time did pass, and it would heal the scars it left behind. The bruises would fade. She'd embrace the future with eager, wiser arms. She had all she needed: a talisman for strength, a patch of wool for luck, and a ring full of love. What more did she need.

Him. She needed him. Alice shook the thought from her mind.

Simons came to stand next to her. "We'll be heading off soon as the skiff is lowered. Ye'll want to be in Cape Henry before the last coach leaves. Should be landing at the Whitmore Plantation by sundown."

"I'm ready."

"Shouldn't be long now."

Simons left to see to last-minute things. Alice allowed herself one final look down the length of the beautiful *Scarlet Night*. She couldn't help scanning the decks once more for the towering man with the sun-bright hair. He wasn't there.

Alice took a slow, deep breath. "Good-bye, *Scarlet Night*. Good-bye, Gavin."

Climbing down the rope ladder to sit in the back of the long skiff, Alice then faced Finch, Simons, White, and Summer who waited to set their oars and row the small ship to shore. Alice had to smile at the looks upon her dressmakers' faces. They congratulated one another on how well the garment fit her—especially the length.

But her amusement was fleeting. As the men were put to oar and the skiff moved away from the side of the ship, it took all she had within her to keep her spine straight and not look back. Would he be standing there watching her leave? Was he waiting for her to turn and wave farewell?

No, she wouldn't look. What if he wasn't there? What if he was in his cabin raising a glass to the good fortune of finally being rid of her? What if he gave her leaving little more thought than a brief notation in his precious ship's log. No, she had made a vow to herself long ago not to look back, and no time was it more important to keep that vow than right now. She had said her good-byes.

* * * *

Gavin stood in her spot at the tip of the bow and watched as the skiff carried her away. He kept his posture casual, hanging on to a bit of rigging, yet he refused to move until he could no longer see her clearly. Giving a nod of his head as if satisfied all was done, Gavin turned back to the task of returning his life and his ship to some sense of normalcy.

He hadn't been the only one watching Alice leave.

MacTavish stood with his thick arms crossed over his broad chest. "Permission te make a wee comment, Capt'n?"

"When have you ever needed permission, MacTavish?"

"Well, beggin' yer pardon, Capt'n, but yer the biggest horses arse I've 'er set me eyes upon."

"Mind your own business." Gavin moved past him.

MacTavish called to his back. "We're it my business, I'd not be fool 'nough te lose the lass, ye bloody fool."

Gavin swung back. "Your only business is to make sure we've enough powder should the British Navy find us sitting here with our backsides hanging out. Or doesn't a price on that handsome head of yours mean anything to you. I suggest you mind your tongue and get back to your duties."

"Aye, aye, Capt'n," MacTavish grumbled. "Yer still a horse's arse."

Chapter 19

The skiff's bottom grating across the sand signaled their arrival upon the shore of the Old Dominion. The men scrambled out of the boat and pulled it out of the waves.

Having been on a ship for weeks, Alice struggled to walk on the soft ground. Finch took her arm and chuckled, "Easy does it, Tupper. Ye'll get yer land legs back soon." He helped her up the wide, rock-strewn beach.

Passing through scrub pines and wild sea roses, Alice, Finch, and Simons made their way inland until they reached a traveled road.

Simon's stopped. "Need te say good-bye to ye here, Tupper. British Navy has a stronghold along this coast. Not safe te be seen closer te town less we want te die a few inches taller."

Alice looked at both men. "I didn't realize I was putting you all in so much danger."

"No danger. Less we get caught," Finch added with a wink. "Quicker we get the *Scarlet* away the better."

"Still got yer pistol?" Simons asked.

Alice nodded. "Tucked in my boot."

"Good." Simons pulled a tied leather pouch from a pocket. "Capt'n wanted ye to have this." Alice looked at him in question and opened the pouch. "Be yer share of that fat Spanish fish. Ye earned it."

Alice removed a wrapped parcel that lay upon a healthy handful of gold coins. Unwrapping it she gasped at the sparkle of emeralds and gold that tumbled into her hand. She recognized it at once. A necklace fit for a queen.

Quick to rewrap it, Alice handed it back to Simons. "Return this to Captain Quinn. Tell him, I didn't earn this."

"Must 'av wanted ye te have it." He pushed it back at her.

She stared him down. "I can't accept it no matter what the reason. Please. See he gets it back."

"If ye say so." Simons returned the necklace to his pocket with a shrug.

Alice added the few items from MacTavish to the pouch and closed it tight. Standing in clear view of the road was making her nervous. If it were true and the British were heavily guarding the area, not only were they in risk of being caught, but Gavin and the *Scarlet Night* were sitting in dangerous waters. "You should head back. I'll be fine from here."

"Won't forget ya." Finch shuffled his feet in the dirt.

Simons nodded. "Been a fine member of te crew, woman or no—"

The pounding of horse's hooves coming down the road had the men scrambling back into the safety of the tree cover with barely a backward glance.

"Bye, Tupper." The men called as they disappeared into the underbrush before the team of horses rounded the bend.

"God's speed," she whispered before moving off in the opposite direction along the shaded road. The cart approaching slowed to a stop. Calling for the horses to, "Whoa," the gentle older couple driving the wagon inquired as to whether she needed a lift.

As luck would have it, the couple knew of the Whitmore's Plantation. It wasn't too far out of their way, and after the startled expression when the woman first looked upon Alice, they didn't hesitate to agree to take her there.

Alice had forgotten about her blackened eye. By their reaction, she must look a fright. Fingering it gently she claimed clumsiness as she climbed into the wagon. The elderly man nodded his understanding, but his wife's shrewd appraisal came with a sad shake of her head and squeeze to Alice's hand. What would they do if they learned she'd earned her "shiner" in the midst of a pirate skirmish? The poor old woman would faint.

Leaving the shore road behind, the wagon passed field upon field of farmland. Alice closed her eyes and breathed deep of the warm fragrant air. Thankfully, her traveling companions were not of a more curious nature. Conversation was kept light, and Alice soon relaxed in the warmth of the sun and the steady gait of the horses.

As the sun's rays began to stretch into the last shadows of the day, they made a wide turn into a beautiful tree-lined lane. The old man announced, "Whitmore Plantation."

Alice insisted they leave her at the end of the lane. They'd already gone far enough out of their way, and it would be dark before they reached their own farm. It was important to her to make this last small leg of the journey alone. She thanked the couple for their kindness and watched as they turned their wagon toward home.

Smoothing her makeshift skirt, Alice ran a hand over her hair and started down the lane. The sun was still very warm even this late in the day. Her hems kicked up the dust from the road. Walking on solid ground still proved odd. Maybe it had something to do with the pistol in her boot chaffing against her leg.

On either side of the lane, past the rich row of trees and lawn, fields of deep green rolled on as far as she could see. Wide-leafed plants grew waist-high in perfect rows. After weeks of endless blue sea, the patchwork of every shade of green was a beautiful change. Up ahead she could make out the grand front entrance of the Whitmore estate. Large white pillars gleamed in the fading light beckoning her closer.

The impressive estate featured a deep-shaded porch, decorated with huge urns of even more foliage and bright flowers to welcome its visitors. A line of inviting chairs rested in the cool recess closest to the house.

Staring up the wide set of stairs, Alice had a moment's panic. What if, after all this time, the position of governess had been filled? She was weeks late. Would they have gotten word the *Pennington* had been captured? They were sure to think the worst. What if the job had been given to another and she'd come all this way only to be turned away?

Alice clutched the small bag containing all her worldly possessions. The small cache of gold gave her some measure of assurance. She wasn't destitute, but where would she go? One thing was certain, she was firmly on dry land, on the opposite side of a wide, dangerous ocean, and she intended to stay put. Regardless of what waited for her beyond those doors, she was never returning to England.

She straightened her spine, tugged on the tails of her blouse, lifted the hem of her skirt, and climbed the broad steps. Ornate double doors stood before her. Leaded prism glass flanked each side and caught the fading light. A gilded bell pull hung down. She gave it a sharp pull, and held her breath.

A gloved servant opened the door. He was formally dressed and his quick appraisal of her was followed by a stern frown. "State your business."

"Good afternoon, may I speak with either Mister or Missus Whitmore please?"

"I should say not." He gave a quick shake to his head and began to close the door.

"Wait." She blocked the door with her foot. "I believe they are expecting me."

He sniffed. "I doubt that."

Impatience urged her to push past the man and find the Whitmores herself, but she needed to remember she wasn't on a pirate ship anymore. She needed to conduct herself with some gentility. "Please." She forced a small smile. "If you'll tell them Mistress Tupper has arrived. I believe they'll wish to see me."

The man's eyebrows rose. "Tupper?"

"Yes, Alice Tupper. Perhaps I should have started with that. I'm sorry. I was coming here to take on the position of governess." She was unsure how to briefly explain the events of the last few months. "I was…detained."

"Mistress Tupper." He broke into a wide smile and opened the door wide. "Missus Whitmore has been most distressed. She'll be relieved to see you. Please, come in." He stood to the side and ushered her in. "They call me Drummond, Miss."

Relief washed over her. "Thank you, Drummond."

Entering the coolness of the foyer, Alice was struck by the sheer size of the mansion beyond. Tall cream walls held gilded-framed portraits. Brass finials cupped thick beeswax candles. A gleaming round table featured an arrangement of flowers, which looked like an entire garden planted in the center of the space. An elegant sweep of a stunning staircase resembled an hourglass as it narrowed then flared into an upper hallway and traveled in two directions. Turning around, Alice could see a railed galley ringed the foyer. Large sets of double doors flanked on the right and left. She could only imagine what could be found behind them.

"If you'll follow me, you can wait in the master's study. I'll tell Missus Whitmore of your arrival."

Following the man's rigid back, Alice's original fears surfaced again. "Drummond? Could you tell me, is the position of governess still available?"

"It is indeed." He stopped, opened another door and stood aside. "Make yourself comfortable, Mistress."

Stepping into the lofty study, Alice sighed at the rich splendor of the room. Floor-to-ceiling bookshelves filled the walls. A tidy desk sat within a bow of stately windows, which looked out upon colorful formal gardens. Lush burgundy leather chairs created cozy seating areas around the room and before a small fireplace. Its firebox, cleared for the warmer months, housed a thriving plant of some sort.

Alice walked about entranced by all the books like a man lost in the desert looking upon a grand lake of water. Beautiful volumes with tooled leather covers followed one another on the shelves. She pulled one down and breathed in its scent before reverently slipping it back into its appointed space.

Running her hand along the rich spines, she remembered the last book she'd read. Gavin had told her to take it with her, but she'd left it behind.

Bringing it would have only brought her heartache. Alice crossed to the windows and stared unseeing at the mosaic of color beyond. She was disappointed she'd never had the chance to look through the expensive books they'd secured from the Spanish ship.

Secured. Alice shook her head. Stolen was the proper word. She'd been among thieves lest she forget. They'd been more interested in the silvered corners than what fascinating reading could be found inside.

And the letters. Beth's letters. They were something she would never forget. Those hauntingly beautiful letters written in Beth's gentle scrolled hand. No, she'd never forget them, or the man they'd been written to.

Alice pulled another book from the shelf and flipped through several pages before closing her eyes. Gavin. She held the image of him in her mind. His face, the fineness of his light hair, the way his eyes darkened before he kissed her. She'd remember it all. The arguments, the tender times, the passion of a stormy night. It was all part of the story. Their story. She imagined their words filling page after page. But like all true love stories, it had its heartbreaking finish. Happily-ever-afters were works of pure fiction. Fairy tales. Better she keep both feet planted firmly in the truth. The story of she and Gavin Quinn was over.

Turning to the last page of the book in her hands, Alice traced the words *The End* with the tip of her finger before closing the cover and returning the volume to the shelf.

Behind her, the doors flung open and a lovely woman rushed into the room. No more than ten years Alice's senior, she wore a gown of pale lavender in a light airy fabric. Lace trimmed the deep, squared neckline and puffed at each elbow. Her hair, piled high, was the color of honey. Wide blue eyes captured hers. Seeing Alice, she clasped a hand over her heart. "Miss Tupper!"

Alice bobbed in greeting, "Missus Whitmore."

"I insist you call me Isabelle. When Drummond announced you, I swear I nearly fainted. We thought you were dead. Good Lord, look at you. You've been beaten. My dear child." She slipped her arm through Alice's and led her to one of the groups of chairs. "You poor thing. Look at your clothing. I can't begin to imagine what you've been through."

Her slight accent and the high singsong pitch to her voice had Alice straining to catch each word. She spoke so quickly, Alice didn't have a chance to respond.

"When we got word you were coming aboard the *Pennington*, Carlton, that's Mister Whitmore, of course, we were thrilled. But then, to receive word the ship had been taken by pirates. Well, you can't imagine how upset we were."

The scene of Rasher killing Captain Fredericks flashed in Alice's memory. "Yes, that was...quite upsetting."

Isabelle gasped and fanned her cheeks. "How did you ever get away? Were they ruthless cutthroats? No, don't tell me. I couldn't bear to hear it." She clutched Alice's arm. "How awful for you. And yet, here you are. It is a miracle. Wait until Carlton hears. He's sure to be as stunned as I. How relieved, he'll be. He's been hounding me for weeks to fill this position, but I was so upset, I couldn't bring myself to do it. I was sure we'd never find a suitable governess for the children." She gasped again. "Oh Lord, the children. They can't see you like *this*. We'll need to get you cleaned up. A new gown." She reached for Alice's cheek and winced. "A bit of powder upon the bruise about your eye, certainly."

She gave a curt nod. "I'll put Millicent to the task. She's my personal maid. A godsend, truly. She can see you settled and bring you anything you may need. A lovely bath and a hearty meal perhaps, then a good night's rest. The children can meet you in the morning over breakfast."

Isabelle stopped and beamed. "You'll love the children. Everyone does. Rebecca is bright as a new penny, and Brighton is his father's son, so serious and reserved, but smart as a whip. I cannot wait for them to get on with their studies."

Alice sat wide-eyed. Isabelle Whitmore had been talking nonstop since she entered the room. Alice didn't know what to say. Which question she should answer. What to comment on. She gathered herself. "I look forward to meeting the children. I'd appreciate the chance to clean up before meeting them or any more of the household. Indeed, a bath sounds like a bit of heaven, but I don't wish to burden your maid."

"Nonsense." Isabelle flipped a hand, rushed to the door, and called for Drummond. "Ask Millicent to come here at once." She turned back to Alice. "The children are out riding their ponies with Mister Whitmore." She stopped and tipped her head, hesitated. "I should say, Brighton is riding. Rebecca is terrified, poor thing. The horses frighten her so. Carlton has been trying for weeks to ease her fears, bought her the sweetest pony, but she wants no part of it. Even so, if we're quick we can get you cloistered away to your rooms before they return.

"Your quarters are up the stairs to the right. I've arranged for you to be in the east room adjoining the nursery. For now," she winced again, "we should keep the doors closed. Just until we can make you a bit more presentable, of course. But in the future, you will have your own private entrance into the children's rooms. Wait until you see the lovely nursery. We had a decorator come all the way from France."

A quick knock saved Alice from, no doubt, a ten-minute explanation of wall coverings and drapes. "Millicent, this is our new governess, Mistress Tupper. As you can plainly see, she's been through quite the ordeal to reach us. Please see to a bath and something hearty to eat. She'll need a suitable gown. I think the pale yellow from last season should do well, and of course, some night clothes."

"Yes, ma'am, at once."

Isabelle dropped her voice to almost a whisper. "Some of my tinted face powder as well, don't you think?" She shot a glance back at Alice.

"Yes, ma'am."

Alice cleared her throat and interrupted. She disliked being talked about as if she weren't in the room. "You're most generous, Missus Whitmore. I can't begin to thank—"

"Please, it's Isabelle. And don't be silly, it is we who should be thanking you." She pulled Alice in for a hug. Over her shoulder she added, "Millicent, be sure to add some lemon verbena to the bathwater and give her some of my lovely French soap. *Quickly.*"

Chapter 20

Alice's head was spinning as she followed the maid's quick strides through the foyer and up the elegant staircase. More potted plants filled corners. Portraits of soft landscapes lined the hallway. At the end of the hall, Millicent stopped and opened the last door on the left. "Your rooms, Mistress Tupper."

Alice stepped inside as Millicent rushed away. The large airy rooms were huge relative to those of an English manor, and palatial given her slice of storage hold aboard ship. A chambermaid was already pulling dust covers from the furniture and opening the tall windows. She, too, scurried out before Alice could thank her.

A bed thick with feathered ticking and crisp white sheets sat between the windows. One door opened into a dressing area along the right side and another door, presumably led to the nursery off to the left. She must have passed the children's rooms on her way by without noticing. A tiny fireplace graced the back wall with two crewel-embroidered armchairs done in soft blues and yellows. Sheer blue curtains danced at the windows. Even a small writing desk, complete with ink and quill, stood pertly by the hallway door. Fresh flowers had already been placed on her bedside table and the night's candles lit.

Alice walked about the grand room silently touching each thing as if to assure it was all real. Moving into the dressing room, she gasped as she caught her reflection in a mirror. No wonder Isabelle Whitmore had been afraid for her to meet the children.

Alice looked a positive wreck. Her eye still held some swelling and was the color of a faded plum. That was bad enough, but it was not the only bruise she wore upon her face. Alice traced each one with a fingertip as the vision of a falling mast with its stiff sails and tangle of ropes flashed through her mind. It explained them all. She was almost afraid to look at the rest of her body.

A quick knock upon her door announced the arrival of a large copper tub and a small parade of maids with pails of steaming water. Millicent led the charge with arms full of drying cloths and various toiletry items. A young girl behind her carried a dressing gown and the aforementioned gown of yellow. They quickly filled the tub, laid out an array of soaps and creams, and a handsome tortoiseshell brush. The gown was hung in a beautiful carved armoire and a pretty dressing gown edged in pink was laid out upon the bed.

Alice was growing more and more uncomfortable with all the fuss and attention. Even before her time spent with uncivilized pirates, she was used to being the one doing the serving, and not the one being served. Led to a chair, one of the maids dropped to her knees to help Alice remove her shoes. The look on the young girl's face when she saw tall men's boots was almost comical. Alice stopped her before she could raise her skirt enough to find her pistol. Millicent gave a quick order and another servant rushed off to bring Alice a proper pair of shoes.

When one maid's hands worked at the braid in her hair, another's removed her belt, Alice stopped them all. "Please. I-I can't catch my breath. Thank you, but I'm sure you all have much more important matters to attend. If I could have some time to myself…." She didn't want to come across as ungrateful. "It's all so wonderful. My head is spinning."

"Of course, Miss, I understand. You've been through quite enough." She scooted everyone out with a quick clap of her hands. "I'll have a tray sent up in an hour. Until then, enjoy your bath and your peace."

Alice secured the lock behind them and slumped against the door. She'd survived two bands of pirates, weeks at sea, battles, storms, and yet Major Millicent and her band of militant maids had nearly done her in.

After stripping out of her ship's clothing, she stowed her things on the floor of the armoire. Her boots made the perfect hiding place for her pistol and gold, but she was happy to find the wardrobe came with a lock—and a key. Alice buried everything under the rest of her clothing.

She lowered herself into the warm, lemon-scented water. A grateful sigh escaped her. Dipping her head beneath the water, she used a bar of soap shaped like a seashell to rub suds into her long hair. The smell was delightful. A fat sponge spread the fragrant bubbles over her body smoothing the rich lather over the swell of her breasts. At the brush of her nipples, Alice couldn't help but think of Gavin. His touch, and the way he seemed to delight in teasing the tips to pebble against his palms.

She closed her eyes remembering his mouth upon her. The building sensation when his tongue circled the rouged bud of her nipple before drawing it into his mouth. Her body pulsed at the memory. Beneath the water, she skimmed the sponge across her stomach.

"No." Alice sat up so suddenly, water sloshed from the end of the tub. "No." She refused to allow her thoughts to carry her away and leave her wanting what she couldn't have. It was over. He was gone. She was here. The sooner she folded up her memories and locked them away like her blasted boots, the better it would be for her. She took the bar of soap and lathered the sponge once more. Using it like a scrub brush, she removed the last layer of her past.

* * * *

Early sunlight peeked through spotless windows. It took Alice a moment to remember where she was. When was the last time she had slept so deep? Dreamless. She stretched like a spoiled cat, languishing in the glow of the sparkling morning. It was an important day.

Rising, she brushed her hair before applying the odd colored powder Millicent had brought the night before. It didn't cover the bruises on her face and neck completely, but it made them far less noticeable. She slipped Tao's lion tooth over her head—for strength—and her ring onto her finger, kissing its face—for love and luck.

The borrowed yellow dress was a bit short in the skirt and tight in the sleeve, but it would serve its purpose until Alice could secure some clothing of her own. The shoes, however, fit like a dream. After shuffling along in boots three sizes too large, it was a simple treat not to clump when she walked.

Back at the looking glass, with her hair braided and secured in a tidy twist at the back of her head, Alice gave a small, sad smile. There she was, the Alice of old. Neat. Tidy. A proper servant. And yet, the familiar green of her eyes seemed different. Wiser? More worldly? Wounded? Like her bruises, under a dusting of powder, she could hide it all from the rest of the world. All her secrets. No one knew them now. Only her and her image in the mirror. And she wasn't talking.

It was still early when she left her rooms, but she was anxious to begin the day. Perhaps a stroll through the gardens would ease some of her nerves before meeting everyone at breakfast. But on her way down the hall, Alice passed the nursery and was drawn to the delightful peal of children's laughter.

Tapping lightly, she opened the door and peeked inside. The boy, Brighton, was crawling about on his hands and knees with his sister, Rebecca, riding on his back telling him he was a good pony and she wasn't afraid for him to gallop faster. Brighton reared back to the squeals of delight of his sister as she clung to his neck to keep from falling.

An older woman dressed in starched whites with hair the color of pewter turned and scolded them for playing too rough. She caught sight of Alice in the doorway and scrambled, fussing over the children to stand up and brush themselves off.

"Please, let them play. I heard the giggles of happy children and couldn't wait another moment to meet them. I'm Alice Tupper, the new governess."

"Our pardons, Mistress Tupper. I'm Susanna, the children's nurse. We heard you'd arrived. This isn't the way we should have met you."

The two children looked up at her with wide eyes. Rebecca was a miniature version of her mother with honeyed hair and soft blue eyes. Brighton was darker in his coloring but he, too, had his mother's eyes. She smiled at them both. "I was the one to barge in. My manners are a bit rusty."

Susanna pushed Brighton toward her. "Good morning, Mistress. I'm Brighton Edgar Whitmore. I'm eight years old." He held out his hand with all proper seriousness.

Alice shook his hand and replied with a serious face. "A pleasure to make your acquaintance, Brighton."

He tugged on his sister while their nurse worried the bow in the girl's hair. "This is Rebecca. She's five." The child stuck her thumb in her mouth, which Susanna was quick to remove with a gentle pat to the back of her hand.

"I'm happy to meet you Rebecca. I'd be happy if you'd call me Alice. I think we're going to have a wonderful time getting to know each other, don't you?"

"You were lost." Rebecca pointed at her.

"I was indeed, but I've found my way here, at last. I'm sorry I was so late."

Brighton gave her a stare. "Father said you were captured by pirates."

"Brighton," scolded his nurse.

Alice held up her hand. "It's true. I did spend some time with pirates." Both children's eyes got as large as tea saucers. "Bad pirates?" asked Rebecca.

Alice sat on a low chair. "A few were not so nice, but some were very kind. They made sure I got to Virginia."

The children crowded her and peppered her with questions. "Were you scared?" "Were there cannons?" "And swords?" "Did you cry?"

"Brighton. Rebecca." Their nurse scolded them and tugged them away from Alice by the scruffs of their necks. "Give the poor woman some room."

"You're curious. I like that. Would you both like to see something special? It was a gift from a special pirate friend." Alice tugged on the chain about her neck and held out the lion's tooth for the children to see. "Do you know what this is?" She leaned forward allowing them to get a closer look.

"No." They both shook their heads.

"This is the tooth from a fierce lion. Do you know what a lion is?"

"I do," Brighton boasted. "It's the king of the jungle."

"That's right. A lion is a big, wild cat that lives far, far away."

"Why did the pirate give it to you? Was it your birthday?" Rebecca blinked up at her with crystal-blue eyes.

Alice smiled. The child was already warming her heart. "It was a good-bye gift. He told me it would bring me courage."

"So you won't be scared."

Alice cupped the girl's cheek. "That's right. You're both so smart."

"May I touch it?" Brighton asked holding out a curious finger.

"Me, too?" Rebecca chimed in.

"Of course." Both children ran a finger over the smooth ivory curve. "When we start our lessons, we could learn more about lions."

"Or pirates," added Brighton.

"We'll see. Right now, I need your help. You live in such a grand house, I wouldn't want to get lost again trying to find the dining room."

"We'll help you, Alice."

Alice smiled at the children as they each took one of her hands. She nodded to their nurse. "Is that all right?"

"Of course, Mistress Alice."

"Well, let's go? I'm starving."

They pulled her from the room. "Didn't the pirates feed you?"

"Did they eat cakes and cream?" asked Rebecca. "I love cakes and cream."

Brighton peered around Alice to correct his sister. "Not for breakfast, Becca."

The children chatted away happily about their favorite things to eat, and those horrible things their nurse makes them try. Green things seemed especially loathsome.

As the three entered the bright dining room, Rebecca let go of Alice's hand to run to her mother. "A lion gave his tooth to Alice."

"Not a lion," rebuked Brighton, "a pirate."

"Children, please, sit at your places." To Alice, she apologized, "I see my chatterboxes have met you."

"I heard wonderful fun coming from the nursery. I couldn't wait." Alice took her place at the table. So much silverware glittered next to her plate. On one hand, she was worried she wouldn't remember the difference between a teaspoon and jam spoon. On the other, she was ashamed to wonder about how much silver it would all melt down to be.

Amidst the happy commotion of settling the children and the tangle of servants and trays, a well-fashioned man joined them. "Good morning, family."

The children chimed together, "Good morning, Father."

Isabelle rose and kissed his cheek, "Carlton, *this* is Alice Tupper." Her pale hand swept in Alice's direction. "Alice, allow me to introduce my husband, Carlton Whitmore."

Alice was on her feet. "Mister Whitmore." She nodded her head.

Carlton Whitmore wasn't much taller than his wife, even with his heeled shoes. Lines about his eyes told her he was several years Missus Whitmore's senior if Alice were any judge of such things. A kindly man, given the way he greeted his wife and children, but there was a shrewdness to his stare. Alice supposed a man didn't get to the position of plantation owner without a keen eye for business, as well as people.

"Mistress Tupper, when Isabelle told me of your arrival, I'll admit to being quite bowled over. Of course, we're delighted you have reached us safely."

Alice was seated at the table. "I had serious doubts at times that I would ever see Virginia, but I'm happy to be here. You have a charming family."

He sat and placed his napkin in his lap. A footman poured his tea. "I'm anxious to hear the details of your trip." He gave her a pointed stare. "The circumstances are disturbing to say the least. I have some specific questions I'd like to ask."

"Carlton," Isabelle interrupted, "you'll have to forgive him, Alice, he trained as a solicitor before becoming embroiled in local politics." She shot Carlton a sharp look. "Let the girl have her breakfast before you begin interrogating her."

"I'm not interrogating the woman." He turned back to Alice. "But the situation here is tenuous regarding shipments and colonizers reaching our shores. The increased activity of these so-called privateers is a concern to us all. Any light you could shed might be of some use in stopping these bloody thieves."

"Carlton, the children," Isabelle admonished. Both Brighton and Rebecca were quiet and listening intently.

"I'll tell you whatever I can." Alice took a sip of her tea, then cursed the slight shake of her hand as the teacup rattled back to its saucer. She steadied it with two hands.

Carlton nodded. "Good. Let's talk privately in my study after breakfast."

Alice forced a small smile to her lips. "Of course."

He clapped his hands together, and spoke to the children. "Do I smell Harriet's famous cornbread?"

Boisterous conversation erupted around the table. Plans were made for the day. Following her meeting with Carlton, the children would give her a quick tour of the property taking care not to venture into the fields. After their post-lunch rest, Isabelle and the children would take the carriage into town and see to Alice's meager wardrobe. Would they like goose for dinner?

Alice smiled and nodded in all the right places, but inside she was screaming. What exactly did Carlton Whitmore need to know? She found him studying her each time she glanced in his direction. Would he be able to see through her to the truth? How could she avoid giving him any information that would bring the Virginian authorities closer to capturing Gavin? What about her own head? She had a pouch full of Spanish gold and a pistol hiding in a pirate's boot that could very likely put a noose around her own neck.

The delicious-looking breakfast of fresh eggs, fat sausage, and the famous corn bread turned to ash in her mouth. It took three cups of tea to wash it down. By the time the meal was over, Harriet's corn bread weighed like an anchor in her stomach.

Chapter 21

Alice followed Carlton Whitmore into his study. Drummond stood at the ready to open the doors for them. As the hasp clicked shut, a wave to dread washed over her.

"Please, Mistress Tupper, have a seat."

The fine leather creaked as she sat. He moved to sit in the tall chair opposite her. From a humidor next to him, he pulled a long, thin cigar. "Do you mind if I smoke?"

Alice stopped twisting her ring and tried to still her hands "Not at all." She worried at her lip. "Your collection of books is quite impressive."

"Dusty old things. Isabelle's responsible for most of them I'm afraid. She says they're one of the benefits of owning an estate like this. You're free to borrow the lot." He rolled the cigar between his fingers and lifted it to his nose. "This is a better benefit of my estate. Shame I can't offer you one." He went through the motions of lighting his cigar with a spill. It wasn't until a cloud of pungent, blue smoke circled his head that he spoke again. "I'm still quite amazed to have you here, Mistress Tupper."

"Alice, please."

"As you wish." He frowned. "I was certain you were dead."

"You're not the first man to believe that." She swallowed. "I'm beginning to think I'm like a cat with nine lives."

"You were aboard the *Pennington*, were you not? That was the word we received."

Alice twisted the ring on her finger. "You're correct. I boarded in Portsmouth."

Between puffs of his cigar, he stared at her intently. "I understood the ship was attacked."

"Yes, sir. The *Delmar* boarded under the guise of seeking aid, and within moments killed our captain."

"You were a witness to this?"

Alice nodded as the memory of staring into the dead eyes of Captain Fredericks flashed in her mind. "They slaughtered all the men on deck, captain, crew, passengers. Most were dead before anyone could react."

"And the women?" He swept a hand in her direction. "It's obvious they spared the women. What of the others?"

"The crew of the *Delmar* spared no one." The leather of her seat creaked as she shifted. She met his frown. "The women were…not killed immediately."

"Good Lord." He stood and paced to the windows. The smoke from his cigar followed him. "I'd heard of these atrocities, but to listen to the telling." He shook his head.

Alice was confident he wouldn't ask the question that burned in his mind. Had she been raped? A proper gentleman would never ask. He'd assume. She waited.

He returned to his chair. His cigar had gone out. It sat cold and forgotten between his fingers. "I'm sorry to make you retell these events. Isabelle was horrified at the bruises about your face last night. If she should learn about this."

"I won't tell her."

"I'm grateful." He nodded, took a draw on his unlit cheroot and set it aside with a grimace. "How did you manage to escape with your life?"

Images and explanations swirled in her mind. She couldn't tell him the truth. The look on Rasher's face with the hilt of her cutlass protruding from his belly. Rummaging through the pockets of a dead man to retrieve her ring. "I-I… The *Delmar* was captured."

"A second ship? A Navy vessel?"

"No, it was captured by the captain of the *Scar*—"

A man burst into the study. Coat tails flying, red-faced. "Those thieving bastards! The *Scarlet Night* was sitting on our very doorstep and they let them get away."

Carlton Whitmore was on his feet at the intrusion. Alice's heart dropped into her shoes.

The man continued his rant. "The dolts had them. Sitting in Everett's cove. Bold as brass, but by the time the alarm was raised in town and the fleet responded, the ship had vanished. They'd never dared come this close to land before. That whoreson, Quinn, has crossed a dangerous line this time. Bloody prick—"

"Emerson." Carlton Whitmore stepped to one side so the man could see Alice now standing behind him. "Show some decorum, man."

The man stopped short. He huffed a sharp breath and planted his hands on his hips. "I had no idea you were with someone." The muscles in his jaw pulsed as he gathered himself. Pushing a hand through his unruly dark hair, he straightened, buttoned his jacket, and gave a polite nod in her direction. "I owe you a thousand apologies, miss."

Alice's heart thrummed in her ears. *Gavin.* They were after him. He wouldn't have been close to shore if not for her. She became light-headed.

Carlton brought the man a finger of brandy. "Emerson Blake," he waved a hand at her, "Alice Tupper."

Emerson set the drink aside and helped her to sit. "Mistress Tupper, I am a cad and an oaf. I've upset you."

"Alice, you're not a well color," Carlton insisted. "I'd offer you a drink of water, but all I have is brandy."

Reaching past a concerned Emerson Blake, Alice snatched his abandoned glass and swallowed its contents in one fiery gulp. The men exchanged astonished glances.

"Mister Blake...a pleasure to meet you."

Carlton Whitmore's eyebrows nearly knocked the wig from his head. A wide smile spread across Emerson Blake's face. "Good Lord, woman, who the devil are you?"

"I'm Alice Tupper. I'm the Whitmore's new governess. And the reason why the *Scarlet Night* was so close to your shores."

"Bloody hell."

Carlton Whitmore poured them all a drink. "Of all the ships. The *Scarlet Night* is reputed to have the most vicious murderers and thieves there are. They pluck whole ships from the seas."

Emerson continued. "And there have been new reports. I was due a dozen new slaves last week. Quinn is said to be attacking the slave ships now and liberating the cargo."

Alice balked at his use of the word cargo to describe those poor men and women of the *Delmar*. "If you had seen the way those poor souls were treated aboard that ship, perhaps you'd understand why—"

"What I understand is Gavin Quinn and the crew of the *Scarlet Night* are operating outside their Letters of Marque and Reprisal. They're no longer under the protection of the crown. In fact, the price on all their heads is growing daily." Emerson moved to stand by the windows.

Alice set her drink aside, this one untouched. She needed to keep her wits about her and answer their questions without giving them any more ammunition against Gavin.

Carlton leaned forward in his chair. "You're speaking a bit like their champion, my dear girl. Surely you can't be defending these men? After the way they treated you? Your bruises."

Emerson spun to look at her. "They beat you?"

"No." A growing sense of panic began in her belly. She wasn't going to change these men's minds regarding Gavin. They had already tried and convicted him. No matter what she told them, Gavin was still a pirate. And a pirate who was personally interfering with their way of life.

Emerson came to stand over her. "Are you asking us to believe a band of murderous cutthroats suddenly gained a conscience when you arrived? I don't believe it. There's no need to hide the truth from us."

"Emerson, the girl has been through enough. I don't wish to have her relieve the horrors that befell her. We have all the facts we need to gather our own conclusions."

"I'm sorry, Mistress Tupper. Carlton is correct. You don't need to explain your ordeal. Tell me this, where is the *Scarlet Night* headed?"

"I have no idea," she lied.

He raised an eyebrow. "They didn't mention *anything*? A direction? A port?"

"If they did, I don't remember. Captain Quinn just wanted me off his ship." At least in that she spoke the truth.

Emerson and Carlton met each other's eye and gave a satisfied nod. "Well then," continued Carlton, "we'll not speak of it again. I'll pass what little information you've given us on to the authorities. I trust they'll not wish to interview you themselves unless we can think of something else."

"Thank you, Mister Whitmore. I'm sorry I couldn't be more helpful. I'd really like to put it all behind me and be grateful I've arrived. A bit battered and bruised, but alive." Alice stood and smoothed her skirts. "Mister Blake...."

He took her offered hand and kissed the backs of her fingers. "I must say, Mistress Tupper, I can't remember a time when I've met such a fascinating woman. I look forward to getting to know you better. Perhaps I can cajole Carlton into a few dinner invitations."

Alice left the study on shaky legs. Once in the foyer she leaned back against the closed door. Through the crack in the door, she heard Emerson Blake question Carlton, "Those bloody bastards stole our slaves. She has to know something. Do you believe her?"

"I don't know. She obviously suffered unspeakable horrors. You saw the way she went down when you mentioned them. I say give the foolish girl some peace. In time, maybe she'll remember something that will help us stretch a few necks."

Alice pushed away from the door and hurried back upstairs to her rooms. She checked the lock on the armoire. Dropping into a chair, she put her face in her hands and stifled a sob. They wanted to hang Gavin. Thank goodness he slipped away. With any luck he was far, far from here.

Carlton Whitmore had to believe she didn't have any more information. If he learned the whole truth, what would he do? Ordered her shot at dawn? She was no better than any other member of the *Scarlet Night*. She had helped free those slaves and killed a man in cold blood. Killed more men in battle. And, she was in possession of stolen gold from a Spanish merchant ship. Could she be any more of a pirate?

Above all the rest, she had fallen in love with Gavin Quinn, pirate captain. A wanted criminal. Carlton had called him vicious and ruthless. To her he was neither of those things. Even though he broke her heart, she feared for his life. She feared for her own should anyone discover her secrets. And while part of her longed to look into Gavin's steely gray eyes again and revel in the strength of his arms about her, the other part of her was willing him to go as far from her as he could get.

Chapter 22

Gavin paced the decks. For the last twenty-four hours he'd done little but look over his shoulder. He'd evaded half the British fleet to get away from the eastern shores of Virginia. It was fortunate for him, he knew where they'd look, it meant they'd never find him.

He'd sailed the *Scarlet Night* through the Needle's Eye. Water washed from the sea through a narrow, hidden channel protected by rocky shoals into an unknown cave known as the Needle's Eye. Inside, the space opened into a skylit cavern large enough for a dozen ships their size. A fool's gamble at low tide, it was just wide enough for the *Night*. Navy warships were far too wide in the berth to follow them even if they had known of its location, and only one way in made it easy to defend should anyone be lucky enough to stumble upon them. The only other captain who knew about this particular hiding place was busy living his new life as a lord in Weatherington, England with his wife, Annalise.

Slipping in two steps ahead of the British, the *Scarlet Night* spent the night tucked into the high-walled cave. A few days there would have guaranteed the British dogs chased their tails, but food was in short supply, and without the proper materials to fix the damn front mast, they were riding heavy and slow. They had to slip past unawares and make their way to a protected port before they were forced to start roasting bilge rats.

Leaving on the first tide, luck had been on their side. The winds were strong coming from the west. They set course due south and headed toward the Caribbean.

Unease crawled over the ship as they left Virginia. The crew was uglier than usual, and the ship was limping. Gavin's own temper was quick to ignite. He relieved the helmsman and took the wheel. Gripping the thick wooden pegs, he gathered a small measure of command when everything else seemed out of his control.

They'd lost Bump for a time. Gavin hadn't seen the boy for hours. He feared he'd fallen overboard without anyone's notice. He'd called a ship-wide search. No one could locate the boy.

Gavin had finally found him curled up tight under Tupper's cot. It was the third time he'd looked for him in her spit of a room. He'd found her book the first time. The second time, he'd been blindsided by the memory of kissing her there. He was at his wit's end when he searched for the third time, but there Bump was. Had he been there the entire time?

The boy was miserable, and Gavin didn't know what to do to comfort the lad. How do you explain with no words? Frustration raged. Why the hell did he take on the role of nursemaid anyway? He missed her as much as anyone, dammit. The child needed to learn the cold, hard facts of this life. This was a pirate ship, not a lady's parlor. Life was hard and brutal, and the sooner Bump learned that the better.

The ship groaned against the tight hold Gavin had upon the wheel. He had to ease off. The ship and the boy. "Bloody hell," he whispered.

Gavin took a deep breath and watched the moonrise spill its silvery shimmer over the water. It was the night after the full, its perfect circle missing one edge. Memories flooded his senses. The same moon was watching Alice as she slept.

Would the light fall across her bed? Across her hair fanning the pillow? With the moon so bright, he could see it all in his mind. The rise and fall of her breathing. Her body naked beneath the thin sheet. One perfect breast exposed. One long leg. She'd wake when he came into the room, hold back the bedding in invitation, and he'd slip into her arms, pulling her body against his, drowning in the smell of her skin and the sweet taste of her mouth.

"Bloody damn, blasted hell." Why couldn't he get her out of his mind? His body still pulsed with want. Having her only made him want her more. He was thankful for the length of his coat. Gavin slipped a hand into a wide slashed pocket and wrapped his fingers around the heavy parcel. His gift to her. The necklace she refused.

He'd carried it since Simons returned it to him with her message. Gavin hadn't shown any reaction, but simply dropped it in his pocket. And there it would remain. A weighty reminder of her time with him. His thumb traced the edges of the large stones as green eyes flashed in his memory.

Gavin handed over the wheel at the next bell after he barked at the helmsman for being late to his post. Storming off the quarterdeck, he made his final rounds before heading below. His body was taut with heated frustration. Entering his quarter, he snatched a fresh bottle of brandy and a glass before he caught sight of Bump. The child was asleep in his chair hidden away beneath a gray hat with a white feather. "Dammit...she's ruined the lot of us."

Settling the boy, Gavin returned to his desk. Another endless night stretched out before him. The brandy stood waiting. He pulled Beth's letters from their hiding place and untied their leather lace. Lifting the first envelope, he traced his name with a fingertip.

"Do you have any idea how many times I've read your words, Beth? I can recite them by memory. I treasure them. I hate them." He pulled the cork from the bottle. "Eleven years. I've held them and poured over every page trying to understand. How could you have loved me like you professed and done what you did? I know, the babe." He gave a heavy sigh. "I know I can't understand the pain, but you never gave me a chance to carry some of that grief. He was my son, too. I loved you with everything I had. I would have walked into hell with you and found a way out. I never got the chance. You stole that from me. When you took your life, you took mine too."

Gavin recorked the bottle and pushed it away. He ran a weary hand over his eyes. "Eleven years, Beth. I've honored the love I shared with you for all that time. I've mourned and grieved and been eaten alive by guilt until the only things left for me were empty, hollow memories and a stack of yellowed letters."

Gavin pulled the necklace out of his pocket and unwrapped it. The gems caught the light. "I love her, Beth. I love her, and I pushed her away because of my loyalty to you. I had to keep her safe. Not only from this brutal life, but from a life with me. I failed you, but I wasn't going to fail her too." He crushed the necklace tight, the edge of the gold cutting into his hand. "So why doesn't it feel like I've done the right thing?"

His arm swept the surface of his desk. Letters scattered. The glass shattered when it hit the floor, but the thick bottle of brandy stayed intact and rolled back to rest against his boot.

Gavin shut his eyes. The strong drink taunted him. Called to him like a siren of the sea. The sweet call of oblivion where nothing mattered. Nothing hurt. It could help him to forget, if only for the night. Brandy had seen him through the first few years after Beth's death, but soon became out of control. He was rarely sober during those times. It was Jaxon Steele who pulled him out of that hellish whirlpooled pit. Beat some sense into him. Dried him out. Gave him back his dignity. Steele had trusted him. Not only with his life but also his ship.

Reaching down, Gavin grasped the bottle as he rose to his feet. He crossed to the bank of windows and threw the thing out to toss in the waves of the ship's wake. The moon's glow washed the sea. And as he had for a thousand times already today, he thought about Alice.

MacTavish was right. He was a horse's arse.

Chapter 23

After the tension of meeting with Carlton Whitmore and Emerson Blake, Alice spent an exhausting morning being tugged about by Brighton and Rebecca. Brighton acted as tour guide, showing Alice all his favorite parts of the estate—the tree he climbed, where he lost his first tooth, and the place where a large black snake had left its skin.

Touring the stables, she was introduced to Champ and Molly, the children's ponies. Brighton warned her about King's Knight, a towering black stallion. He had a nasty temper and was a terrible biter. She wasn't about to get too close. But Starr, a gentle roan mare with a white blaze upon her forehead, was the best horse Brighton knew, second to his beloved Champ.

Their visit to the stable had been quick. Rebecca was indeed terrified of the large nickering beasts. She wouldn't venture any farther than the shade of the wide doorway. As the day progressed, Alice was please to see Rebecca relaxing in her company. Her thumb, while always at the ready, found its way to her mouth less often. The reason, Alice soon discovered, was that Rebecca outrivaled her mother's gift of constant chatter.

Walking past the neat fields of tobacco Alice noted the rows of small shacks to house the field hands. Brighton pointed out the larger house near the head of the fields, which belonged to the overseer, Mister Bishop.

"I don't like him," announced Rebecca. "He likes to yell and…and cusses a blue streak."

Alice cocked an eyebrow. "Where did you hear such an expression?"

"Nurse Susanna. We were walking, and her big straw hat blew off into the fields and we chased it because it was new and nurse said it cost a pretty penny and Mister Bishop chased after us and started hollering and Nurse covered my ears and hollered back at him then she told Mama he cusses a blue streak." One long sentence, all in one breathe. Alice had to smile.

As both children ran off toward the main house, Alice paused to look over the slave quarters again. From what she'd observed, the Whitmore's were good to their help, but the fact still remained these men, women, and children were property. If he and Emerson Blake had witnessed those men from the *Delmar*, she wondered if they would have a different view.

Alice returned the children to the nursery after their noon meal. She would have loved to join them for a rest, but Isabelle revised the day's schedule, and Alice was hurried off to town.

Cape Henry was a bustling seaport, with a variety of merchants ready to service the growing population. What interested Alice more, however, was the strong number of British soldiers and seamen in town. The same sick worry from this morning washed over her. Gavin had risked everything to bring her here. She couldn't bear to think what would happen to him and the entire crew if they were caught.

By the time she and Isabelle returned to the estate, Alice was beyond exhausted. No training aboard a pirate ship prepared her for the ball of perpetual energy that was Isabelle Whitmore. They returned with armloads of packages with more to be delivered later. For each gown Isabelle picked for Alice, she chose two for herself. Lengths of cloth were debated, shoes dyed to match. She even insisted on buying Alice a tiny feathered hat, which perched upon her head like a bird's nest simply because it suited Alice's coloring.

The children were well rested by the time they returned, and after being spoiled with small treats and gifts from their mother, they were eager to spend more time with Alice before nurse would gather them for their baths.

"Why don't I read to you? Brighton, could you fetch us a book? Do you have a favorite story you'd like to hear?" Alice settled them in the shade of the wide front porch.

"Couldn't you tell us a story instead?" Brighton lay on his stomach lining up his new lead soldiers. He popped up. "A story about pirates."

Alice shook her head. "Your mother wouldn't approve."

"Please?" both of them pleaded. Two sets of imploring blue eyes blinked up at her.

"What if I tell you about a little boy?" she countered.

"Are there pirates?" The lad had a one-track mind.

"Yes," Alice promised. Brighton's eyes lit up, and she continued. "He's a few years younger than you, Brighton, and he lives on a pirate ship with bright red sails."

"Was he with his mommy?" asked Rebecca.

Her brother shot her a look. "There aren't pirate mommies."

Alice continued, "He doesn't have a mother or a father, but he has a whole ship full of people looking out for him. Captain, especially."

Brighton had forgotten about his soldiers. "What's his name?"

Alice smiled. "His name is William, but once you become a member of a pirate crew, sometimes they give you a nickname. Like when Brighton calls you Becca.

The girl scooted closer. "What was his made up name?"

Alice tucked Rebecca's fine hair behind her ear. "They call him Bump."

"Bump?" Brighton laughed. "That's not a pirate name."

Alice shrugged one shoulder. "It is. He wasn't used to being on a ship. And when things fall or are swinging, if you aren't watching, you can get a bumped on the head. He got a lot of bumps at first.

"He wasn't careful." Rebecca frowned and pushed her thumb into her mouth.

"He was as careful as he could be, and his friends would shout for him to look out, but he couldn't hear them."

"Was it too noisy?" asked Brighton.

Alice ruffled his hair as she'd done to Bump. "No, Bump can't hear. His ears don't work anymore." The children looked at each other as Alice continued. "But Bump is a fine cabin boy. He's brave and strong. I miss him. Makes me wonder what it would be like if I couldn't hear like Bump." Alice pointed up into the trees. "Can you hear the birds calling to each other? I love to hear the birds. Can you imagine what it would be like if you couldn't hear your favorite sounds?"

"I don't like this story," pouted Rebecca. "It's sad."

Alice laid a gentle hand on her head. "Don't be sad. I want you to remember to be grateful. You're very lucky children, strong and healthy, with two wonderful parents and a beautiful place to live."

"Will Bump get a mommy?" Rebecca asked around her thumb. Brighton reached over and gently removed it from her mouth.

"I don't think so." Alice gave a quick shake to her head.

"I bet he'll get his own pistol," chimed Brighton.

Alice smirked. She could almost picture MacTavish rummaging through the gun bin to find the perfect one as he'd done for her. "When he's older."

Rebecca looked at her brother in disgust. "Mommies are better than stinky old pistols."

"To girls maybe, not boys," he argued.

"Girls can have pistols, too." Rebecca planted her hands on her hips.

"They cannot. Can they, Alice?"

Alice put a hand on each child's shoulder and held them apart. "Only grownups get pistols. Now pick up your things and let's find Susanna. Its time she scrubbed your dirty little necks."

On the way back to the nursery, the children discussed the pros and cons of pistol ownership versus something even better than mommies—puppies. Leaving them in Susanna's gentle care she couldn't help but wonder about Bump.

It had only been a day, and she missed him desperately.

Dressing in one of her new gowns, a lightweight, striped cotton in a soft shade of green, Alice applied a bit more concealing powder. The color of the dress did wonderful things to the green of her eyes, and it fit her like it had been made for her.

Arriving in the parlor, she found Isabelle Whitmore looking lovely in a dress of silvery blue. She was the very height of elegance and grace. A single teardrop of sapphire adorned her throat and dripped from each ear. The perfect hostess, she was pouring the wine.

Alice twisted her ring. It had been months and an entire ocean since she dined amongst gentry. She hoped she remembered which fork to use. "Good evening, Isabelle."

"Alice, dear, don't you look lovely. I knew the color would suit you. So much more attractive than the mud-colored skirt you arrived in." She handed her a glass. "I've just come from seeing the children. They are quite taken with you already. I'm so pleased."

"They were fun today. Both so eager and curious."

Isabelle beamed. "I told you, everyone loves them." She took a sip of wine, and slipped her hand through Alice's arm, steering her toward the back patio overlooking the gardens. "I worry about Rebecca being too timid, but she's young yet. And Brighton takes after his father in so many ways. He's anxious to wish away his childhood so he can do all those grownup things he thinks are so interesting."

They stood catching the first cool breeze of the evening. "It's beautiful here. The children gave me the tour. Tomorrow, Brighton wants to show me the stream."

"It's one of his favorite places. I'll have Cook pack you a basket lunch."

"Well, what have we here?" Carlton Whitmore stepped out onto the patio. "Blake, we've found their hiding spot." Isabelle tipped her cheek as he kissed her. "My dear, you are a vision."

Isabelle scolded, "We weren't hiding, and if you men had any sense of time, you'd not have kept us waiting." She smiled at their guest. "Emerson, I'm so pleased you asked to join us tonight."

Emerson Blake looked much better when he wasn't flying into a study anxious to hang a ship full of pirates. "Isabelle, you're too kind. I forced myself upon you and you're gracious enough not to show me the door."

Emerson kissed her hand. Had she been meeting him for the first time, Alice might have considered him attractive.

"Nonsense, you're always welcome." Isabelle turned toward Alice. "Have you met our new governess, Mistress Alice Tupper?"

"Yes, this morning. My lack of manners precedes me, I'm afraid." He nodded a greeting in her direction. His eyes warmed. "But the idea of spending my evening in the company of two such beautiful women was all the incentive I needed to be boorish once again."

His flight of angry agitation past, Emerson Blake was the vision of a country gentleman. Wig, waistcoat, and walking stick. Dressed in his dinner clothing, he was quite handsome. His dark coloring hidden by a short wig, yet the strength of his brows and the depth of his brown eyes seemed more striking in contrast. When he smiled, a boyish dimple flashed in one cheek. Broad shoulders filled the fine brocade of his wine-colored waistcoat. A froth of lace adorned his neck and cuffs. Slim hips and long legs were encased in a dark gray satin. A proper gentleman down to the silk of his stockings and the buckles on his heeled shoes.

"I would have thought all your evenings would be spent with Harriet Applegate. Rumor has it you've spent a good deal of time in her company. Perhaps we'll soon have news of a harvest wedding?"

"Isabelle," cautioned Carlton, "leave the man be."

Emerson chuckled. "Isabelle, ever the matchmaker. Harriet is a lovely woman, quite proper. Fine stock. A pleasant enough companion. She and her mother are off. Visiting an aunt, I believe. Up North. The summer temperatures don't suit them." He moved closer to Alice. "What about you, Mistress Tupper? Does the heat suit you?"

The way he emphasized the word "heat" put her immediately on guard. "The workers in the fields must suffer terribly on days like today."

He waved a hand in dismissal. "They're used to it."

Alice opened her mouth preparing to congratulate him on maintaining his high standard of boorish qualities, when dinner was announced. Emerson scooped her arm and tucked it in his as their hosts led them into the dining room. He gave her fingers a squeeze and whispered, "I've been looking forward to this all day."

"Dinner?" she countered. Emerson laughed as Alice tugged her hand away from his arm.

Five long courses later, Alice was ready to step in front of a cannon and yell, "Fire." Emerson Blake was relentless in his attention. He dominated the conversation. When he wasn't asking questions about her life in England, he was regaling her with stories about himself. Each charming anecdote ending with some subtle yet pointed mention regarding his wealth, prestige, or standing in the community.

Alice nearly wept with joy when Carlton suggested he and Emerson retire to the study for their brandy and cigars.

"Wonderful idea, Carlton, I can tell you about the two new racing stallions I acquired. Fine stock." He rose and smoothed his vest. "Excellent meal, Isabelle. Thank you." He gave a quick bow. "Mistress Tupper. I trust we'll see one another again."

"I fear it's inevitable." Her parting shot flew clear over his bow. It hadn't even ruffled his wig.

After the men left, Alice begged off tea with Isabelle claiming the children had worn her out. She needed nothing more than a quick breath of fresh air before seeking out her bed.

Pale moonlight lit the graveled garden paths. The air, blissfully cool. Alice took a deep breath, willing the tension to leave her shoulders.

A faint whiff of cigar smoke met her before she heard the footsteps in the walk. "Perfect end to a perfect evening." Emerson's voice reached out to her in the moonlight. "Mind if I join you?"

Alice screwed her eyes shut and refused to turn around. "Actually—"

"Staring into my brandy just now, I couldn't get a particular image out of my mind." He had come to stand beside her, took a pull on his cigar, and blew a cloud of smoke above their heads. "Aren't you going to ask what image?"

Alice waved the smoke away from her. "I'm assuming you'll tell me."

"You. This morning. Swallowing my brandy as if it were mother's milk."

"Did you bring me another?" She looked at his hands before raising her gaze to his all-seeing eyes.

"Afraid not." He grinned. His eyes twinkled with amusement.

Alice crossed her arms and dropped her chin. "That's probably for the best. It's not a proper thing for a lady to do. Swilling brandy."

"All I can offer you is a smoke." He smirked holding his smoldering cigar toward her.

Alice plucked the cigar from his fingers. "Do they taste as horrible as they smell?"

"You've no intention—" He reached for it, but she was quick to pull it away from his reach. Lifting it to her mouth she took a puff, grimaced, and handed it back to him.

"Worse than I imagined." She wiped at her mouth with the backs of her fingers.

Emerson threw his head back and laughed. "Who the devil are you?"

Lisa A. Olech

"Poor stock. Not a proper lady, obviously. But a tired one. Good night, Mister Blake."

"It's Emerson," he called after her.

Chapter 24

"Come on, Rebecca, you can do it," coaxed Alice.

The child stood in the dark, wide doorway of the massive stable and sucked her thumb. Alice crouched down and rubbed at the child's arm. "I'll be right here and Starr is very gentle. She'll love the apple you brought her. Let's go give it to her. I bet she'll whisper 'thank you' in your ear."

"I need the tooth." Rebecca lisped around her thumb.

"I left the lion tooth in my room, but you don't need it. You're already brave and strong like that old lion. Come on. Starr is hungry."

Alice cajoled and nudged the girl enough to enter the stable full of intimidating horses. Rebecca could either be afraid all her life and swoon at the sight of a spider, or she could inherit some of the determined fortitude of her father and brother. It was in her to become a strong, capable young woman, if she'd allow herself to be.

When the child walked those last few feet and lifted the offered apple, Alice silently whooped like a pirate swinging from the rigging.

Before long, Rebecca was climbing trees and bringing Starr apples and carrots each afternoon. She even knocked her brother on his backside after he'd stolen one of her toys.

Isabelle noticed the change, too. She mentioned it at dinner one evening. "I see you're teaching my daughter to be as strong as my son."

"Rebecca is every bit as strong as Brighton. She's coming out of her shell." Alice frowned at the concerned look on Isabelle's face. "Is that a problem?"

Isabelle shook her head. "No, I think it's wonderful she's becoming less timid, but there are proprieties that need to be remembered as well. A man rarely chooses a headstrong woman to be his wife. Rebecca needs to learn the proper etiquette for a young woman."

"I agree. There's no harm in helping her find a bit more self-confidence. Brighton is such a strong boy. He tends to over shadow her. Encouraging Rebecca also teaches Brighton things like respect and compassion for others."

"I hadn't thought of it that way. It's a wonderful prospect for both of them," smiled Isabelle. "You are a wonder, Alice."

"I'll draw the line if she suddenly wants to wear britches."

* * * *

Weeks passed, and Alice finally begun to relax. Her bruises had faded and she'd not heard any news from Carlton or Emerson Blake regarding the *Scarlet Night* or Gavin. They'd questioned her again as to whether she'd remembered anything more. She told them Gavin may have mentioned a sister living near Boston. No doubt, at this very moment, at least one British Naval ship was headed north in search of a wild goose.

Gavin headed south for sure. All the safe ports for him are there. By now, the mast had been repaired. She imagined he'd be heading back to intercept more slave ships and fill his coffers again. After witnessing a slave auction last week in town, men and women chained like animals, giving Emerson Blake any tiny tidbit of misinformation well justified the lie in her mind.

Neither Carlton nor Emerson was pleased about the fact Gavin and his crew had escaped the hangman's noose. They grumbled about it often. Alice would nod sympathetically, all the while relieved they were well away from danger. You'd have thought that fact alone would help her sleep at night.

Her days were packed full of activities with the children. Alice would fill the hours with a busy array of lessons and walks, trips to the stream, picnics. All so when she dropped her exhausted body into bed, her nights might be filled with dreamless sleep.

Gavin only whispered into her thoughts during the day; however, he would ride full-sail into her dreams at night. The passionate images were so vivid she would awaken certain she was not alone in her bed. Realization would collapse atop her heart and punch the air from her lungs while frustration and want raked across her body. Try as she might, she couldn't put him from her mind. He was there each time she closed her eyes.

Today she and the children secured a basket lunch from Cook. Taking fishing poles and a wide-mouthed jar of earthworms, they headed down to a small pond near the very back of the property. The day was crystalline clear, the sky a cloudless swath of vivid blue. Alice and Rebecca wore straw hats and drank cool, tart lemonade from a thick stoneware pot. Brighton hunted frogs and skipped stones over the dark, flat surface of the water.

Following their lunch of cold chicken, fresh apples, and leftover cornbread from breakfast, Brighton was patient in showing his little sister the proper way to stick a worm on a fishhook. All were proud when Rebecca mastered the maneuver with no squeamishness at all.

Hours later, the trio rushed happily into the manor house. Brighton was so excited about the three fat fish he caught, he couldn't wait to show his father. Rebecca had caught one small sunfish, but by the look upon her beaming face, you would have thought she'd hooked a whale.

Both children raced through the house calling after their father, holding their prize catches high. Alice hurried after them. "Keep your voices down. Don't run in the house."

Ahead, Brighton ignored Alice's warnings and burst into his father's study.

Carlton Whitmore jumped to his feet. "Brighton, don't you knock, boy?" scolded his father.

"Sorry, Father, but look." He held up his fish.

Rebecca was right behind him. "Father, me too, look."

Alice was less than three strides back and came up behind both children. "I'm terribly sorry," she huffed, out of breath. "The children were excited." Emerson Blake stood. Since the night in the garden, she'd done all she could to avoid the man, but he seemed a constant visitor. "We didn't mean to disturb you."

She patted the children's shoulders. "Say 'good day' to Mister Blake, children."

"Good day, Mister Blake," they repeated before excitement caught hold again. "Aren't they the biggest fish you've ever seen?" Brighton insisted. "I caught mine all by myself, Father," Rebecca added.

As Carlton examined the children's prize catch, Emerson stepped closer to Alice. "We were actually just talking about you."

Uneasiness washed over her. She focused her gaze on the children and tried to keep the rise in her breathing under control. "Me? I can't imagine a less interesting topic. What were you saying?"

"The subject of pirates came up again."

"And you were wondering if I'd ever scaled a yardarm or sported an eye patch?" She gave him a quick smile and watched his dimple flash. "Children, your father has seen your fish, and we're being rude to Mister Blake." She tried to pull the children back out of the study.

Carlton Whitmore smoothed the front of his waistcoat and smiled at his children. "Those are the finest fish I have seen in quite a long time." He leaned forward. "They look delicious. Why don't you take them to Cook and ask her to fix them for our dinner?"

"Cook makes the best fish dinners," agreed Brighton while beaming with pride.

"But, Father," cried Rebecca, "my fish isn't for dinner. I want to keep him. He'll be no trouble. He's quiet, and he only eats worms."

Alice bit her lip and soothed Rebecca. "Let's talk about this outside and let your father get back to his meeting with Mister Blake."

Carlton walked them to the door. "Thank you for sharing your good fortune with me, children."

Rebecca frowned. "They're not fortunes, they're fish."

"Come along." Alice ushered the small fishing party through the doorway. She kept her gaze away from Emerson. There was no telling what he'd read on her face. "I am sorry we interrupted you."

Children and fish were delivered to their respective places. After debating with Rebecca, she agreed perhaps a drawing of a fish was better than a dead fish. Even if he was quiet. They found him a shady spot in the garden as his final resting place.

Using the children's respite, Alice found her own shady spot. Taking a book she'd borrowed from the Whitmore's library, she settled herself beneath one of the huge oak trees that graced the edges of the garden. Beneath its wide shadow, it was blissfully cool and comfortable.

Alice plucked at the clover next to her, rolling the tender stalks between her fingers. Dropping it into her lap. Try as she might, she couldn't concentrate on the words within the book. Her encounter with Emerson Blake still nagged at the back of her mind.

Perhaps she was being paranoid, but the way he looked at her at times, was most disconcerting. They were talking about her. In what context?

Alice turned the page without reading a single line, and picked another stem, absently twirling the small round blades of its leaves like a top. Perhaps they were still determined to capture Gavin. Had something else happened? Seems there were new reports of pirate activities all along the coastline and throughout the outer banks.

She sighed in worried frustration and leaned her head against the rough bark of the oak. She even tried to convince herself it wasn't just Gavin she was concerned about, it was everyone. MacTavish, Robbins, Bump, and the rest. But in her heart she knew the truth of it. The ache of Gavin's rejection had lost some of its edge. She understood why he'd pushed her away. Had the boot been on the other foot, she might have done the same thing. If she had been the captain of the *Scarlet Night* and feared for a member of the crew, she'd have put them ashore, too.

So why didn't that knowledge and conviction ease her worries more? Because of the one thing all the rational thought and distance and practical understanding couldn't explain away? The love. What was she supposed to do with that? Try as she might, she couldn't stop loving him. In fact, if anything, her feelings for Gavin had only grown since she'd been here.

She missed him with all her heart and even missed that infuriating look he would give her when she had exasperating the hell out of him. But it was the look in his eyes the day they had made love. He never said the words, but she saw the hunger and passion in his eyes.

It was in his touch and his kiss. The way he put his lips to the scar upon her thigh before lowering is mouth to—

"A picture of quiet contentment." Emerson Blake's voice startled Alice out of a dream.

She leapt to her feet, heart pounding, brushing bits of green from her skirt. "I-I didn't hear you approach."

"I'm sorry, I didn't mean to frighten you, but I'm most anxious to speak with you."

Short of shimmying up the tree to escape him, she couldn't think of any way to avoid him. "What did you want to talk about?"

"May I sit with you?" He indicated the grass.

"If you wish." They sat upon the soft ground. Alice kept her back to the stout tree trunk with her book in her lap.

Emerson sat facing her. "That was impressive earlier."

She gave him a questioning glance.

"The children." He smiled.

"They run faster than I." She lifted one shoulder.

"You handled them brilliantly. Carlton and Isabelle rave about you."

"They're not difficult to *handle*." She plucked another piece of clover. Curiosity made her ask. "Did you finish talking about me after I left?"

Emerson's smile tipped up on one side. "Actually, yes. Carlton and I were celebrating a small victory. The British have agreed to increase their patrols along the coast, and we heard the *Scarlet Night* was spotted leaving port farther south. With any luck Captain Quinn will sail right into their hands."

A cold finger of fear ran down Alice's spine. She fought to remain calm. Struggled to think of what she could do without bringing the entire British Navy down upon her head. Her heart thundered in her chest while Emerson Blake kept chatting away. She'd lost track of what he was saying. Something about safe futures and higher profits on shipments.

Emerson leaned forward. "I'm a man of action." He reached for her hand, crushing the clover's tender stem she held between her fingers. "I work hard. When I see something I want, I take it. I'm direct. It's my nature. I want you, Alice."

She jerked as if he'd struck her. How had the conversation moved from Gavin being captured to this? "I b-beg your pardon?"

Emerson released her hand and stood. "It's no secret. I want a wife. I want children."

Alice's mind spun. She was back on a pitching deck trying to find her footing. "Weren't you courting Harriet Appletree?"

"Applegate." He smirked. "She's a fine woman. Everything I wanted in a mate." He knelt before her and lifted her hand. "But then I met you."

Alice tugged her hand away and stood, dropping her book. She stepped clear of him. "You're confused. You hardly know me. I'm sure once Harriet returns, the two of you—"

"I don't want her. I want you." He reached for her again.

Alice dodged his hands. "Stop saying that." She turned her back on him and placed her hand over her pounding heart.

He moved to stand behind her. "It's true. I find you captivating."

She spun, catching her skirts as they brushed his legs. "Proper. You said she was a proper woman. Fine stock, remember?" Alice took another step back, shaking her head. "I'm neither of those things."

"You're a rare find, Alice Tupper. Intelligent. Strong. You know your own mind."

"Translation," she laughed. "Odd. Opinionated. Stubborn."

Emerson smiled. The dimple in his cheek flashed. "I can be just as stubborn." He closed the space between them. Alice moved to step back and met the tree. "I realize you're unconventional. Spirited." His gaze lowered. This close he had a clear view into the top of her gown. She was breathing so hard, he was getting quite the show. "It may be against my better judgment, but I don't care. I've decided." Emerson's voice was low. He was so close. Alice could smell his cologne. The lingering scent of cigar smoke on his clothes. The brandy on his breath.

If she moved a fraction of an inch, he'd be kissing her. "You're drunk."

His eyes locked with hers. "I've never been more sober in my life." His gaze moved to her mouth. "I can offer you so much. I have land. Wealth." He moved to touch her, his fingers a whisper away from her skin. "I'd never raise a hand against you. Never hurt you." Emerson closed his eyes and released a deep breath. "You don't love me. I know. But in time."

She waited for him to lift his gaze before she shook her head. "Emerson, you have no idea who I am."

He eased back, opened his arms wide and smiled broadly. "I'll learn. I'll court you. You'll see, I'll win your heart."

Alice pushed away from the tree and skirted him. Picking up her book, she held it to her chest. "That's impossible."

"I don't know the meaning of the word." He caught her arm as she tried to leave. "Nothing is impossible."

She pulled out of his grasp. "I'm afraid this is."

Chapter 25

The flowers began to arrive within the hour. An invitation to tea interrupted the flow of blossoms. Alice replied with a curt refusal together with an insistence Emerson cease sending her flowers.

At dinner that evening, Alice apologized for the uproar caused by the persistent Mister Blake.

"I've told him to stop, but he is determined."

Carlton laughed. "You've underestimated him. Emerson is like a dog with his teeth in a new bone. He can be relentless."

Her patience snapped. "I'm not a dog's bone, Mister Whitmore. His proposal is ridiculous."

"I wish you luck persuading him otherwise." Carlton chuckled. "Tell her, Isabelle."

Isabelle dabbed at the corners of her mouth with her napkin. "He's right, Alice. Emerson can be most single-minded. But in truth, he's a wonderful man. He's the most eligible man in the county. You'd want for nothing. He'd make you a fine husband."

Alice couldn't believe she was hearing this. "I just became your governess. Now you want to marry me off?"

"Of course, we'd hate to lose you as our governess, but the opportunity to marry a man like Emerson doesn't come along every day. We could still be the best of friends. We'd still see you all the time."

The fish course was served. Brighton's fish. Alice fiddled with her fork. How could she get them to understand short of telling them the truth? She'd need their help in dissuading Emerson from this ridiculous notion. She'd make as fine a wife to Emerson Blake as Rebecca's fish would make a lovely pet.

Isabelle took a sip of her wine. "If he's planning a wedding after the last harvest, that wouldn't give us much time to make all the proper arrangements." She turned to Carlton. "People would need sufficient notice and travel days. I suppose we could put some of the wedding guests up here."

Alice muttered around the food in her mouth, "Wedding guests?"

"I'll have to make a list for Cook. Oh, and we would need to contact the dressmaker at once. And the minister." Isabelle shook her head at Carlton. "You men rarely think of the time it takes to plan these things."

Trying to swallow and object, the bite of fish took a wrong turn in her throat. Alice choked and started coughing. Violently.

Isabelle was on her feet, "Carlton, do something."

He rushed over and gave Alice several quick raps on her back, until, with eyes watering, she lifted her hands in surrender. She grabbed for her water and took a drink to clear her throat.

"Alice, are you all right?" Isabelle fussed.

"No," Alice coughed.

"More water, Carlton," Isabelle insisted.

Alice caught his arm and stopped him. "No, I don't need more water." She coughed once more and stood. Catching her breath, she pressed a hand to her stomach. "There will be no need to contact a dressmaker, or give a list to Cook. I'm not marrying Emerson Blake." She dropped her napkin to the table. "I don't care if he is mule-headed, nor do I care if he has all the money in the world and buys me gowns of solid gold. I don't wish to insult a friend of this household, but I'm telling you, I'll not wed him."

"Foolish girl," sputtered Carlton.

"Why ever not?" asked Isabelle. "Any other woman would jump at the chance to marry Emerson. Does this have something to do with your voyage here?"

"No." Alice took another breath and fought the urge to scream.

Isabelle would not be quelled. "What reason could there be?"

Carlton held up a hand. "Isabelle, it is no business of ours. If the girl doesn't wish to marry, so be it. For goodness sake, she was taken by pirates. She's been traumatized. She's hardly in her right mind." He took his seat again. "If you'll think about it, it is actually rather amusing. Watching Emerson Blake *not* get what he wants for the first time in his life?"

"Excuse me. I've lost my appetite." She didn't wait for a response, but left the Whitmore's to the remainder of their dinner.

Entering her room, Alice was overcome with the dizzying smell of dozens of flowers that had been placed there. She opened all the windows and resisted the urge to hurl them into the back garden. After moving them into the hallway, Alice dropped to lie across her bed.

What in hell was wrong with men? Were they all daft or simply the ones she happened to cross paths with? When had the word no come to mean something other than no? When had yes become yes, but only for a day? Or a night? Do they speak a different language? How had so many words become convoluted? Want. Need. And what about love? Is it even in their vocabulary? Why were men either making her crazy or trying to kill her?

Alice sat before her mirror and pulled the hairpins from her hair. Tugging the braid loose, she attacked it with her brush. She shook the brush at her reflection in the mirror. "I know the fastest way to dissuade Mister Emerson Blake and remove the infuriating twinkle in his eye. He wants to get to know me? Let him get to know me. I'll bet his fascination would shrivel like grapes in the sun once he learns his sweet, unassuming wife-to-be is actually a murderer, a thief, and a liar. It would serve him right to wed him. Perhaps I'll wait until he carries me to our wedding bed before I announce he's taken a pirate for a wife."

No sooner had the words left her mouth, there was a quick knock on the door. If it was more flowers, she was getting her pistol. Alice opened the door to find Isabelle standing with a tea tray.

"I'm sorry to disturb you, but your light still burned and you didn't eat much of your dinner."

"That's kind, but—"

"I wanted to apologize for our behavior earlier. I know we upset you. Please. I won't sleep with this hanging between us."

Alice stepped to one side and let her come in.

Isabelle set down the tray. "Are you sure I can't tempt you? Cook sent along some of her delicious cookies."

"I do love Cook's baking." Alice gave her a small smile.

The women settled into the matching armchairs. Isabelle went through the motions of pouring them both a cup of tea. "We did upset you at dinner, didn't we?"

Alice accepted the steaming tea. "It wasn't your fault. I'm frustrated that I can't seem to make Emerson realize I'm not the right woman for him."

"Don't you want to get married? Keep a fine house? Have children of your own?"

Alice shook her head. "Marriage is *not* in my future."

"But here is your chance." Isabelle offered her a plate of cookies.

"It's not that simple." Alice bit into the soft molasses round.

Isabelle gave her a long look. "I bet I can guess the problem."

Alice chuckled. "I'd be shocked if you could."

Isabelle leaned forward and placed a gentle hand on her knee. "All women hope for a love match when it comes time to wed. You barely know Emerson. You don't love him. But he's a fine man. There's a good chance for you to come to love one another. When Carlton proposed to me, I was still a child with fanciful ideas about love and marriage. I wasn't in love with him on our wedding day. But our love grew as we came to know each other. We began to forge a life for ourselves. Then came the children." Isabelle gave her a serious stare. "You do want children of your own, don't you? You're so wonderful with Brighton and Rebecca. You'd make a fine mother."

Alice set her cup aside. Fear she might have carried Gavin's child had already been dismissed. "Isabelle."

"You could fall in love with Emerson as easily as you could fall in love with someone else."

Alice took her hand. It was the one truth she could share. "I've already done that."

Isabelle blinked with wide eyes. "You're in love with another man?"

Alice couldn't deny it.

Isabelle gave a little gasp. "I can see it in your eyes." Concern etched her face. "Who is he? Why aren't you with him? Did you leave him in England?"

"I can't talk about him." Alice chewed at her lip. "Caring for him the way I do, I couldn't make promises to another."

"Of course." Isabelle tsked, and sat back to drink her tea. "How awful. For you both. Did you leave him with a broken heart, as well?"

Alice envisioned a stack of old, yellowed letters. She picked up her tea to sip away the sudden lump in her throat. "Yes, his heart was truly broken."

Chapter 26

"Fire!" Gavin screamed through the smoke. Chain shot exploded from the port cannons taking down their main mast. The falling sail and rope crippling the men on deck.

The British warship had caught up with the *Scarlet Night* somewhere off the coast of the Province of Carolina. Word had spread about the increase in patrols. The British bastards were making wider sweeps, covering more ocean to protect the growing traffic along the sea's routes. Traps were set and nets hauled. Rewards had doubled. Hanging pirates was becoming a popular pastime.

Because of that, Gavin made the decision to stay clear of open seas for a while. Scuttling along the shoreline was safer. More places to hide, and even if someone was watching on the beaches, by the time the warning was sounded, the *Night* would be miles away.

Running into the fourth-rate frigate, the *Hampshire*, had been an unpleasant surprise for both parties, but it didn't take long for them to wage battle. Luck was on Gavin's side, however. The *Hampshire* was fighting into the glare of the setting sun. But his luck was fading fast.

The captain of the *Hampshire* was playing it smart. By keeping a steady bead on the *Scarlet Night's* starboard side, they were forcing her closer to the shore. This area was known for its shallow sand bars and rocky shoals that would snag a ships keel and stop her dead. As the coastline made a decided crawl toward the east, the *Scarlet Night* was being squeezed.

Gavin lowered his spyglass. "Need to take out their forward mast before we lose the sun. If we wait till they come into range, we'll be swallowing their port cannons."

Simons alerted his attention to the standing boulders off the bow. "Hull busters ahead."

"They mean to wreck us," Quinn growled.

"Ain't no channel leeward," Simons reported. "We turn hard to miss the rock, we cross their path. Those foregunners got us dead to rights. Either way, we're done."

"We're not done yet." Gavin shouted to the rear gunners to fire at will. Over the roar of the blast, he commanded Simons to turn to port.

"Capt'n, there ain't no channel. At this speed—"

"Turn! And when I give the signal, turn back full to starboard." No time to waste passing the order up ship. Gavin took off running. "Drop the mainsail." That would slow them down some. There was one shot. He knew only one man who could make it.

"Robbins," he bellowed above the fray.

The ship began to head straight for the reef. "Capt'n, the rocks!" Robbins pointed.

"Aye, fire on them."

Robbins's mouth dropped open. "What?"

Gavin slapped his shoulder. "Billiards, Robbins. Let's play billiards."

Robbins shot an anxious glance to the rocks and back to the *Hampshire*. "Can't work."

"Aye it can. You're putting it in the right back pocket. Take down the forward mast."

"Ye want me te cushion off the rocks?" His eyes were wide with disbelief. "Capt'n, no."

The rocks were getting closer. They were running out of time. "I've seen ye play, lad. Ye beat every bastard in Port Royal." Behind them, the *Hampshire*'s forward guns began to fire. "Aim for the biggest stone and make the damn shot."

Robbins checked his position. Angled his gun. Checked his position again. Adjusted his aim. Holding the slow match over the touchhole.

"Now!" Gavin covered his ears and turned away from the blast.

Robbins's cannon exploded hurling the shot to bounce back off the rocks. Through the smoke and gunfire, Gavin watched as the mast of the *Hampshire* jerked with the blow. Son of a bitch, Robbins had done it. The six-pound ball hit its mark. But the force of the shot wasn't powerful enough after angling the ricochet to shatter the mast.

They were dead men. The British were upon them. They were out of options. Did they take their chances and crash the *Scarlet Night* into the shoal or let the *Hampshire* blow her out of the water?

There was only one way for a proper pirate to die. Lord help them all, they'd go down swinging. Gavin shouted, "Simons, hard to starboard. Raise the mainsail. Starboard gunners, prepare to fire."

Over his command, a sharp *crack* reverberated across the water. Gavin raised his gaze to watch as the *Hampshire*'s leading mast snapped under the weight of canvas, rope, and wind to crash forward obliterating the crew in the bow.

Through a final blast of cannon fire, the *Scarlet Night* dodged the rocks and left the *Hampshire* floundering in a cloud of red smoke as the sun dropped behind the bluffs. Men slapped Robbins on the back and cheered. They called him "Ricochet" Robbins. Rum flowed free that night.

Their party was short-lived, however. Less than two days later, the British were at it again. Only this time, a heavy bank of fog kept them at bay throughout the day. They'd caught a glimpse between breaks in the haze and could hear them getting closer.

Gavin passed an order from man to man to man. The sails were lowered. The *Scarlet Night* slowed to a crawl and silence was the command. Not a word. Not a whisper. All lanterns doused.

Not long after dark. Robbins found Gavin in the gloom. "Capt'n," he whispered. "Bump's hurt."

Gavin followed him as he groped his way along. Even below deck, they kept their voices quiet. "What happened?"

"Fell half down the ladder way. Let out a yelp like a kicked cat when he hit. Arm looks broke te me."

Gavin's gut twisted. "Where is he?"

Robbins hitched his chin. "Yer cabin."

"I'll go. Fetch the surgeon. Bring him to Tupper's old space. No windows. Least there we can light a lantern and see what we're doing."

Moving quickly through the utter darkness, Gavin stopped inside his doorway. Alone, hurt, couldn't hear, couldn't see. The boy must be terrified. He imagined the layout of the room in his mind and crossed to the bed. Bump wasn't there. Damn it. It wasn't as if he could call out to him and have him answer. Where else would he be?

Gavin checked his chair. Under the desk. No luck. He feared in his stumbling he'd fall over the lad and injure him more. He stopped mid room. Straining his eyes and his ears, he heard it. The tiniest of whimpers.

Bump had found his way into a narrow space behind the bed. There was no way Gavin could squeeze in to reach him. He gave the wall three hits with the heel of his hand. Bump shifted, but he didn't come out. If Gavin grabbed for him... *Wait*. He knew how to get him out. Where the hell was it? Gavin prayed it was still where he'd last seen it.

Tupper's hat. With its foolish feather, he could tickle the boy's arm and maybe he'd come out. After a few sweeps with the hat, the boy emerged. Gavin slipped a gentle hand around the boy's waist and lifted him. Bump buried his face in the hat.

But when they reached the space where Tupper had slept, Bump wrestled out of Gavin's hold. Robbins and the surgeon pushed into the room. Raising the wick on the lantern they carried, Bumped blinked against the sudden onslaught of the light. He looked about the room in a panic, then back at Gavin.

The look of confusion was replaced with one of disbelief. Did Bump think Tupper had returned in the mist? Tears washed his wide brown eyes. Seeing Robbins and the doctor behind Gavin, Bump screwed his eyes tight and dropped to sit on Tupper's cot.

Gavin knelt to comfort him, and Bump turned away. He flinched when Gavin tried to touch him. Without realizing it, he had betrayed the boy. Using the hat to coax him out, he'd inadvertently raised the boy's hope that Tupper had returned. The hurt on Bump's face broke Gavin's heart. Bump's pain reached past the broken bone in his arm and Gavin had made it worse. He was an idiot. How could he find a way to explain?

As the surgeon worked on Bump's arm, the boy never made another noise. He twisted his face in agony as the bones were set back to rights, but remained silent. Splints of wood and a wrapping of bandage held the arm in place. After rigging a sling of sorts, the surgeon left.

Gavin tried once more to get Bump to look at him. Find some way to say he was sorry, but the boy wouldn't have it. Turning to Robbins, Gavin ran a hand over the ache between his eyes. "Stay with him. If he needs anything, come to me at once."

When the sun rose and burned off the last of the night's mist, the British ship was nowhere to be seen. Sails were set. Gavin gave the helmsman the order to set course at full sail.

MacTavish came to stand with Gavin in the bow. Checking the sky, he huffed. "We be heading north?"

Gavin stood with his arms crossed over his chest. If he thought he could walk away from this conversation, he would. He set his jaw. "None ever accused you of being stupid."

"Ney, but ye are." MacTavish pushed into his line of sight. "What ye thinkin' man?" He jabbed a finger toward the open sea. "The king's bastards are over the next crest sippin' tea, just waitin' on yer arse."

"I know what I'm doing."

"Do ye?" MacTavish shook his big oxen head. "Without Bellamy and Jessup te keep things in check, ye been makin' some decisions of late we ain't gonna survive." He jerked his chin toward the bowsprit setting the braids in his beard swinging. "They have the nooses tied. One fer every man and *boy* on this here ship. How many times ye plannin' to dodge 'em?"

Gavin turned away and headed aft. "They haven't caught us yet."

MacTavish pushed in front of him again, blocking his exit. "How many lives ye think we got? Ye pushin' yer luck. We should be runnin' due east. Gettin' back te what we know. "

Gavin refused to back down or stand for any more insolence. He stared into MacTavish's florid face as he rested one hand on his pistol. "Who's the captain of this ship?"

MacTavish watched Gavin's hand before raising his gaze back to Gavin's eye. "Ye are, Lord help us."

"Then I suggest you mind your own business." Gavin shoved past him.

"My neck *is* my business."

Gavin kept walking. "Soon as we make the next port, you can take your neck and your precious red smoke and leave my ship."

"She won't have ye. Not after the way ye treated the lass."

Gavin spun on him. The muscle in his jaw threatening to turn his back teeth to dust. "Shut your mouth."

"Ye were right te send her away. Let her live her life. Safe. She don't belong on this tub. She's better than all of us lowlife bastards. Change course 'fore ye get us all killed chasin' somethin' ye got no right te have."

Gavin pulled his pistol, cocked the hammer, and pointed it into the face of Malcolm MacTavish. "Shut. Your. Bloody. Mouth."

MacTavish didn't flinch. He didn't even blink. Instead, he narrowed his eyes and held his arms wide. "Don't be threatenin' me. Shoot me if yer gonna shoot me. But ye ain't gonna. 'Cause ye don't shoot a man fer talkin' the truth." MacTavish turned and walked away.

Shoving the pistol back into his baldric, Gavin glared at the man's back. Last night's scene with Bump in Tupper's quarters had confirmed his decision. He wanted her back. Bump needed her. He needed her. But was it worth watching the crew hanged? Watching the boy hanged?

There was a price to pay for living this life. Gavin had already paid that price with his heart—twice. He'd lost Beth. He'd rejected Alice. Cruelly cast her aside as if she meant nothing to him. Washed away any feelings there might have been. There was no guarantee after swimming through shark-infested waters to reach her that she would ever forgive him.

Moving back to the quarterdeck, Gavin changed his earlier command. "Set a new course. We're heading east."

Chapter 27

The air was sultry and oppressive. Heat and humidity built throughout the afternoon. Rebecca and Brighton had been cranky and argumentative all day. By the time Alice delivered them back to their nurse for baths and their evening meal, she wanted nothing more to do with this day.

Emerson Blake only added to the day's oppressiveness. The flowers had stopped arriving. Thank goodness. But the man was everywhere. She and the children had seen him and Carlton in the stables this morning. Running errands in town later—whom should they meet? While reading to the children on the wide front porch, he'd stopped and shared their lemonade. The man would be the epitome of infuriating if he wasn't so damned charming. Respected. And so well liked that to complain about his attention was comparable to showing the king your bare arse.

While Isabelle understood her initial refusal, she continued to argue Emerson's merits. After all, he was here. While he couldn't replace the man she'd loved and left behind, he was obviously taken with her. He'd provide a good life for her. She should at least consider him.

It was all too much for one day. A bath awaited her. She looked forward to a simple evening, a quiet meal, perhaps a cooling stroll through the garden, and her bed.

Alice lowered herself into a tub of tepid water and sighed. The water refreshed her after the sticky, gritty film of the humid day. Verbena soap filled the tub with its sweet lemon scent as she washed the stress of the day away. Leaning her head back against the rim of the tub, Alice closed her eyes.

For the first time in weeks, images of Gavin didn't fill her mind and bring a painful ache to her chest. She'd barely thought of him today. Only that once. She'd seen a boy in town with corn-silk colored hair, which shone bright in the afternoon sun.

Gavin's hair was fine like silk slipping through her fingertips. Unqueued, it brushed his shoulders. It tickled her cheek when he leaned over her and kissed her. Trailed along her skin as he moved along her body.

Alice groaned. "Fine. Twice. I've thought about him twice." She dunked her head under the water and blew bubbles full of frustration.

A roll of far-off thunder announced the coming of a storm as Alice dressed for dinner. She'd chosen the lightest weight dress she had in her wardrobe. The top was done in a delicate cream cotton, trimmed in a fall of lace along the neckline that dipped off the tops of her shoulders and ended in a wide lace ruffle at the elbow. The bodice nipped in her waist before flaring into deep rose skirts that fanned into a small train behind her.

Having foolishly wet her head, there was no time to do her hair properly. Instead, she pulled it off her neck, pinned its length atop her head, and left the ends to dry into soft curls.

Warm and flushed, Alice's cheeks were pink when she looked at her reflection. The heat in the room was cloying and airless. Another rumble of thunder gave her hope the storm might bring changing winds.

She hurried into the parlor. "I'm sorry I'm late. Forgive me."

Carlton Whitmore stopped pouring his drink. "Alice, you look lovely this evening. Did Isabelle ruin the surprise?"

"Surprise?" Alice turned to Isabelle.

Isabelle sat on the settee. "That dress is the perfect shade for you." Her voiced pinched. "I adore what you've done with your hair." Isabelle gave her a small tight smile and did her best to study the contents of her wineglass. "D-don't you agree, Emerson?"

Alice spun around to find a dimpled Emerson smiling at her. The royal blue of his waistcoat looked striking against the silver of his vest and the black of his breeches. Her breath caught in her chest, but she was quick to recover. "Mister Blake, I had no idea you were joining us. Again."

He moved to kiss the back of her hand and spoke quietly. "I thought we'd agreed you'd call me Emerson?"

"That was before I realized you would take it as encouragement," she replied as she pulled her fingers from his grasp.

Emerson chuckled. "Touché."

A flash of lightning lit the room followed closely by the sharp clap of thunder. Isabelle rose and went to the window. "Our wish for rain is to be granted. I do hope the storm brings in cooler air." Another bolt cracked the sky. "I should run up to the nursery and check on the children. Rebecca is terrified of thunder storms."

"I'll go," offered Alice. Any excuse to be away from the persistent Mister Blake.

"Thank you, but times like these are sometimes best handled by a mother."

"Of course." Alice nodded.

"I won't be long. Carlton, pour Emerson another drink." Isabelle motioned to a servant. "Have Cook send in a tray of small bites." She patted Carlton's arm as she past. "That will tide you over until I return. I'll hurry, I promise."

Alice moved to Isabelle's place at the window. Dark clouds churned overhead. Lightning still danced within waiting for its chance to bolt to the ground. The winds had risen and whipped at the landscape. Trees bent and swayed like...like a mast.

In the reflection of the glass, Alice relived the scene from another storm. Jessup's sneer, her hands as she clung to the ropes of the rigging. Sliding inch by inch across the yardarm. She shivered. Then waking up in Gavin's arms. When his mouth met hers. The sight of his naked body. The delicious sensation of his skin against hers. "Okay, three times," she muttered under her breath, "I'm not counting anymore."

"Pardon?" Emerson stood behind her with a glass of wine. He handed it to her.

Alice took hold of the goblet, and turned away from the window. "Nothing."

Emerson's gaze swept her face. "You look miles away."

"Thousands." Alice took a strong swallow of her wine.

He scanned the clouds himself. "I enjoy a good thunderstorm, don't you?"

Alice stepped away from him. "Oh, yes. Of course, it's one thing to experience it watching from a parlor window. Quite another aboard a rolling ship."

"Did you have many storms on your crossing?" asked Carlton.

"There was one I'll never forget." Alice swallowed more of her wine.

A tray arrived and Carlton attacked it hungrily. Both Alice and Emerson shook their heads when he offered the appetizers to each of them. He popped another morsel into his mouth. "All the more for me."

The wind outside grew stronger and lifted the sheer drapes at the window. Then the rains came, pouring hard and fast. A heavy gust carried it into the room through the open window. Alice was quick to shut out the sudden flood.

Isabelle was back wearing a bemused expression. She smiled at Alice.

Alice raised her eyebrows in question. "Are the children all right?"

"More than all right." Isabelle retrieved her drink. "I don't know what you've done with Rebecca, but in the short time you've been with us, she's gone from a timid waif to being quite plucky. I haven't seen her suck her thumb in days." She spoke to Carlton, "I went upstairs expecting to find her upset and crying. She's always so frightened by the thunder. What I found was she and Brighton debating whether thunder was God throwing rocks or clouds yelling at one another. She told me she believed it was the clouds because everyone knows they cussed a blue streak."

Alice smirked behind her wineglass.

"That reminds me," added Carlton. "Stable manager told me he found Rebecca happily feeding carrots to King's Knight yesterday. Said the beast was gentle as a foal with her."

They all turned to look at Alice for some explanation. "Rebecca just needed to find her courage. I simply planted the seed. She's blossomed."

"Like a magnolia tree in June," puffed Isabelle. Catching sight of her husband snatching more appetizers, she took his arm and steered him toward the dining room. "Please, let's go into dinner before my husband eats the painted flowers off the platter."

Alice was grateful for the width of the Whitmore's grand dining room table to keep the ever-present Mister Blake on his side of the room.

"Did you tell them we ran into each other in town?" Emerson cut into his entrée of tender sliced beef. Alice shook her head. To Carlton he added, "The navy's presence there was much more obvious today. Shop owners say it's been a boon to their business. That was before the news came regarding the *Hampshire*, however." He took a bite of his meal. Dabbing his mouth with his napkin, he continued to explain. "The *Scarlet Night* struck again. Crippled the *Hampshire* and left her adrift off the Carolina coast."

"Can no one stop these freebooters?" demanded Carlton.

Emerson continued, "There have been half a dozen pirating ships caught since the patrols were increased. Quinn's been lucky up until now. His luck is about to run out."

The smug arrogance in his tone triggered Alice's temper. "Did you ever think perhaps it isn't luck that keeps the *Scarlet Night* from being captured? Captain Quinn and his crew are just more skillful than you give them credit for."

Emerson gave her a patronizing smirk. "I'm sure to you, it might appear that way, but I assure you there is no greater force than the British Navy."

She raised an eyebrow in his direction. "Evidently not, if they can't catch one small ship."

Emerson leaned forward and pointed at her with the tip of his knife. "Just because they rescued you from the *Delmar* and didn't slit your lovely throat doesn't mean they deserve any of your loyalty, Alice."

"Emerson, I'm sure Alice holds no loyalty to those scoundrels." Isabelle attempted to soothe the conversation.

Alice shrugged a shoulder and went back to dinner. "I respect them for being accomplished seamen and for treating me kindly."

"You can't be serious." The man snorted. "They're vicious cutthroats."

Alice tightened the grip she had on her fork. The man was insufferable. "How cutthroat must they be if they let me go?"

Emerson stopped eating and looked at her as if she were mad. "Isabelle saw your bruises when you arrived. How was that treating you kindly?"

"My bruises had nothing to do with them," she shot back.

He used his knife to flick her comment aside. "They only let you go because you were worthless to them."

Isabelle's gasp gave sound to the force of the slap behind Emerson's words.

The storm outside had gone as quickly has it had arrived. As had the minor skirmish at the table. An uncomfortable silence descended upon the room. The only sound was that of cutlery meeting china.

Alice emptied her wineglass and stood, dropping her napkin into her chair. "I'm sorry Isabelle. I need some air."

"Alice—" Emerson was on his feet.

She held up her hand to stop him. "Please."

Outside, the winds had made a decided turn. The air was crisp. Clean as crystal, while the last of the sun's rays sparkled in the rain-scrubbed landscape. Flowers in the garden bowed, heavy with their drinks. Alice lifted her skirts to keep her hems dry.

Lights from the house spilled into the shadowed pathways and drew her away. Away from Emerson and his infuriating dimple. Sanctimonious twit. Alice stopped and closed her eyes and let the evening's calm wrap around her.

Some tiny creature chirped in the fading light, and the cool breeze brushed the stray pieces of her hair against her neck. Alice folded her arms and dropped her chin to release the last bit of tension from her shoulders.

"Alice, I'm an opinionated bore. Forgive me."

She hadn't heard Emerson approach. She stifled a groan. "I don't want to discuss it anymore."

"Can you forgive me?"

Alice stepped away from him. "Fine, I forgive you."

He followed her. "You know, I cannot remember the last time I argued with a woman."

She stopped and spun on him. The man knew how to irritate her. She'd give him credit. "No, I'm sure you prefer your women to keep their mouths shut and their comments to themselves."

"It wasn't meant as an insult." He raised an eyebrow at her and tipped one side of his mouth. The dimple flashed. "I rather enjoyed it." He took an unwelcome step toward her.

Alice held up a hand. "You need to stop right there."

"I can't. You've bewitched me." His eyes swept from the top of her head to her hems and back. "From the first moment. You're quite unlike any woman I've ever met."

She shook her head at him. The man needed to get this ridiculous notion of any kind of romantic future out of his mind. "Emerson—"

"Let me finish. For surely, if I do not say it now, I'll lose my nerve." He took her hand and dropped to one knee on the sodden ground. "Marry me, Alice."

"No." She jerked her hand away.

"Why not?" He looked stricken.

Alice covered her eyes with her hand. "Where shall I start the list?"

Emerson rose. Mud stained his knee. "Tell me your objections. There's nothing we cannot overcome."

"Let's start with, you're crazy." She made another attempt to walk away.

He called to her retreating back. "Men act irrationally when they lose their heart."

Alice stopped and sighed. She turned back to him. "You can't love me. You don't know me."

"I know enough. I know you're beautiful." His hand swept the length of her. "Tonight, in this light, you take my breath away."

"Beauty fades."

"You're intelligent and strong. I need a woman like you by my side. Together we could do great things."

Alice chewed at her lip. "I'm not the type of woman you should wed. You're a prominent member of this society."

"Society be damned." He flipped a hand.

She gave a bitter laugh. "You say that, but there's no truth in it."

"Is it because you're employed by my friends? This isn't England. Our class system is much less rigid." He shrugged. "I don't care about any of that. It's you I care about."

"Emerson, you have to believe me. You know nothing about me. There are things…in my past. Things I can't undo."

"You've made whatever it is larger in your mind. I can't believe you'd do anything so damning. Tell me, please, I'll ease your worries."

"I can't tell you this. It jeopardizes my life"—at his frown, Alice lost some of her bravado.—"here. It jeopardizes my life with the Whitmore's."

"The Whitmores adore you." He moved closer and stroked her cheek with the back of his finger. "I adore you."

Alice turned away, holding her forehead in her hand. "You're not going to stop, are you?"

"No, my darling, I'm not. If it takes the rest of my life to convince you we are destined to be together, so be it."

She lifted her chin and spoke directly into his eyes. "I love another man." Alice could see her statement had given him pause.

He held her gaze. "Are you wed? Promised?"

Alice gave a quick shake to her head. "No, but—"

"Then he has no claim. Does he share your feelings?" When Alice said nothing in reply, a wide smile spread across Emerson's face. "Then there is no problem other than the man is an idiot." He took her hands again, kissed their backs, and looked deep into her eyes. "I will love you, Alice Tupper, and in time you—"

"It's Gavin Quinn."

Chapter 28

"What did you say?" Emerson's hold on her hands tightened.

Alice's gaze never wavered. "I'm in love with Gavin Quinn."

"You can't be serious." Sweat made his forehead glisten.

"I am. Captain Gavin Quinn of the *Scarlet Night*. I love him." The words had rushed out. She'd only meant to shock him, but once the words had claimed the air, they breathed life into her heart. It was foolish. The declaration would change nothing as far as Gavin was concerned. It certainly was going to cause a new barrage of interrogations from Emerson, but she didn't care. She was happy someone else who knew. Even if it was Emerson Blake.

A darkness crossed his face. "The pirate who beat you?" His voice rose. "You *love* him?"

The deadly look upon Emerson's face caught her short. She was quick to defend Gavin. "He never beat me."

He shouted. "The bruises—"

Alice rushed to explain. "I told you. No one beat me. We were fighting a skirmish with another ship. They caught the tip of the main mast with chain shot. I pushed Gavin out of harm's way, but the ropes and sail came down on top of me. That's how I got my bruises."

"Did you say, 'we'?" He dropped her hands as if they were covered in filth. "You said, 'we.'"

Alice rubbed at her hands. "I wasn't a captive."

"You're one of them?" Emerson tipped his head as if he hadn't heard her.

She swallowed the sudden wave of dread threatening to choke her. "It's complicated."

"It's not," he snapped. "Either you are or you aren't."

Alice was in too deep to back out now. "I never signed the ship's Articles, but—yes, I served as a member of their crew during my time aboard."

He glared at her for a long moment in silence before narrowing his eyes. "I don't believe you. Is this is an attempt to distract me from marrying you?"

She held up her hands in surrender. "Short of fighting you with a cutlass, I don't know how to convince you. You wanted the truth. There it is."

Emerson studied her face. The line between his brows deepened. "My Lord, you're a *pirate.*"

Alice shrugged a shoulder. "Technically, they were still under the protection of their Letter of Marque and Reprisal, so it would make me a privateer."

Emerson snapped, "Is this a joke to you, woman?"

"No, of course not."

He stormed away from her only to storm back. "You can be hanged." He paced some more and stopped short. "The Whitmores need to know about this at once."

She grabbed for his sleeve. "Please, Emerson, don't do anything rash."

"There are children involved here." He glared.

Alice's jaw dropped. "I would *never* bring harm to those children. You know that."

"I know nothing anymore." Emerson jerked his arm from her grasp.

Alice reached for him again. She had to get him to see past the anger. "Please, Emerson. You have every right to be upset, but you need to understand." She took a deep breath. "A series of unfortunate circumstances threw me into that life. I did what I did to survive. But it's in the past," she reiterated. "I'm no threat to Brighton or Rebecca, I swear to you. It's over."

"You're in love with a pirate. It's hardly over."

Alice heard the hurt over the anger. She shook her head. "He's thousands of miles away. He doesn't want me."

He looked into her eyes. "But you want him."

"Moot point."

"Hardly." He pulled away, but his anger had begun to cool.

"Emerson, whether or not I want him has nothing do to with my life here, now. It has to do with being honest—with you—about any hope of a future as your wife."

He snorted. "Oh, I don't think there's any question as to that now."

"Good. You're a fine man, and you can provide a wonderful life for some lucky woman. It just can't be me."

He gave a bitter laugh. "Obviously."

The quiet of the night surrounded them. She wished she could read his mind. He still controlled the ax hanging above her head. Given his hurt and anger, and his hatred of pirates, Alice was ready for him to pull a rope from his back pocket and hang her right there. "What are you going to do?"

Emerson heaved a heavy sigh. "By law, I'm obligated to bring you before the town governors. Carlton and Isabelle must be told. I couldn't possibly keep this from them. Perhaps when you explain the 'series of unfortunate circumstances,' they and the law will be lenient."

She crossed her arms over her chest and dropped her chin. The fuse had been lit. Whatever happened now was out of her control. "And perhaps, I'll hang as a pirate."

He shook his head sadly. "You never signed the Articles. A good solicitor could argue you were held against your will."

"I won't lie about what I've done. I need to face whatever consequences that brings." Alice straightened her shoulders. "Do what you believe is right. I can't change what's happened and I won't blame you for what's to come. I'm glad you know the truth. And don't worry, I won't prey upon your fondness for me. I'd never ask you to compromise your integrity." She gave him a small smile. "You are a decent man, Emerson. Had I been a better woman...." She shrugged.

Emerson looked toward the house before meeting her eye. "The hour is late. Perhaps my integrity can wait until morning."

He stepped closer, lifted her chin with his finger, and placed a soft chaise kiss upon her lips. "I was correct about one thing, Alice Tupper. You *are* fascinating and one of the strongest women I have ever met." He took a deep breath and stepped away. "Come, I'll walk you back."

"If you don't mind, just a few more minutes? After tomorrow, it may be a long time before I stand in such a beautiful garden. I won't linger too long. I promise."

Emerson hesitated, but then nodded. "I'll see you at first light."

Alice watched him leave, then closed her eyes to the quiet of the garden. She rubbed at the tightness at the back of her neck, but when she envisioned the knot of the noose snapping her spine like a twig, she wrung her hands as she walked in a small, tight circle, unsure of which direction to run.

Good God, this was it. She was going to die. There was no way Emerson or Carlton would let her walk free. Come morning, she'd be arrested. Thrown into some prison. Put on trial for treason against the Crown and piracy. Hung.

Alice walked deeper into the garden, lifting her hems as she turned and headed back. She'd seen the gibbons along the docks where they put the tarred bodies of pirates to serve as a warning to others. Putrid corpses left to bloat and rot in the sun. Alice covered her mouth as bile rose in her throat. As hideous as the possibilities of a gruesome end, a tiny part of Alice was at peace with what was to come.

This chapter had been coming since she pulled a cutlass from a scabbard and planted it in a duke's neck. She was no innocent victim. She was a pirate, but she'd been a murderer first. It was time to pay the price for her sins. She'd run as far and as fast as she could, but there was almost a relief in being caught. It was a crazy feeling, but there it was. Liberation. No more running. No lies. No regrets.

Shouldn't she be more afraid? Maybe she was insane. A sane person would be pleading for her life. Begging for mercy. Not pacing in a garden calmly accepting her fate.

Her thoughts turned toward the children. Poor Rebecca and Brighton. She prayed they would understand. Would Carlton and Isabelle even tell them what's happening? Would they let her say good-bye? Perhaps they'd lie and tell them she'd been called back to Engl—

A hand reached out of the darkness and clamped over her mouth, muffling her scream as an arm wrapped about her and hauled her backwards against a solid wall of chest. Alice flailed, scratching at the hand on her mouth, bringing her elbow back to deliver a sharp blow to the man's ribs. The wind rushed from her attacker's lungs.

With her elbow planted, she swung her fist straight down to deliver a punishing blow to the man's groin, but he shifted enough to deflect the punch.

"Blood hell, Alice. It's me," he hissed.

Alice spun about. Adrenaline pumped through her body. She pounded him on his chest with her fists. "Gavin? What are you doing? Oh, God, it's really you." She grabbed fistfuls of his shirt. His clothing was damp. Had he stood here through the rain? "Oh, God, you have to leave. You can't be here." She looked frantically back at the garden path. "If they catch you—"

"Alice, stop." He gripped her arms.

"You don't understand. You're in terrible danger."

"Alice," he wrapped his arms around her and pulled her to him, "could you stop talking for a second and kiss me?"

He didn't wait for an answer. His mouth claimed hers. One arm slid higher pinning her to his chest as he persuaded her lips to part under the insistence of his tongue.

Alice was lost to the long, deep, ground-shattering kiss. Her heart pounded. She clung to his shoulders as her legs weakened. Gavin's arms tightened around her. When the kiss came to a breathless end, he continued to hold her tight to him. His breathing labored, Alice could feel his heart keeping time with her own.

Sanity returned. She pulled back. "What are you doing here?" she whispered.

He cupped her cheek and lowered his mouth again. "Isn't it obvious?"

She stopped him, taking a step back. "You risked your life to come kiss me?"

"It was one hell of a kiss." His gaze traveled down the length of her. "Were you always so incredibly beautiful?" Gavin reached out to tease a loose curl of her hair before tracing a fingertip along her ear.

"Not always." His simple touch was making her thighs shake. "Stop, Gavin. Why are you here?"

"I came back for you." He tipped his chin toward the house. "And by the looks of it, I arrived just in time."

Alice reached out to touch his face. His lips. Her brain was having trouble registering what her eyes were seeing. "How much did you hear?"

"Every word."

"Then you heard how much danger you're in. British—wait, you came back for me?"

"Aye, I couldn't stand another second without you. Only danger that worries me is not having you again. Spent weeks trying to forget you. Trying to find a way to live without you. I couldn't. I miss you. Everyone misses you. Crew's sick of my foul mood. MacTavish threatened to maroon my sorry arse. 'Course he's laid money on the fact I won't be able to convince you to come back." He stroked her cheek. "I need you. Bump needs you. Boy's been miserable."

"But you said—"

"Forget what I said, I was a bloody bastard. I'm not leaving without you so you can save all the arguing for when we're back aboard. Sail away with me, Alice. Tonight. Now."

Her mind was a jumbled mess. Did this mean he loved her? If he heard every word between her and Emerson, he heard her declaration. Hell, she'd said it three damn times. Was he here to get her for Bump or himself? When she hesitated, he threatened, "I'm prepared to toss you over my shoulder."

Suddenly, it didn't matter what his motivation was. He was asking her to go with him. Be a part of his life, whatever that happened to look like. "Wait here. I'll go change."

Gavin smiled in the dark. From inside his coat, he pulled a small bundle. "You'll travel faster in britches. Robbins says you'll owe him." Running a finger along the wide neckline of her gown, he added, "But I like this a lot, too. Bring it along."

Whispering, alone in the dark, with his fingertip skimming over the tops of her breasts, Alice began to shiver again. "It-it doesn't belong to me."

He fished two gold coins from his belt and pressed them in to her hand. "It does now. Pack the dress."

His eyes sparkled as she slipped the coins into her bodice. She traced the smile on his face. "Don't let anyone see you. I'll be back as quickly as I can."

"Hurry."

Alice nodded and pushed him back into the deepest part of the shadows. Gavin pulled her in after him and kissed her near senseless again. "Hurry," he whispered against her lips.

Her heart soared as she moved quickly back to the house. Before she entered, she slipped on the breeches beneath the skirts of her gown. There would be no explaining were she caught with them, but there was an odd comfort to wearing them again.

The lamps had been lowered, as most of the staff had already retired for the night. She didn't run, although fear and excitement pressed at her. Should there be anyone awake, she would behave as if all was as it should be.

All the while, her mind sang. He'd come for her. There was a secret thrill that he was out there waiting in the dark shadows of the night to take her away. Save her. He hadn't said. Had he come to love her?

"Alice." Carlton Whitmore stood in the doorway of his study holding a large glass of brandy. Beyond, she could see Emerson Blake waiting within.

Chapter 29

Carlton Whitmore ushered her into the study and locked the door behind them. Cold fingers of panic ran along her spine. She had to get out of this room and warn Gavin. If she could think of a signal he would understand. Something. Think.

Alice met Emerson's brooding stare. She glared at him. "First light has come early."

"I couldn't risk you fleeing into the night." Emerson drained his glass. "Like a common criminal."

"So much for your integrity." Alice turned to Carlton. "Please forgive me, Carlton, I can—"

Carlton's face was practically fuchsia. "How dare you?" he spat. "How dare you come into *my* house, sit at *my* table, care for my *children*? Did you think we wouldn't discover who you are? *What* you are?" He screwed his face as if he'd tasted something spoiled. "A pirate? You've lied to us since the moment you arrived."

She notched her chin. Anger lessened some of her fear. "You're right. I lied. I spared you the truth about my journey here and what happened to me." She folded her arms over her chest. "Did you really want to hear how the captain of the *Pennington* was shot through his neck at close range right in front of my eyes? Or how after the crew of the *Delmar* killed everyone in sight, the deck became so slippery with blood, I couldn't stand?" She turned on Emerson. "How about having to fight off men who wanted to rape me? Do you want to hear that truth?"

Both men simply stared at her. Cold and unmoved. Oozing with judgmental arrogance "How would you like some more truth? The *Delmar* was carrying slaves. *Your* slaves. Half of them dead already. Stuffed into a hold like animals. Shackled to one another. The living attached to the dead. I watched a man die after the iron band around his leg cut straight through to the bone. That man's death is on your hands." Alice planted her hands on her hips. "Gavin Quinn is a lot of things, but he's the only one who cares about protecting them. You want to live in your perfect world and believe you're better than everyone else? You're no better than I am. You're certainly no better than him."

Emerson mirrored her stance. "We are not going to debate the horrors of the slave trade with you. I treat my people well."

"And that makes it right? Is that what you tell yourself so you can sleep peacefully in your nice clean bed at night?" Alice calmed the racing of her breath. She could sense the walls of the trap closing in. She needed to compose herself, find a way out.

She turned back to Carlton. His face had gone from florid to ashen. Alice continued to plead her case. "I'm not proud of some of the things I've had to do, but I did them to survive. I came here to start a new life. Put it all behind me. I love those children. I love Isabelle. I have done nothing since I arrived to bring my past to this house, until tonight. Yes, I'm a pirate. If you have to bring me to justice, then I'll face whatever is to come."

Carlton rubbed a shaky hand over his jaw. "I certainly didn't imagine it would come to this, but we have no choice. There are laws."

"And I'm guilty." She lowered herself into a chair.

Carlton and Emerson exchanged a look. The room breathed a silent pause. Emerson knelt before her for the second time tonight. The look he gave her spoke of heartbreak and sadness. "You've told me you love Gavin Quinn. As much as it hurts me, I have to accept your declaration for the man. But I can't watch you dragged off to the gallows. It would kill me." He looked stricken. "I know how hard this is, but, darling, if you have some information we could use, anything against Quinn. It might be enough to save you. Are you sure there's nothing?"

Alice stared at her hands, fiddled with her ring, and chewed at her lip. Emerson placed his hand over hers. "I beg you, tell us."

She sighed and looked between the two men. "There may be something."

* * * *

"What took you so long?" Gavin cupped her cheek and kissed her.

"I had a few loose ends to tie. I'll explain later. We need to get out of here."

"We haven't much time." He took her bundle, grasped her hand tight, and headed off into the night.

They didn't speak as she followed his lead. The only whisper was their footsteps through the thick trees and brush, and the rush of their breathing. They'd been walking over an hour when Alice began to smell the salty tang of the ocean. They had to be close. Soon the brush seemed to part, and Gavin stopped.

Standing on the edge of the dunes, Alice could hear the waves as they broke upon the shore. With only a slight crescent to the moon, it was hard to see.

"Dammit," he hissed.

"What is it?" She clutched at his arm.

"They're gone." He pulled a small scope out of his coat pocket and scanned the sea. "Damn." He huffed out a breath. "They were spotted."

"Gavin?"

"Thought the Royals might be a problem. They've push more patrols along this stretch. I left orders. If this spot wasn't secure, we'd meet up with them farther down the coast."

"The Royal Navy?"

"Aye. Come on. We need to be away before daybreak. After that, our chances of getting away without a fight are slim."

Alice grabbed at the fabric of his sleeve. "You've risked so much. If anything happens to you because of me...."

He turned in the dark and found her mouth, kissing her before laying a warm hand over hers. "Don't worry. I know every cove and inlet along this coast. I won't let anything happen. I'm not losing you again. Let's go. If we're to meet up with the *Scarlet Night* before dawn we have to be quick."

Gavin kissed her once more before turning them back into the trees. Alice needed to run at times to keep up with his long-legged strides. He moved with little hesitation, certain of where he was headed even in the dark.

When he broke back through the tree line to stand at the edge of another cove, they were both out of breath. Alice bent at the waist, pressing a fist into the painful stitch at her side while she gasped for air. Gavin pulled his glass and tried to still his own breathing so he could hold it steady. Dawn was coming. The faint lightening of the sky told her they were running out of time.

Alice prayed they'd found the ship.

"There she is. We need to climb down to the water line and get their attention. Follow close and watch your footing."

The high bluff surrounding the cove made for a slow descent, but soon Alice and Gavin stood upon the coarse sand. Gavin began gathering bits of driftwood and making a small pile. "Need a fire to signal for the skiff. With the rain earlier, the wood is damp. Hope we can get the blasted thing to light."

Alice searched for dry grass and small sticks to use as kindling. When she returned, Gavin was crouched alongside working with a flint. He added what she'd gathered and got a spark to catch. Smoke became flame, and soon a tiny fire struggled to catch the larger pieces of wood.

"Son of a blind bitch. They'll never see this."

The sky was growing lighter by the second. Alice looked about in a panic for more dry wood, and then a thought struck her. "I know what they'll see."

"What are you thinking?"

Alice rummaged through her bag and pulled out the small pouch of powder. "If this works, there'll be no living with MacTavish. I'm not sure how much to use. You might want to stand back."

Gavin did so as Alice tossed the entire pouch onto the fledgling fire. The resulting explosion and red fireball lit up the beach and threw them both back on their arses.

"Bloody hell," shouted Gavin.

Thirty minutes later, Gavin and Alice, together with a six-member crew, were racing back in a skiff as the first pink of daylight began to creep along the horizon. "Put hard to the oars boys. The Royals couldn't have slept through that."

"There's my bonny lass." puffed MacTavish as he pulled Alice back aboard the *Scarlet Night*. Hearty welcomes came from the rest of the men. White, Finch, and Summer led the cheer.

Alice tossed Robbins a small bundle. "I brought you a present."

He held up a pair of fine black breeches and raised a brow. "Satin?"

Their good-natured reunion was short-lived as the call from the crow's nest confirmed everyone's fears. The *Scarlet Night* wasn't the only one to witness MacTavish's red magic.

"Ship off of starboard. Coming fast."

* * * *

Gavin swung over the gunwales and began shouting orders before his feet hit the deck. "Get the skiff secured and raise the anchor. Full sail, Simons. Glass." He was handed the largest scope and fixed it upon the coming ship. "Four masts. She's flying Jack and looks like she plans to blow us out of the water. Hoist every inch of cloth we've got, our only chance it to outrun the bastards."

A cannon blast from the huge navy warship's largest gun fell short of the *Scarlet Night*, but it was a clear warning for them to stand or suffer the consequences. Gavin watched the ship get larger in the glass.

Above them, the sails of the *Scarlet Night* filled, and the ship leapt through the water. They were riding high and empty, and they could outrun the heavy warship, but they were seriously outgunned. If the bastards got close enough, their front-mounted cannons could turn the *Night* into floating kindling with one blast.

"I've an idea." He grabbed Alice's arm. "Go below and put on that gown I just paid for." At her puzzled look, he gave her a gentle push. "Be quick. And let down your hair. Get back up here fast."

The rigging began to hum as the *Scarlet Night* gained momentum. Another shot from the Royals fell short. "They're getting closer. We're going to need every bit of speed we can squeeze from her, men."

In no time, Alice was at his side having followed his orders to the letter. Her hair was wild in the wind, and her gown was barely on.

"I didn't have time to lace up the bodice."

"Perfect." He grabbed a rag. "There's no time to explain. Put this in your mouth like you've been gagged."

Alice's frown quickly melted into a smile. "You're bloody brilliant." She put the rag in her mouth.

"Only if it works. Climb into the main rigging, midship. Put your hands behind you like they're bound and grip the ropes tight. I'll keep a hold on you, too. Understand?"

Alice nodded as he pulled her along after him, and they settled themselves in the ropes.

Gavin tossed his glass to Simons. "Keep an eye on the commanders, and those lead gunners."

Slipping his arm around Alice's waist, Gavin pulled her tight against him. He drew his pistol and placed the tip of the barrel under her jaw. "My beautiful captive," he murmured in her ear. "Let's hope they see you before they fire those guns."

"Gunners are at the ready," Simons called out.

"What about the officers?" Quinn asked.

"Got their glasses on us. Wait. One lowered his sight and pulled it back quick. He's pointing. Seen ye, Tupper. Smile pretty. Got three scopes trained on ye."

"Struggle against me, then tip your head back like I made a grab for your hair." He pulled her tighter and growled low. "This would be much more fun if the bastards weren't trying to kill us."

Behind the loose rag in her teeth Alice said, "I have another idea."

Gavin's mouth was close to her ear. "What do you suggest?"

"Use the butt of your pistol. Lower the top of my gown."

"Bare your breasts to the bloody British Navy?"

"Just the right side. Show them I'm truly a woman. Don't worry, my left one will still be yours alone."

"Bloody hell, woman," he growled.

"Gunners leveling the barrels, Capt'n," shouted Simons.

Alice nudged him with her elbow. "Best be quick about it. If they ruin this dress...."

Gavin pressed the brass end of his pistol's hilt to her skin and dragged it down catching the edge of her bodice and pulling the wide lace trim past the peak of her right breast. With her flagrantly exposed, he pointed the barrel of the gun to her heart. "First man on this ship to so much as glance in this direction is dead."

"Damn wind," Alice mumbled against the rag as she shivered pretending to struggle.

"I'll warm ye later."

"If we have a later."

"Five glasses now," called Simons. "Shoutin' orders. Gunners at ease. They be droppin' two mainsa'l. They're fallin' back."

Chapter 30

A cheer went up as the *Scarlet Night* began to add distance between them and the British. Adrenaline pumped in Alice's veins. The hum of the rigging set off a humming within her. Gavin kept a tight hold on her as he lifted the top of her gown back into place and they moved down out of the rigging.

He called the order. "We're going to thread the needle. Simons, pull every ounce of speed we've got."

God, she'd missed him. His commanding presence, the way he captained his crew. The strength of his jaw. The smell of his skin. "Can I kiss you now?"

"They're still watching." He jerked her closer and moved toward the ladder way. "They won't shoot on us now they've seen you, but they'll pursue us to attempt a rescue. If we can lose sight of them long enough, there's a place we can lie low. Let them chase their tails for a few days."

"Foolish men, don't they know I don't need rescuing?"

"Go below. I'll be down soon."

Alice slipped back into the rest of her clothes in the galley way where she'd changed in haste. Activity top deck rumbled down as the men sent the *Scarlet Night* flying over the water. The clamor was like coming home. The creak of the wood, the rush of the sea. She was back.

But what did that mean? Indecision crept over her. She and Gavin hadn't shared more than two score words between them. Yes, his kisses left her knees weak, but he'd pushed her away one too many times to assume they meant anything more than a moment's desire. He'd come for her, but there were still many things left swinging in the breeze.

There was one thing she was certain of, however. Alice went in search of Bump. Regardless of what happened between her and Gavin, she would not be leaving that sweet lad again.

She found him tucked away in a corner of Gavin's cabin polishing a pair of Gavin's boots—one-handed. What had happened to his arm? He hadn't noticed her when she entered, and so she stood in the doorway and waited.

His face looked thinner. Dark smudges visible beneath his eyes. His hair stuck out in every direction. The sight of him filled her heart and made her want to scoop him into her arms and never let go.

Bump looked up from his work. His eyes met hers and he frowned. Rubbing them with the back of his hand, he looked at her again. Bump jumped to his feet, knocking the boots to the floor, and ran to her. Midroom, he came to an abrupt stop. Eyes wide, he stared.

Alice stood her ground. She'd rushed to him before and embraced him against his will. She needed to be patient. Tears pinched the backs of her eyes. She opened her arms out to her sides and held her breath.

Bump tucked his chin, gave a great sigh, and leapt into her arms. He encircled his good arm around her neck and held tight. Alice wrapped her arms around the boy as she buried her face into his slight shoulder and wept.

Gavin entered a short time later. Alice lowered Bump to his feet and wiped at her face. "This was not coddling."

"I didn't say it was." Gavin touched Bump's shoulder, and when the boy looked at him, he made a few odd gestures with his hands. Bump smiled and gestured back before giving Alice another quick hug and leaving the cabin.

Alice wiggled her fingers. "What was that you did?"

"Do you remember the books we acquired from the Spanish merchant ship?" Gavin lifted a book from his desk. "I found this." He handed it to her. "Priest, named Bonet, has a way of talking to the deaf."

Alice looked through the book. Each letter of the alphabet represented by a different position of the hand to spell out words. She practiced forming the letter *A*. "This is wonderful."

"It's slow, and in Spanish, but it's a start. Bump's smart. He's catching on."

Gavin hung up his coat and baldric. Set each in its proper place.

"What happened to his arm?"

"He fell. It's healing well. Bump being Bump." Gavin loosened the stock at his neck. Pulled the lacing from his hair.

Alice hugged the book to her chest. All the bravado from before faded away to nothing. The chasm between them still stood. She drew a shaky breath. "Have we outrun the British?"

"Aye." The neck of his shirt open, Gavin stood with his hands on his hips. He was the most handsome, beautiful man she'd ever seen. She wanted to go to him. Kiss that place where his neck dipped into his chest. Feel the beating of his heart beneath her lips. But if he put her aside, pushed her away again, it would destroy her. She'd endured torture, beatings, attacks. She'd faced down fierce pirates and an evil duke and swung her weapon in battle. But standing here, wanting him like this, it was a battle she wouldn't survive.

Gavin poured a healthy measure of rum. "Had you not secured your place among this crew before, you've surely done so now. You were… amazing." He handed her the glass. Gray eyes held her gaze. "Of course, now I'll have to hunt down five British officers and kill them for ogling you." The corner of his mouth twitched.

He gave a slow shake to his head, before he ran the backs of his fingers along her cheek. Slipping his hand beneath her hair, he brushed it over her shoulder before capturing the back of her neck and drawing her mouth to his. "Dear Lord, I do love you."

Alice released a small cry as his lips claimed hers. He tipped her back, deepened the kiss, and erased any doubt in her mind as to his true feelings. Gavin's arm circled her waist and pulled her to him as his mouth continued to ravish hers. A deep groan rumbled from his throat. He ground his hips against hers. The firm ridge of his desire pressed against her belly.

She was beyond thought. He had to feel the pounding of her heart as it tried to burst from her chest. Alice dropped the book and the glass to the floor. Rum ran between the floorboards as the glass rolled away. She wrapped her arms around his neck.

Gavin ran his hands down over the roundness of her and lifted her off her feet. In breeches, she was free to wrap her legs around his waist as he carried her to his bed.

They came together like a storm. Clothing tossed aside in haste. Hands and mouths, grasping and tasting. A sexual fire consuming them both. Nothing mattered but being joined with him. Alice cried out when he drove into her. Joy bursting in her heart. Passion surged through her veins as he pushed her higher, sending her full sail into the blinding light of the sun. She screamed his name. Gavin continued to thrust into her until the heat of his release flooded her.

He kissed her, panting. Rested his forehead against hers. "I love you so much." He raised his head enough to look into her eyes. "I'm sorry I sent you away. Never again. You're never leaving me again." He kept shaking his head. "I only wanted to protect you."

"Gavin—"

"No. Let me finish. This is my life. I've lost so much already." He kissed her. "Promise me I won't lose you, too."

"You can't shield me against everything, Gavin. I know the dangers, but I belong here. With you. I don't want a life away from the *Scarlet*

Night. I choose you." She held his face. "I'm a pirate in love with a pirate. I can't promise to live until I'm old and gray, to die peacefully in my bed. I can only promise I will love you as long as the moon pulls at the tides and there is water in the sea."

"Be my wife," he whispered.

Alice blinked at a sudden flood of tears. She sniffed back all the emotion before it poured out and embarrassed them both. She hid it behind a sassy smile. "Is that an order, Captain?"

Gavin held her cheek and used his thumb to wipe the tear away from the corner of her eye. He shook his head, as he looked deep into her soul. "No. It's a plea."

* * * *

When the *Scarlet Night* dropped anchor within the protected shelter known as the Needle's Eye, the entire crew stood witness to their marriage.

"I, Alice Louise Tupper take you Gavin Quinn to be my husband." She wore a skirt the color of mud with red stripes down the back.

Gavin promised to love her 'til death do us part.' He slipped a stunning necklace of gold and oval emeralds around her neck. It was all she wore to bed that night.

Some time after eight bells, Alice insisted on signing her name to the ship's Articles. Arguing that Alice Tupper was no more, she signed her name in a large, flowing script: Tupper Quinn.

Epilogue

"Damn it man, untie me." Emerson Blake choked after the gag was removed from his mouth. "Not my ankles, you idiot. Start with my wrists!" He shook his hands under the servant's nose.

Carlton Whitmore tossed the strips of sheeting to the floor. "Drummond, saddle the horses. I'll take King's Knight. We'll go after her."

"Are you joking? She's been gone for hours. We'll never catch her now." Emerson rubbed at his chaffed wrists.

"We have to do something," Carlton insisted. We can't let her get away with this."

Emerson's head pounded, and he needed to punch something. The whole thing was humiliating. "This is your fault."

Carlton raised his eyebrows and straightened his wig. "Mine?"

"You sent for the chit," Emerson barked.

"How was I supposed to know she was a pirate?" Carlton shook his head and pushed a finger at Emerson's face. "No, what happened tonight was your fault. It was your brilliant idea we get her to turn over Gavin Quinn to us. Your charm is not as persuasive as you imagine. How are we supposed to report this now? We'll be laughing stocks."

Emerson knew the something he was going to punch. "You insisted we follow her upstairs so she wouldn't try to escape." His wrists burned. "Did you have to tie the restraints so damn tight?"

"The woman had a loaded pistol pointed at my head. Do you think she really tried to behead a duke?" Carlton gathered the scattering of gold coins that littered the mattress. "At least she was good enough to reimbursement me for her passage." He held up two coins, "And a gown."

"How perfect for you." Emerson ripped the cover off a pillow and attempted to wrap it around his waist. He reached over and snatched one of the coins from Carlton's hand.

"*This* will pay to replace my bloody pants."

Meet the Author

Lisa A. Olech is an artist/writer living in her dream house nestled among the lakes in New England. She loves getting lost in a steamy book, finding the perfect pair of sexy shoes, and hearing the laughter of her men. Being an estrogen island in a sea of testosterone makes her queen. She believes in ghosts, silver linings, the power of a man in a tuxedo, and happy endings. For more please visit lisaolech.com.

Within A Captain's Fate

Be sure not to miss Lisa A. Olech's sequel to *Within A Captain's Hold* and *Within A Captain's Treasure*:

Read on for a special sneak peek of the next book in the Captains of the Scarlet Night series!

Learn more about Lisa A. Olech
http://www.kensingtonbooks.com/author.aspx/31711

Chapter 1

June 7, 1692
Port Royal, Jamaica

A wicked grin tugged across Henry "Ricochet" Robbins's face. The *Scarlet Night* sat secure at the dock, and he was the first one off the ship after the captain dismissed the crew. His boots hit the wide, weathered boards of the pier and he set his sights on spending the next twenty-four hours drinking as much sweet rum as he could hold and enjoying the lusty pleasures of Port Royal.

The last time he was here was over the winter's careening of the *Night*. He'd filled his pockets with winnings from the billiards tables and caught the eye of a dark-skinned beauty who worked as a bar wench at the Rogue Wave Tavern. Ah, Teja. Did she have a last name? Didn't matter. They'd spent four wild days and nights in her bed. She was the kind of woman a man could lose himself in and take a month finding his way out. Silken hair the color of midnight, whiskey-colored eyes, the sweetest mouth that could do the dirtiest things, and ample curves. More than ample. Just the way Ric liked his ladies. Soft, round, and plentiful.

After being aboard ship for months, regaining his land legs had put an extra swag in Ric's swagger. The noise, heat, and smells of Port Royal welcomed him home. This was his town.

The *Scarlet Night* and Captain Quinn were on top of the heap, and he was the best swivel gunner there was. He could thread a six-pounder through a knothole at two hundred yards. He'd earned his nickname by cushioning a cannon shot off a rocky shoal and taking out a British mast—that, and he was in the habit of bouncing from woman to woman.

The day had dawned sultry. After the constant breeze aboard ship, the airless swelter of Port Royal laid steamy upon his skin. Pushing his way through the crowds loitering about the docks, he headed straight for the Rogue Wave.

Port Royal had become an interesting mix of humanity. A pirate haven, it teamed with society's dregs. Thieves and murderers. Whores and connivers. Lately, it was also seeing an influx of English influence.

Beyond the city, the British hold was gaining strength. Plantations and colonies were becoming more established. Of course, you'd never catch a proper British gentleman wandering the fermented streets, not without good reason, and certainly not at night.

Ric pushed into the dim tavern. The smells of stale ale and rank bodies meeting him head on. It took a moment for his eyes to adjust after the brightness of the morning. Time was irrelevant here. Patrons from last night lay passed out in their chairs and littered upon the floor. Other's played cards. The billiard tables were active and revelers still crowded the bar.

He sidled up and ordered a rum. "Make it a double."

"Ric Robbins." A cluster of men at the far end of the bar recognized him. "Ye bastard. Back to take more of me gold at the tables?"

"No time to fleece ye again, I'm afraid, I've a mind to spend my shore leave in the arms of my luscious Teja." He downed his drink and dropped a coin in payment.

The men burst into laughter, jostling one another. Snatching the coin off the bar top, the bartender snapped off what was owed him, and shoved the remainder of the gold back across the bar. "Ye be a mite too late there, Ric. Teja done hooked herself a captain."

They all laughed louder. One of them leaned toward him. "Captain Black." He gestured to the back corner of the tavern. It took Ric a second to register what he was seeing. A couple kissed. The deep, long, wet kisses of lovers. Captain Black had a hand pushed up under Teja's skirts and had bared one of her full breasts.

"Captain Black?" Ric choked. "*Pandora* Black?"

Roars of laughter erupted around him. "Guess the great Ricochet Robbins bounced her right over te the other side."

At the commotion, Teja and Black ended their kiss. Seeing Ric over Pandora's shoulder, Teja adjusted the neckline of her blouse to cover the dark peak of her nipple and smoothed down the front of her skirts.

Pandora Black turned a lazy look over her shoulder. Dressed as a man, Ric wouldn't have guessed she was a woman had he not known her by name. A fierce captain, she would fight any man who made the mistake of underestimating her. And she only took women into her bed.

She pierced Ric with an icy blue stare and hauled Teja back against her body. Holding Ric's gaze, she lifted her hand and licked her fingers.

Hoots, catcalls, and uproarious laughter followed Ric out of the tavern. "Son of a bitch," he growled. "I should 'ave known. She was wearing the same britches as me."

"Someone's in your trousers again, Robbins?" Gavin Quinn laughed as he and Bump approached him. Bump was another crewmate from the *Night*. A lad of less than a dozen years, Bump had been like a little brother to Ric since they brought him aboard. Sharp as a honed blade, the boy had become a first-rate seaman. Given the fact he was stone deaf only made his accomplishments more impressive.

"Damn women in my pants," he grumbled to Bump. "Story of my life." He shook his head and gathered what was left of his pride. "Nothing, Capt'n. Rum in the Rogue Wave leaving a bitter taste in my mouth."

"Forget the rum, stick with Bump while I meet with Fin Willy. I'm heading now to seal the deal. Soon we'll be sailing the *Scarlet Night* and the *White Witch*. Add that to the *Raven Wing;* more ships, more bounty to share."

The trio maneuvered their way past the array of taverns and brothels lining the docks. Urchin children picked the pockets of the unaware. "Congratulations, Capt'n. Gonna give Tupper a chance at the helm of her own ship?" Robbins asked. Tupper Quinn was the former Alice Tupper. She and Gavin had married and spent the last six years pirating their way back and forth across the Atlantic.

"Doubt it." Gavin dodged a puddle of filth. "Wouldn't care to be apart from her. Not now that I've grown so used to her being at my side."

Ric jostled past a group spilling out of a doorway. "Ye could always make me captain."

Gavin chuckled. "Another year or two under your belt and maybe the crew'd be ready to vote you in."

A crowd had formed into a tight knot of bodies surrounding the town's auction block. Gavin stopped. A fierce defender of the abolishment of the African slave trade, he hated these auctions. Men, women, and children being sold as property was abhorrent to him. Ric had been with him long enough to see him hunt down and track slave haulers to deliver their human cargo back to the safety of their own shores. The number of those he saved must have reached a thousand in all these years.

By the look, today's auction wasn't for Africans. A line of woman, chained together like dogs, was being dragged before the crowd. Young, old, weak, strong. The mob jeered and shouted lewd comments as the chained group was towed up onto the block. Sex slaves. Bought and sold into prostitution, life as concubines, some into harems or simply to satisfy the lust of the owner. The youngest and prettiest went to the highest bidder.

Quinn scowled before turning away. "It is a good thing Tupper loathes Port Royal and is still aboard the *Scarlet Night*. She'd be drawing her sword and taking on this whole crowd to set those women free." He slapped Robbins on the back. "I've kept Fin Willy waiting long enough. I'll meet you and Bump back on board. Tonight we celebrate the new addition to our fleet." Quinn made a few hand gestures to Bump who nodded in agreement before Quinn headed off to his negotiation for the *White Witch*.

Ric barely noticed. Over the heads of the pack of bystanders, he caught the panicked gaze of one of the women up for sale. She'd been scanning the throng before her. Her face ashen beneath a tangled mop of dark curls. Dirt and scratches marred her face and neck, and one sleeve of her blouse had been torn from its seam at the shoulder.

He moved closer to the block. The noise and energy of the crowd seemed to make the ground tremble. Bump gave a sharp tug on Ric's arm. He paid him little notice, as he was too absorbed in the scene before him. The raven-haired captive held his gaze. It was as if she were reaching out to him alone. Looking for some tether. Perhaps a sympathetic face in the mob to keep her from tipping into the abyss of insanity.

Whatever the reason, she had found him amongst the dozens of faces and held onto him. Pale frightened eyes seemed to silently plead with him to stop this madness as the bidding began.

Ric's world narrowed to a pinhole. A buzzing sounded in his ears. His brain screamed at the craziness of his thoughts. *Save her.*

Her tenuous bond was broken when she was jerked to the forward edge and became the next victim to be auctioned off.

"That one be mine," slobbered the fat man standing next to Ric. He smacked his thick lips and opened a sack of coins.

Ten gold pieces was the starting bid. An auctioneer scanned the crowd for any takers. Ric shoved his hand into his pockets and curled his fingers around the rough coins held there. "Ten," he shouted. His gaze never leaving her.

The man next to him bid fifteen, another yelled eighteen. Soon the bidding passed twenty-five gold pieces.

"Thirty," Ric bid, knowing full well he didn't have more than twenty gold pieces on him.

"Thirty-five," barked the fat man, narrowing his eyes at Ric before scratching at his crotch.

"Fifty," Ric countered. In his mind he knew he couldn't keep this up. Even if he managed to scrape together fifty gold pieces, what would he do with this girl?

The auctioneer smiled an oily grin as if he could sense a bidding war commencing. Turning back, he tore at the woman's blouse exposing her breasts to the audience. "Show 'em what they be buyin', Frenchie."

A black rage flooded Ric as the beast next to him frantically counted coins and raised the bid to seventy-five.

"Eighty."

"Ninety."

Blood rushed in Ric's ears. He shook with anger and the rush of indignation. His stomach turned at the thought of this man laying his fat, filthy hands on her.

Bump tugged on him once more trying to pull him away. Ric scowled at the boy's imploring gaze and shook his head. No, he wasn't leaving. He wasn't going to back down. There was no way he was going to lose her.

"Three hundred!"

Printed in the United States
by Baker & Taylor Publisher Services